Tango of water and flame
fantasy+sci-fi+romance+crime
Anna Molman

Copyright 2019 Anna Molman
Published by Anna Molman Amazon

Amazon Edition License Notes

This book is licensed for your personal enjoyment only. All the money, earned on this book will help me to control my 1 type diabetes and tell you new interesting stories. If you would like to share this book with another person, please purchase an additional copy for each recipient. If you're reading this book and did not purchase it, or it was not purchased for your enjoyment only, then please return to Amazon.com or your favorite retailer and purchase your own copy. Thank you for respecting the hard work of the author.

Prologue

Two tired healers were sitting in the lounge of the capital city's maternity hospital for mothers-to-be with pathologies.

"I poured all my magic reserve into him," the black-haired man said faintly.

"I saw it, Professor," quietly answered the slender gray-haired woman. "We all tried our best to save him, but when the magic streams are not adequate there's nothing you can do."

"The point is that this pathology could have been corrected at around the fifth month of pregnancy, but we still haven't learned how to detect it in time," the healer seemed to blame himself for the imperfection of the diagnostic techniques.

"So it's not your fault," his colleague replied gently. "You did everything you could. You're exhausted now and can't even raise your hands. Please, drink some sweet juice to restore your magic reserve. Because if you don't you'll fall asleep in no time."

"Yes, you're right, Mrs Clara, thank you!" the man raised his hand heavily and took a mug from the table. One of the nurses filled it with orange juice for him. The man's hand was trembling and the drink was splashing. Professor noted sluggishly that he couldn't even remember who had taken care of him. "We still need to talk to the parents. I can't fall asleep just now."

"I'll deal with the father," the woman suggested.

"Mrs Clara, I can't let you carry this burden," Professor objected.

"Oh, just stop it, please," his colleague was annoyed. "I shift the worst part on your shoulders — you have to talk to the mother."

She got up from her chair unsteadily and slowly moved to the exit of the doctors' lounge. She wasn't as hard hit today as Professor was. A black-haired young healer has aged fifteen years that morning. That wasn't such a big problem, the man would grow younger after getting some sleep. He'll definitely start breaking girls' hearts again.

A stumpy man in his forties was sitting in the waiting room. He was fiddling with something and seemed to be gazing somewhere deep inside himself. Upon noticing the healer the man got up and rushed to her.

"I'm so sorry," said Mrs Clara gently. The man's face fell, and the woman hastily added: "Your wife is fine now. But we couldn't save your son. We had almost lost our Professor, he gave the boy all his magical reserve. Each of us had tried our best. But your son had a pathology which could not be mended during the labor. It should have been corrected in the second trimester---"

"Murderers," the man said, looking at the tired woman with hatred. Mrs Clara recoiled from the darkness that seemed to be coming from him. "I'll take revenge on you for my son, be sure."

"Security!" yelled the woman.

"Oh, please," the man smiled disgustingly. "I'm leaving. You can live. For now."

Chapter 1

I was sitting on the roof and thinking about what I should do next. My shift in the hospital ended a few hours ago, but it was not yet time to go back home. Today I had to make a decision that could change my whole life. On the one hand, there was my peace of mind, and on the other — my feelings and a new job, unimaginably interesting, but dangerous. I had been dreaming about this job for thirteen years. I became a professional in my field thanks to this dream. I could remember how it all began as if it was yesterday.

"Helga, come here!" my Dad called me. He gave me my first magic cucumber that day. No, in fact this vegetable is called Colligit Truncis, but we were simply calling it a magic cucumber among us. You just have to bite off a piece, and the magical flow concentrates in one place, which allows you to use it more efficiently, without wasting your time and energy on collecting grains all over your body. I turned twelve that day, and it was The Day of the first magic initiation for me. Therefore, I needed a piece of this vegetable, which looked like an indigo-colored gnarled gherkin.

"Don't be afraid, baby," suggested my Father. I timidly bit a little piece and almost spat it out. What a bitter thing!

"You may not chew it, but you have to swallow it," patiently explained my Dad. "It's good that cucumbers are so bitter, otherwise people would eat them in excessive quantities. Such consumption of magic plants is harmful for the body."

After being tortured by a bitter blue botanical oddity, I quickly ran to my school, where I handed a pass to the testing room over to security guard. I was admitted quickly to save time. The effect of the cucumber is not endless and nobody really wants to chew it again because of one's own sluggishness. Well, at least I thought so in my twelve.

My school was a huge complex of buildings, including different lecture halls, training facilities, a laboratory department, a sector of magical experiments, a testing room and a greenhouse where magic plants grew. There were also different technical rooms such as a dining room, locker rooms, showers, and the first-aid post. The testing room was slightly away from the main lecture building. This small room was isolated from any influence. Neither sounds, nor external lighting, nor magical flows could penetrate it. Nothing could affect the first initiations of students.

I was met by a young woman in a pretty and stylish gray dress. Miss Kathy wasn't very beautiful, but the ability to choose stylish clothes to her fit distinguished her from other women. This is what girls from senior courses said about her, and I've absolutely agreed with them. Miss Kathy told me to sit down on a comfortable soft chair, put a helmet on my head and opened a special screen in front of my face.

"Relax and close your eyes please," she suggested. "Breathe in a little through your nose at your usual pace. Then open your eyes and look straight ahead. Pictures will appear on the screen and helmet sensors will read your reaction to these images. At the end of the test I'll tell you the result."

As for me, I didn't see any sense in this test. My parents knew that I had a big talent to be a healer. Such talent can be seen from the moment a child learns to speak and begins to ask questions. But I thought that if it was necessary, I should do this testing. I followed the instructions of the tester.

"Healer!" proclaimed Miss Kathy after testing. I sighed in relief and grunted. As I said earlier, I'm a doctor. "But your Gift has considerable inclination to the martial magic based on fire."

I almost fell off the chair after these words. How could I possess any martial magic? I'm scared of spiders! I love mice. I love all animals, even vipers. All of my family members are like that. My Father specializes in magical botany, my Mother specializes in pediatrics and my Brother specializes in magical zoology. All of them are healers. Myself included. But spiders, like the rest of insects, are on a par with evil spirits for me. And martial magicians fight with such evil spirits. In addition, martials also become the guard or soldiers. In any case, such sphere of activity is definitely not for me. There's a legend in our family that my great-grandfather was working for the secret service of the King.

Officially, it's believed that he was also occupied with healing. But Mom hinted a couple of times that something was not true there. Perhaps it was he who had thrown this "present" into my genetic magic card.

Feeling doomed, I took a piece of paper with my verdict and trudged to the dean of the school.

"It's curious," said the dean, rubbing his chin. "Well, Helga, my congratulations on the initiation and selection of the future training program! What do you want to specialize in?"

"Healing!" I blurted out. "I don't want to be a martial magician! I'm scared of spiders! And I don't like to fight!"

"Oh, yes, I see," the dean grinned. "Well, let healing be your main direction. But we can't ignore the second direction, which is very strong in your magical gift. Therefore, some disciplines that are mandatory for militants will be included in your individual training program. You'll start studying it from the new school year. You can go home now and celebrate your birthday. But please return to your classes tomorrow."

It's easy to say 'Celebrate'! I could only think about all these tough martial magic exercises. No, I wasn't afraid of weapons and exercises. All students have trained their bodies during usual sport classes, and I saw a lot of benefit for myself in such training. But there were all these classes about overcoming fears, where the teacher had to force me to fight against my personal fear — a giant spider...

When I came home, my Mother asked me about my bad mood. I told her all about my new training program. Mom winked at me mysteriously and pulled me into my parent's bedroom. She took an old photo album out of the safe deposit and opened it in the center.

"Oh, I've never seen this album before," I was surprised.

"Of course, you haven't! Who'd have shown such horror to children?" said Mom and pointed her finger at one photo. "Look here."

I looked at it. It was black and white, without any movement or volume, very old. And there was a picture of my great-grandfather surrounded by strange creatures. They did not resemble spiders, but they also didn't have much in common with the magical creatures of our planet. They were closest to snakes and octopuses. As for me, they were looking like scaly octopuses with big weird eyes.

"These are the Grenons," said Mom. "They are top secret. I just know their name and I have just seen this picture. Only martial healers can work with them. And there are some other... m-m-m... entities in the same category. I've always been very interested, but I'm not a martial healer. But you are. And you'll have the opportunity to get access to this secret. Well, do you feel better now?"

It was a wonderful birthday gift for me! The Grenons didn't inspire fear, although I understood that they are probably dangerous. They inspired awe, aroused curiosity and the desire to become closer to their world. Looking at them, I suspected that they're intelligent, but their mind is alien to ours. I thought that I would study hard just to come closer to this secret.

I must say that all the people in our world have some magical potential. There are more gifted and less gifted people, but no one is completely devoid of magic. Directions vary of course, but after all, people's talents differ as well. A magical gift allows us to work with planetary bowels, weather, living matter, atoms and electrons, plasma . . . And it does not determine the profession. The weatherman can go to study and become an ordinary doctor, and the atomic magician can choose the path of a baker. However, usually those who possess the magic of fire and plasma become bakers.

Actually, healers become doctors, botanists, zoologists, microbiologists, veterinarians and reincarnation specialists (whom evil tongues sometimes call necromancers). Before talking to my Mom I wanted to become a doctor. And what was the name of a profession which I was thinking about from that day, I didn't know.

Chapter 2

Next nine years of studying were very difficult for me. Yes, my teachers didn't train me according to the full program of martial magicians, but taking classes in two specializations at once was not easy at all. The matter was complicated by the fact that I'm not a very outgoing and sociable person, so it was difficult to ask for help from my peers. I had to do everything myself. That was probably good, because the information is better absorbed this way. But it was hard.

Thirteen more years have passed since my initiation. I was studying carefully in both specializations, hiding the reasons for such zeal from everyone. After school I went to work at the city's main maternity hospital for women in labor with pathologies. A healer must be present at every birth to correct any problem that ordinary obstetricians can't handle. In our maternity hospital there was a whole team of healers led by Professor.

There were only three men among us — a hefty and bald obstetrician-gynecologist; a young thin nurse, who had considerable strength in his sinewy hands to easily shift women in labor on stretchers, if it was necessary; and Professor. He was of a medium build, not too tall for a man, young, incredibly handsome and single. The whole unmarried part of our team was ogling him. Even some women in labor blushed at the sight at our leader. It felt like there was some kind of inner strength in him, nourished by the healer's magic. And this strength was insanely attractive for women.

I'm not a naive nymph batting my eyelashes at the sight of men. My character is secretive, I don't open my soul to all winds, but I also don't avoid communication and companies. I was dating one of the martial magicians of my age when both of us were in the last school year. My parents even allowed me to live together with him. But the relationship didn't last long — it ended after the first head of the hydra which I saw one day when I opened the refrigerator in the kitchen. The guy didn't even understand why we'd broken up.

Professor had been supervising my practice for all four years — right after my school graduation. For two years I had been receiving skills in all major areas of medicine, including traumatology and anesthesia. I used to hand Professor all the relevant reports at the end of each part of practice. At that time we saw each other very rarely — once a month or two. For the last two years I've been working in the hospital and was seeing him almost every day. I used to greet him without raising my eyes, because I was shy to even look at my boss. Mom told me that I'm beautiful, but I had always waved her words off. It is my Mom who's beautiful! She's a slim, petite, even fragile woman with refined features and a pitch black hair without a touch of gray. I could never understand what she had found in my Father. Dad's a very tall, heavy-set, even stoutish man with red hair. I inherited considerable height from him. Five feet and ten inches for a woman — that's a bit too much as for me. Especially in comparison with my Mother's five feet and three inches. I looked at men including Professor as an equal, and I've become insecure and bashful because of that. In my opinion, a woman should be much shorter than a man. But I have to say that I received from my Dad a real gift — luxurious copper-brown hair, for which I've never been ashamed. In general, I used to consider my appearance to be average, and therefore I tried to look independent and communicate with Professor only for work.

But today was a holiday, we all drank a little (it was impossible to drink a lot, expectant mothers do not choose when to give birth, and our team had to always be in working condition) and cheered up quite a bit. I went into the doctors' lounge and saw Professor there, looking out the window thoughtfully.

"You know," I told him, "today is the anniversary of our acquaintance. Exactly four years ago right after my school you interviewed me here in this very room, and in the evening you added me as a friend on a social network."

Professor smiled. I looked down, because looking at him when he smiles is painful. Not a single female eye can stand this radiance. At least my eyes couldn't.

"Tell me please Helga, why did you agree to undergo a complete medical and magical examination at my request? Few people agree to this. Almost everyone wants to have the confidentiality of personal information and hide it from other people. And the procedure is not so pleasant, frankly."

It seemed to me, or did I really hear the excitement in his voice? He asked a weird question in response to my remark about the anniversary, but ok. . .

"I trust you," I simply answered. And then he stepped towards me, quickly hugged and kissed me. I didn't understand immediately what was going on.

We were kissing self-forgetfully. I enjoyed every moment. The mixture of enthusiasm, magic, wine and disbelief in what was happening was almost explosive. I broke the kiss, barely sensing the insistent knock on the door, breaking through the veil of madness. Professor sat me down at the table carefully, facing the window, back to the entrance. He straightened his disheveled hair and went to open the door (when did it get closed?). I found one of the medical cards on the table and buried myself in it, hiding my kissed lips.

"Did the lock break down again, closing the door?" our overweight obstetrician muttered grudgingly when Professor opened the door. "And I've left the key in the pocket of my jacket. I have to move it into my uniform shirt."

He was muttering, rummaging through the closet and paying no attention at us. Professor was sitting on the edge of my table, looking at my embarrassment mockingly. I guess I was really funny with my nose buried in paper like a shortsighted old woman.

"Let's get out of here," he whispered to me when the obstetrician dived into the closet again, looking for his missing key. We ran out of the doctors' lounge and went up the hospital roof.

"What if they are going to need us?" I asked.

"They'll call us," Professor drew me to his body, kissing again.

You probably know how all this happens. We felt neither coolness nor time. I didn't know how many days, hours or seconds had passed.

"You're so independent!" he was whispering to me between kisses. "You're so proud! You were walking by and never even looked at me. I was exhausted! I smiled at you, and you looked down. I was sad about it, and you asked if everything was good with women in labor! I got sick, hoping to get your signature broth from your hands. You've cooked it for every ill colleague. But not for me! You're my cruel star."

I laughed and kissed him back. And he continued:

"And today was a real miracle! You spoke to me! Anniversary! Oh, Lord! Am I not just a boss? I said to myself: 'Kiss her! Well, maybe she'll slap you, but at least you'll get the kiss, finally! Maybe she will not have time to hit you?'"

After the end of my duty at the maternity hospital, I was sitting and thinking on the roof of my parents' house, which was wet from rain. A cool April night full of joy and romance didn't allow me to tune into serious thoughts. I wasn't cold, since my element of the martial magic is fire, so I can warm myself with it anytime. Some teenagers were sitting with a guitar on a bench at a small square near the house. They were quietly playing something unobtrusive. Echoes of other people's emotions, layered upon mine, came to me from there. At some point, a huge striped cat sat next to me. All the people on our street fed this cat from time to time. It has rarely allowed somebody to stroke it, but for some reason it condescended and succumbed to me tonight and even purred a couple of times under my hand. It was stroking the cat that had finally helped me to concentrate. I suspect that pets too have some kind of magic, despite the official refutation of this assumption by the magic science. My experience has told me that these creatures always take away excessive emotions, both negative and positive.

Honestly, I was supposed to come back from my job five hours ago, but I didn't have the strength to go home. I switched off my phone. I could see from the roof how my

Father went somewhere restlessly, probably looking for me. But I wasn't worrying about it too much. Family members can feel each other at a distance. Kidnapping is a completely impossible situation in our world as everyone will immediately take alarm in that case. Dad knew that I was safe, that nothing was threatening me. Yes, it was very weird to him that his daughter didn't come back home and didn't answer calls. But it was nothing to worry about.

Even if my Father was going to visit the hospital, I've warned everyone there that I want to have some time for myself. Colleagues would repeat these words to my Dad, and he would come back home. And I'll get the necessary time to put my raging hormones, emotions and magical flows in order.

It wasn't even about the kisses. In the end, I'm an adult woman and it was the right time for me to start a relationship. There was no sense in hiding this fact from my parents. The point was different. After the passions calmed down a bit, Professor admitted that I was soon to be transferred to another job.

"It must have something to do with those Grenons. . ." I thought out loud.

"How could you know that?" Professor was surprised. "Yes, it's about the Grenons. And it's about the Clevres, and the Lonquies. There are too few martial healers on our planet. They've been gathered all over the Earth in one place. This is a unique combination of magical flows. Usually martial magic is not compatible with healing. But such people exist and have been invited to work with the creatures that are too important for humanity. People's magical field maps are similar to theirs. We look for common ground and when we find it, we develop new abilities in human beings, such as vitality, magical potential, the power of thought and so on."

"My great-grandfather was a martial healer, I saw his picture with the Grenons. When it comes to me – I get it, but how do you know about it?" I asked him.

"Did you think you'd practice here without supervision?" Professor grinned. "Well, as I said, there are very few martial healers. Each of us is like a diamond. If you agree to accept this offer, tomorrow you and I will be redeployed to another place. And there will be another professor here."

"How can I object when there are so few of us? Do I have a choice?"

"There is always a choice. You can stay here as a doctor. The new job is complicated, dangerous, often nightly, because the rhythms of our life do not coincide with the Grenons and the Lonquiest."

"My family will be against my night job. . ."

"You can't tell them about it. But if all your objections consist of the dissatisfaction of the family with the work schedule, then this can be easily resolved. The Department has a special procedure for such cases. Employees are usually married off. Martial healers generally come to work in the Department at a young age, and the wedding procedure is often the easiest way out. The family usually has no questions about what the employee is doing at night. However, there are always some exceptions to this rule. Anyway, there are several specialists in legends and cover at the Department, so we'll figure it out."

"Did you marry someone too?"

Professor cheered up.

"My mother is a martial healer. I'd known what kind of job I was being prepared for since childhood, and my family members had never asked me where I hang out at night. And it's easier for a man to hide his business. Usually we're not so patronized by relatives as women."

So now I was sitting on the roof and thinking. The new job has been attracting me like a magnet since the day of my twelfth birthday. But getting married? Professor said with a smile that he's ready to play the role of my fiancé and husband, but I didn't want him to. His words poured over me like a cold shower. I didn't want to get married for a job. Not with him. And what if all of this madness today was just a fight for the sake of a loyal healer? I indulged in my feelings like liquid honey, but what if he's just succeeded to persuade a new employee to take up a dangerous night job? I was trying not to think about how many times Professor was married before me.

However, what was there to think about? The Grenones, the Clevres, and the Lonquies (how do they look, these Clevres and Lonquies?) have been captivating me since my childhood as the most unattainable dream. And I could figure out my relationship later.

"Yes?" I heard Professor's voice on my phone.
"I'm in."

Chapter 3

The next day my supervisor was no longer at the hospital. His place was taken by a dry elderly doctor who brought peace into the souls of the female part of the staff, but greatly ruined the mood of some young employees. It became clear immediately who had an eye on the former boss.

I was only glad, because I wanted to leave my old job quietly and without any negative feelings. Our young ladies would quickly know that something was happening between me and Professor if he was to stay at the hospital for longer. And now the girls were upset, they've concentrated on discussing the new professor, and so I was sent off with the greatest possible warmth. I handed over the cases and formalized all the necessary permits for my new job. My transfer documents came very quickly, literally in the morning, and the change occurred without a hitch.

Three days later Professor came to our house with flowers for me and my Mom, and alcohol for my Dad. I warned my parents about the upcoming visit but they were clearly dumbfounded by what was happening and didn't have time to get used to the new situation yet. At the same time my Mother and I set the table, chasing the nervous Father and my impudent cat out of the kitchen. A little later there was the solemn presentation of the fiancé to the family. We were sitting at the table; the future groom was joking and gazing lovingly at me. Even my picky cat that hated strangers changed his usual strategy of behavior and perched on Professor's lap. I tried to drive away this insolent fellow that was spoiled by our common family attention, but the guest stopped me and kept stroking a whiskered muzzle all evening. Parents were happy, the cat was purring. I was diligently playing my role too, habitually lowering my eyes when Professor smiled at me.

"How did you meet?" Mom was asking standard things which are probably interesting to absolutely every mother in the world.

"At work, Mom," I said tiredly, because the answers to such questions annoy probably every daughter in the world.

"Oh, Helga is so independent! I didn't know how to draw her attention to me," Professor was in good humor. He gazed at my lips and smiled again. It seemed that he, unlike me, was sincerely enjoying the dinner and the conversation. "I had to go on the offensive and kiss her immediately."

"She's the same as her mother at this age!" Daddy said proudly. I looked at him in surprise. I have never heard this part of my parents' story. "Her mother had walked around me in a huge arc for several months, until I waylaid her in a dark alley with flowers in my hands. That evening I got a kiss and a black eye. Weren't you beaten, young man?"

"Your daughter didn't have time to hit me," laughed Professor. "Although for the sake of truth, all this didn't happen in the dark alley and Helga was in good mood after a small party. In a different case I would have probably got a bruise too."

I smiled at him. No, he wouldn't.

Mom began to ask Professor about the peculiarities of working at the hospital (as if my stories were not good enough for her) and soon they began to discuss some topics related to pediatrics. Dad didn't intervene, although he was listening. But he was looking at me attentively, and I was trying to pretend that it was also incredibly interesting for me to participate in the discussion about the nuances of the pediatrician's work.

After dinner, my fictitious fiancé asked my parents to let me go out with him tonight.

"We'll ride around the capital," he lied to my family. "I promise that in the morning Helga will come back home safe and sound."

Mom laughed and winked at me, Dad frowned but didn't mind. It seemed to me for a brief moment that my Father saw my sadness, but I dismissed this thought — as far as I knew, he had no magical gift of a mentalist. I went to change for a walk. It was necessary to choose something that would pass as both the clothes for a date, a work uniform, and also as a flight set. Upon further thought I decided to wear dark green trousers and a white fitted shirt with a stand-up collar. I put on a raincoat on top. April nights weren't warm enough yet.

"Do you think they sensed it?" Professor asked me when we went up on the roof and rushed into the sky.

"I'm sure they didn't," I said sadly. My companion took my hand, gently squeezing my fingers. I hastened to change the subject of our conversation. "Listen, why was it necessary for me to work at the maternity hospital?"

"Every martial healer has to learn how to control the energies that run at birth. We cannot be present at conception, therefore it's necessary to instill new abilities into people at the stage of birth," Professor grinned. "At this moment a child's magical field breaks away from the one of his mother, and becomes susceptible to infusions from the outside. Only a martial healer can catch the tune for new abilities due to the specifics of the magic of our wards. And he also has to pass them on to the next generation of people, weaving them into the flows of the newborns' magic. It's enough to transfer the new magic technology to five or seven percent of babies and after a couple of generations all humanity can possess this new knowledge. It absorbs into the general magic cards somehow strangely — it doesn't pass from father to son or from mother to daughter by blood, but it's as if it spreads throughout the human race. We just need a certain percentage of those who possess it and by the third generation everyone will already have it. The Department would like to spread it faster, but we can't keep abreast of such pace because there are too few of us. I was passing on the ability of quick regeneration to the babies in our maternal hospital while you were practicing."

"But now the hospital stuff works without us."

"Yes, but I passed on more than enough for now, because we were working at the institution for women in labor with pathologies from all over the country. And now I need to get you to the Department in time. Everyone is looking forward to seeing you. Tomorrow my colleague will go to the other side of the planet to start working on passing the new abilities there. I'll substitute for him at the Department until he comes back."

"Why can't I tell my family? Why is it such a secret?"

"Too many people want to possess new knowledge and abilities single-handedly. At the start of the Department, when all of the information was in open access, our specialists and their family members were bribed and threatened. Then a decision on secrecy was made. Since then it took several centuries to hide everything and there are only vague myths for now which are perpetuated, by the way, by the global network users. The Internet is a useful invention, but there are also some troubles with it for us. We learned how to deal with this oncoming wave. We create our own thought-through myths that have nothing to do with reality. And as a result, people stop believing in rumors that are dangerous for us."

"And what if I haven't agreed to take up this job?"

"We'd have to erase a part of your memory" he averted his eyes and then looked at me again. "But you have agreed, haven't you?"

"Are you kidding? I've been dreaming about this job since my twelfth birthday!"

"Why so?" my companion was interested.

"That day my mom showed me a photo of my great-grandfather with the Grenons."

Professor frowned. We were flying through the night city, heading somewhere to the outskirts, in the direction of the royal botanical garden. Skyscrapers and spires of ancient buildings were flashing by. In many windows the light was on, because it was still not too late. From time to time we met other people who just like us preferred flying to ground traveling. Special streets have been reserved for flights, and there was no risk of catching on wires or coming into collision with a trade sign.

"We have to do something about this family picture," Professor said.

"Oh no, please!" I exclaimed fearfully. "My parents didn't blab for so many years, so I don't think they'll do it now."

"Helga, it's impossible to leave everything as it is, sorry. There can be some very big problems if the photo falls into the wrong hands. We cannot allow even the smallest possibility of it. The very fact that such a photo exists suggests that your great-grandfather has committed a crime. We'll teach you the technique of memory obliteration so that you can take the photo and erase your mom's memories about the Grenons. In this case we'll stay out of it, which will be even better, because the process of memory obliteration involves a trusting relationship. Will that do for you?"

I nodded. There was no reason and sense to object. I suddenly realized what a serious organization this Department was. They wouldn't even ask me. They'd obliterate my memories as well. And Professor would not dare to interfere.

"By the way, what kind of technique is this memory obliteration? As far as I know, our healers don't have it."

"This is one of the abilities that we've acquired from the Lonquies. And by the way, it's one of the most dangerous ones. Nobody knows about it, except for the employees of the Department. We haven't even told the authorities yet, because we think they'll want to use it for their own purposes. Espionage, military tasks, interrogations and experiments — this technology will untie some hands. They have to learn how to act without it."

I imagined the scope of application and cringed.

"So you haven't been passing it to newborns, have you?"

"Of course, we haven't. Neither this, nor several others which are also dangerous for humanity."

"But such a technology could be used for good too — for example, in psychiatry or the rehabilitation of children who saw terrible things."

"It's too dangerous. How can we control its use? If we just give people something like that, they'll begin to employ it against competitors or enemies immediately. We have to find the ways to control this process. Until it happens humanity will have to live without the technique of memory obliteration."

"But maybe it's possible to find a medical institution where experts will work under the supervision of the Department?"

"Yes, in theory it's possible to do so. But only adult martial healers can learn how to use these new techniques. The rest of people have to get this knowledge at the time of conception or birth. And who'll agree to determine the fate of his child immediately and as a matter of fact, to leave the baby at our complete disposal? Do you understand that we'll have to take away the newborn from his parents in order to keep the baby under supervision and bring it up properly?"

"And what about the children of the Department's employees? Nobody would have to take anyone away, everyone is near and everything is under control."

"You can do it when you have your own children," my interlocutor was joking. "We have arrived, by the way."

'Your own children,' he said. Not 'our children', but 'your own'. What a fool I was! What was I was hoping for? I had to make sense out of this fictitious marriage and other stuff.

"So, you have to get ready now," Professor continued. "Our employees are cheerful, they'll greet you joyfully. Sometimes they are too enthusiastic, but don't be afraid. And one more thing — stop calling me Professor, please. I'm just Dun here. Professor! I haven't got used to this title in four years."

Chapter 4

We flew over the botanical garden to its very center. Magical plants were glittering around us like colorful lights, forming a stunningly beautiful composition for the healer's inner gaze. As if the festive illumination was on throughout the garden. I could see this beauty since my early childhood, and this is how my parents had found out about my main gift. I've already been accustomed to this sight, but when the magical plants are gathered in one place it still causes a storm of excitement in my soul. We landed near a huge covered pavilion. Apparently such pavilions were used for conducting experiments with plants. My companion opened the door and we stepped inside a small vestibule with an electronic lock on the inner door.

Dun. Wow! He hasn't got used to the title of professor. And how can I get used to calling him simply by name? All these events were happening so quickly that I didn't have time to adapt.

Meanwhile my companion pressed the button with his thumb and a newly appeared window scanned the iris of his eye. Then another window opened at the door and someone said: "The magical cast of the aura coincides". And only after that they let us in.

"She agreed!" Dun said loudly and the whole building exploded with joyful cries. I was being greeted from everywhere; I saw a whole forest of waving hands. The guard at the door shook hands with my companion and kissed my wrist.

"You said that there are only a few of us," I was very surprised. "And here I can see at least a hundred of employees."

"One hundred and thirty, to be correct," Dun told me. "And right now there is about two-thirds of the stuff. The others have daily work. But there are only thirteen martial healers in the Department. The rest of the employees are the accompanying staff. Here we have security sector and documentation department, lawyers and accountants, laboratory assistants and computer technicians, cooks, cleaners, suppliers, assistants in working with wards etc. Director, for example, is not a martial healer. He's a manager who simply does his job well. He's a mentalist just a bit. This gift makes it easier for him to negotiate. Let's visit him because he stayed at the Department after his day shift specifically to meet you."

Director was a short, respectable man with a tenacious calculating gaze and a protruding abdomen. When we entered his office he briskly jumped out of his table and went to shake Professor's hand and kiss my wrist.

"Congratulations Dun! Congratulations Helga! There are only some formalities left after which you'll start working in our team. Do you want to work with us?"

"Yes, sir!"

"Oh, what a cool girl! Just like the military specialist!" Director was impressed. "Why do you want to work here?"

"This job is incredibly interesting for me!" I admitted timidly. Director was delighted.

"Then it will be easy for you to work with our team. We all are here for the same reason."

"Sir, what formalities are we talking about?" I dared to inquire.

"First, you'll be checked by security guards for loyalty to the fundamental idea and the absence of ulterior motives. Dun has already given us your medical and magical cards, so this step can be skipped. By the way, you have an amazing potential as a fire magician, I'm impressed by it!" Director showered praise on me. I was embarrassed, but he promptly continued. "Secondly, we'll formalize all the necessary paperwork; take your aura cast, a picture of the iris as well as the other access parameters. You'll be given a badge with your name and a photo on it. Safety instructions will be handed over to you in the same department."

"What safety instructions are we talking about?" I asked again.

"Our wards — the Grenons, the Clevres and the Lonquies — have their own characteristics," Dun intervened. "Each species has some dangerous features which every employee must be aware of and take into consideration. The Grenons, for example, live in water and don't have the sense of time. They also leave a hypnotic impression on beginners. That's why they can accidentally drag an employee into the water and drown him. The Clevres are very big and heavy — there were cases of people being squeezed by them---"

"And the Lonquies are mentalists of the highest level," Director intervened into our conversation. "Previously, there were various troubles with our employees, including madness, which happened after communication with them. Therefore, we have developed a whole system of security measures that must be learned by heart. Every martial healer should pass such an exam. After this exam, you'll be taught the necessary magical techniques and allowed to work with our wards. You have to learn how to facilitate the accelerated regeneration, how to use the technique of memory obliteration and so on. By the way, we don't have a single martial healer with the fire element. Since your great-grandfather there have only been four more of such specialists. We're really in need of such an employee."

"I can't believe you remember my great-grandfather," I said incredulously.

"Of course I don't!" Director smiled. "But I must know all the martial healers who work or have ever worked for us. Now go to Julie please. It was nice to meet you, Helga!"

We left the Director's office and turned right.

"Where are we going?" I asked Dun.

"We have to visit the security guards department. The testing is conducted by Julie. Something tells me that you'll like her," he answered.

We walked just a couple of steps and knocked on the white door. "Come in," said a pleasant female voice. It was as if my Mother was sitting behind the door.

The woman who met us in a completely white room really looked like my Mom. She had the same fair skin, jet-black hair and a miniature body constitution.

"Hello, Helga!" she hastened to meet us with a pleasant smile. "I've been waiting for you. Come in! Hi, Dun! And goodbye! Seriously, wait outside the door please. Or better go about your own business."

"Julie," Professor tried to object, but she interrupted him.

"Dun, I'm a specialist of the highest rank. I! See! EVERYTHING! So don't shine around here, please!"

For some unknown to me reason, my companion was embarrassed.

"But will you tell me later?"

"Don't you even dream about it!" said the woman and turned to me. "Come in, darling. Sit here, please."

I sat on the soft snow-white chair which was located in the very center of the room. It was dangerous to argue with this iron lady who spoke to Dun in such a way. In general, Professor lost all his respectability here and began to look even younger. It was evident that in the Department he was just an employee and not a big boss. Suddenly I realized that I don't know the age of my fictitious fiancé.

"Don't be afraid, darling. You have nothing to worry about. I'll just ask you a couple of questions and you'll go to the other rooms," said Julie and then turned to Dun again. "Why are you still here? Out!"

"Damn those professional ethics," he muttered, leaving the office. "Paul will not tell me, and---"

The remark was cut short when the door closed behind him.

"What was he talking about?" I dared to ask the security guard.

"He wants me to tell him what you think about him," Julie said bluntly. "Do you want me to do so?"

"No, please, don't!" I was scared.

"Hush, calm down darling. I won't. Honestly, I don't approve of these kindergarten games nor do I understand them. If he wants to know he should ask, right?"

I nodded and tried to calm down. This man won't ask.

"So, darling, I'm the aura specialist. You and I are going to chat like two girlfriends, and I'll watch your emotions during this conversation. If it makes the process easier for you, I can pour a cup of tea. After the conversation, I'll give an opinion about your loyalty to Director. There will be no details, just a general conclusion. Do you agree?"

"Of course, I do!" I had nothing to hide, so such a procedure wouldn't bother me at all.

"Okay. So, you want to work with us?"

"I absolutely do. I have been dreaming about it since I was twelve."

"Why so?"

"It's incredibly interesting for me. On the day of my first initiation, I was terribly upset that I would be trained as a martial healer. And then my mother showed me a black and white picture of my great-grandfather with the Grenons. It seemed to me that the Universe looked at me from their eyes that day."

"It's not surprising for me, because the Grenons had been the inhabitants of another planet before coming to ours."

"Wow! Where did they come from?"

"I wasn't there at that time, I'm not so ancient," Julie laughed. "But the Department's early archives say that several hundred years ago we had a meteor shower. Among meteorites, strange capsules fell on the ground. Upon touching the soil or water they cracked up, leaving no residue except the contents – which were, in fact, the Grenons. Some of them died. But those who fell into the water survived. Let's continue the procedure?"

I nodded.

"Are you ready to maintain secrecy for life regarding everything related to your work?"

"Yes. I haven't blabbed a living soul for thirteen years. My mother and I have never talked about this again. So I'm ready to be quiet about it in the future too."

"Do you have any hidden motives for getting this job?"

I was surprised.

"What hidden motives can I have?"

"For example, it can be an industrial or military espionage."

"Oh, no, no," I shook my head. "I have no hidden motives."

"I can see that you're being elusive."

"It's still Dun," I blushed.

"And that's true. If this relationship does not work out, will you leave the Department?"

"Never!"

"Well, you already saw the Grenons and they didn't frighten you, which means we can skip this question. What do you think about pigs?"

What a strange question.

"I'm fine with them. Especially with clean pigs. And with dirty ones as well. I dislike people-pigs, but you're not talking about them, are you?"

Julie shook her head and asked the next question:

"And what do you think about lizards?"

"I'm fine with all the animals. I'm afraid of insects, but I love animals."

"Ordinary healers work with insects here. You don't have to if you don't want to. Okay, you can go now. Come here for a final check after your first visits to the wards, please."

"Can I ask you a question?"

"Of course, my dear. Just don't ask me, please, to tell you how Dun feels about you," Julie cheered up again.

"Oh, no. I just wanted to ask why do you all call the magic creatures 'wards'?"

"And how else can we call them? They are not animals, be sure, not evil, not undead. This is why martial healers had chosen such a relatively neutral term. The Lonques, of course, disagree with it. They consider us their wards. But nobody asks their opinion. That's it, go to the next door along the corridor, please. I'll call them now."

I said goodbye and left the white room. Dun was waiting for me in the hallway. His face was thoughtful and I decided that he was saddened or dissatisfied with something.

"Why is everything so white there?" I asked Professor under my breath.

"Why are you whispering?" Dun was surprised, distracted from his thoughts. "Julie's room is completely soundproof. This is how she maintains full confidentiality during the testing. And the room is white, because the changes in an aura are best visible in such an interior. Julie says she can notice the tiniest glimpse of emotion even if someone tries to hide it."

"And does she spend all her time there? How has she not lost her mind in such a sterile colorless place?" I asked. As for me, I would definitely not be able to work in such a room.

"First of all, there's a projector, and she can always project a magical illusion onto the walls. Everything becomes colorful and beautiful immediately. And secondly, Julie spends a lot of time at a security desk. She watches what the employees are doing. So keep in mind that you can't hide from anyone here."

"Dun, how old are you?" I dared to ask.

"Don't you know?" he was surprised again. "I'm thirty-four. And I'll turn thirty-five in three months."

Why did I think he was a little older? Was it the white doctor's smock and the title of Professor that gave him some solidity in my eyes?

Chapter 5

In the next room security made a name badge for me with my photo on it, took my aura cast and fingerprints. Why do photos on badges always turn out so ugly? Although I don't think highly of my appearance, it cannot be compared to the picture on my badge.

Dun was sitting on a chair and talking with security guards about different things, while I was passing all the procedures. It was very interesting for me to know about how often he came here during his work at the hospital. At the end of all the paperwork, one document was handed to Professor for signature. Then security gave it to me to sign as well, I saw that Dun's name was in the column 'Warrantor'. They had a strange system here in general. Will Professor be responsible for my mistakes?

Outside the door I asked this question directly to Dun. He nodded.

"Yes, I'll be responsible while you're on your probation term. But I don't believe that such a situation is possible. Over the years of your practice, you've proved yourself to be an extremely collected and serious employee. Sometimes you were even too serious," my companion said it with a smile.

I decided not to stop at this moment and continued questioning:

"How long is the trial period?"

"Helga, this is just a formality. Not a single martial healer has ever left the Department having failed the probation period. This is just an ordinary procedure for all the employees of the Department, without any exception."

"Dun, I didn't ask you about that."

"The trial period usually lasts three months. We will celebrate the end of it as well as my birthday on the same day. But don't worry; they'll immediately pay your salary at full rate."

Honestly, it wasn't my salary that I was worrying about. Firstly, I didn't want to let Professor down either willingly or involuntarily. What if I can't do my work well? You never know what kind of tasks awaits a martial healer here.

Secondly, being under constant supervision like a small child is humiliating, as for me. And in the case of Dun as a warrantor, it has also been very nervous. I decided to voice this consideration in the form of a new question.

"And will you accompany me everywhere in the Department for all these three months?"

"No, of course I won't. As I said, this is just a formality. But you can always get my absolute attention," Dun whispered the last words into my ear.

Hmm, I felt that having this new job may turn out to be very difficult. But it was great that Professor's mood was good again.

"This is Paul — our Reincarnologist. He is very talented, by the way," meanwhile, my companion introduced me to a young tall long-haired guy in a medical scrub and stylish yellow drop-shaped glasses. I knew that such glasses help reincarnation specialists to see the parts of the other world that are generally available to them even better.

"Hi, beautiful!" Paul blurted out to me. I was embarrassed and he held out his hand. "Nice to meet you, Helga!"

"Never mind," Dun laughed. "He says such words to all beautiful women. But he's been crazy about Lina for a year. There she is, sitting at the computer in a white coat. She's one of our doctors who don't have the admixture of martial magic. We have such specialists here."

"Why hasn't he told her that?" overcoming my embarrassment, I shook Paul's outstretched hand with a smile.

"He has. But she brushed off his compliments. And she did the right thing, because compliments must be given to only one woman, not to all of them. The whole Department knows that Paul is crazy about Lina, but she hasn't become aware of it yet."

I grunted. It was possible that she'd seen everything, but hadn't shown it. I should ask this to her somewhere away from the guys. At least there would be a topic for reflection that I could distract myself from my relations with Professor.

"Let's go to our lab, Helga," Paul suggested. "I'll make you a tour and tell you about our sphere of work, and Dun will take care of his affairs for now."

"Yes, thanks, Paul!" Dun said to Reincarnologist and turned to me. "You can go with Paul, and at the end of the night I'll take you back home and hand you over to your parents. If you have more questions, I'll answer them along the way."

I nodded, and went somewhere deeper into the pavilion with Reincarnologist. By the way, the inside of the building's roof wasn't transparent. The Department looked like a full-fledged fortified building with different rooms, sectors and an extremely strict security system. Each second door had code locks with fingerprint reader buttons. A large surveillance panel with a bunch of monitors and several security guards located near the entrance. Cameras were looking at us from above, turning their mechanical heads and following us. My name badge was also a key to some rooms. I was given a list of codes that needed to be memorized by heart.

"Who's giving financial support to the Department?" I asked Paul. "A lot of money must have been invested in the technical equipment here, as I can see. And someone should pay salaries to a considerable number of staff."

"We're an international organization that is receiving funds from all countries. The sum of money depends on the number of people living in each country. We're not concerned with war, contentions and politics, because governments, thank God, are smart enough to understand our concern for the whole planet. And a couple of hundred years ago, the Department managed to patent the first invention that appeared thanks to our work. Since then, more of such patents appeared and we have received an independent source of funding. Honestly, this opened up a ton of new possibilities for us, and now we decide which magic technologies to transfer to the authorities and which to keep silent about by ourselves. And the salaries are excellent, it's almost impossible to draw over the employees."

"Can you give me an example of a patented invention?"

"The biggest part of the profit comes from cosmetology," Paul winked at me. I opened my mouth in surprise. "Women like to spend a lot of money on all sorts of lotions and creams. But the aura cannot be smeared by cosmetics. For example, you have a very beautiful aura. I can see a lot of love for the living creations in it and it's very warm! Lina, of course, has no competitors, she has sheer joy and fun in her aura, as sunshine--- but yours is beautiful too."

"Thanks! Can you focus, please?"

"So I was saying that cosmetology and perfumery bring a lot of money. For example, we have identified a magic component from the Lonquies. It allows making one's appearance more attractive. The impact is not physical, but rather mental. The Lonquies possess a mental magic and the magic of a soul. I work a lot with them. What was I talking about? Oh, yeah. We add a little of this component to the perfume. People who sprinkle themselves with it seem more attractive to the opposite sex. This perfume is being sold in huge quantities every year!"

"Is there any difference between such a perfume and the one with pheromones?" I asked. The topic was extremely interesting, both from the professional side and from the point of ensuring my own safety.

"Perfumes with pheromones, or whatever their name, are characterized by the unpredictability of reaction. It affects some people, but it doesn't influence the others. Our perfume affects everyone. The sales managers of our manufacturing partners say that men buy it as well."

"Oh my Gosh! But how can I determine whether a person uses such a perfume or not?"

"Healers can see it, reincarnologists can see it, aura specialists can see it. It looks like something alien to the magic field, and it also has yellow color."

"Ahh, yeah! I remember that my martial classmate had something like that. She mentioned a perfume that cost a lot of money. The guys really paid attention to her all the time," I said. So as a healer, I shouldn't worry about my safety. That's great!

"It was one of our products. There are a lot of such things. Come in, please!"

Paul pressed the button on the door with his thumb and had his iris scanned. He had to remove his yellow glasses for this. Apparently, no one checked the cast of his aura this time because it was an internal sector of a common structure. While Reincarnologist opened the door, I asked the last question about the perfume:

"And does anyone in the Department use such a perfume?"

"Of course not! We have so many healers here. We can see such things immediately. And in fact there's no sense in using this perfume. I think that it's only efficient when it comes to the first impression. A beautiful soul should be there under the perfume, and if somebody's attractiveness stops at their appearance then no single perfume will be of help."

Yes, I remembered that the classmate didn't really stay in relationships for a long time. Because she was a stinker.

"Pharmacology is highly developed as well. We work with a variety of extracts of magical plants, turning them into digestible pills or injections. The Department has its own pharmaceutical factory. The specialists who work there don't know anything about the main activities of our organization, so they report only to our leadership. Accordingly, its profits also sustain the needs of the Department. Well, the laboratory sector is perhaps the largest in the pavilion. And this is understandable, because the main work with wards takes place here. The rest of the premises are simply facilitating it. The documentation sector, where the legendary specialists are working, the security services sector, computer technicians, a mini-dining room, the legal department, and the offices of authorities are all secondary compared to the sectors of wards and laboratories," said Paul. We walked into the long corridor with a bunch of doors. Paul opened the first one and we stepped into a small room, where a large white box with a matte cover stood in the center.

"This is a clone box," Paul nodded at it. "It's empty now. We have a lot of them here. They only differ in sizes. We grow the most diverse types of biomass in such boxes. We started with plants, then there were mice, then ordinary animals, then magical animals. Eventually we moved on to humans and have successfully learned how to grow organs for transplantation and material for regeneration. But the process of cloning people hasn't proved successful at all."

"What do you need to clone people for?" I asked fearfully, imagining two identical Duns. I didn't know how to handle even one. . .

"Things happen," Reincarnologist shrugged philosophically. "Accidents, deaths during dangerous missions, disasters, sudden heart attacks etc. If a person dies because of old age — this is distinguishable and normal. The soul goes away quietly, nothing holds it, it's simply on its way to reincarnation. And if something happens — it's hard to watch, but we can do nothing about it for now."

"What's the problem?"

"The soul doesn't return. The body is fully prepared to take it back, but the soul can never enter it again. The halves do not reunite. Once we had almost succeeded. The man died by accident, his wife loved him very much and kept his soul thread. She didn't let him go away completely. But while we were preparing the body, she got tired. It usually takes several days to grow a body. The woman fell asleep for just five minutes and during this time something happened there. It was like someone cut the thread. The men died eventually. The Lonquies then told us that we're trying to catch the wind in a net. In their species the reincarnation occurs almost instantly through babies. They know how to make a mental cast of personality and pass it to the younger generation. While the child is growing up, the adults gradually pour the knowledge of the departed individual in it. By puberty, a young Lonquie looks like as if he hasn't died at all."

"So what, the souls have never been lost?"

"Of course not. They've registered all the souls. They can also see and distinguish them from each other."

"And what about the birth of the new ones? I mean, does the population grow?"

"It does, but rarely. They have a separate procedure for new souls. As far as I know, during the entire existence of the Department there have only been three of such babies. I haven't seen them yet and maybe never will. They told us that our work is nonsense, because we have not mastered the procedure for transmitting a person's cast and track the souls **yet**. But I can't imagine how this can be achieved given our secrecy and the number of people on the planet. And the factor of life expectancy is not taken into account by the Lonquies. If a woman has lost her husband, then she'll become old when a child with his soul and personality grows up. I think that it will be possible to adopt this procedure for human beings when we master the technology of life extension completely and start to live up to three or five hundred years. Then the several decades that are required to grow a new 'old' person will no longer be important."

"So it's impossible to create two identical people by cloning, isn't it?" I voiced my stupid fear.

"Yes, it is. The second one will be just a body without any life and soul. You can, of course, sustain this body with the help of life supporting systems. But what can be the reason for it?"

I breathed a sigh of relief and laughed at myself. Second Dun will not be happening.

"And when will I be allowed to work with the wards?"

"First you have to meet your colleagues and pass the safety measures exam. Without it you won't be allowed."

"Director gave me a whole week for this."

"That's just enough. When you get tired of the instructions, come to our laboratory, we're always in need of doctors. Let's proceed."

We left the first laboratory and went to the others. Paul showed me the work on regenerative processes, experiments in increasing life expectancy (which, by the way, were conducted on insects to speed up the process), attempts to transmit thoughts through distance and so on. Located separately, there were also premises used for the cultivation of magical plants. We went to the cosmetology laboratory, where my colleague secretly informed me that regenerative magic fits perfectly into the new recipe of a rejuvenating cream. I thought that soon the Department would have an additional increase in profits from the avalanche of sales of a new skin care product. I learned that, thanks to the mind-reading laboratory, one hundred and fifty years ago we've got the ability to feel our blood relatives. And thanks to the regeneration laboratory, we do not have unwanted pregnancies. And the ability to fly, as it turned out, has also originated at the Department. Reincarnologist introduced me to staff everywhere, and after a short time all the faces and names began to merge into one.

"You shouldn't try to remember us now," a girl at the life prolonging lab told me. "We all have been in your shoes. You can just smile at us, say hello, but don't strain your memory. Each employee has a name badge on their chest. Look at it and don't be shy. You'll remember all of us eventually."

Hmm, it seemed to me that the experiments on the transmission and reading of thoughts have been fruitful. Or, maybe, I just had everything written on my face? Nevertheless, I decided to follow the advice of my colleague and focused on asking new questions to my guide:

"What do you need ordinary healers for?"

"Has Dun already told you that there are very few martial healers? We're scattered around the world. For example, my homeland is very far from here. Lina came to the Department a year ago, following her brother from the northern part of the planet. Her brother's a martial healer and she's an ordinary one. And Dun's ancestors came here from the Yellow Archipelago. Why are you surprised?'

"He doesn't look like the representative of the Yellow race," I admitted. "Just something distant. Well, hair color, of course. And his name---"

"Ha, that was a few centuries ago. Their blood mixed so many times that you can't even track it. But I got distracted again. There are only a dozen of martial healers in the Department. Some of them work with the wards; others pass the new features of magic to newborns. We have a lot of work here. Someone has to do it. And there are a lot of tasks that don't require our unique abilities."

"And where is Lina's brother?"

"He works day shifts with the Clevres. You'll meet him soon."

"And who're you working with?"

"The Lonquies. And sometimes I visit the Grenons. When Dun wasn't here, I used to come there quite rarely. But now it's time to change my work strategy."

"You haven't seen Dun for all these four years up until this evening, have you?"

"No, that's not true. He came here sometimes. He had to hand over the reports and inform Director about your successes. But in fact, if a martial healer works in the hospital he almost never visits the Department during that period. It's just that in your case both the maternity hospital and the Department are located in the same city. This is why Dun used to visit us sometimes.

"Is it that necessary to be away from our main place of work for all four years?"

"Actually, only those who supervise the newbies take such a long time. This rarely happens. Usually it takes about two years to transfer skills."

"Are you giving me a full tour of the Department?" we left the laboratory and moved somewhere in the opposite direction.

"You don't mind, do you? For example, here we have a gym," said Paul, opening the next door. "An hour of daily training is part of the job for security guards and martial healers. Some of us stay for another hour after their shift in order to train not only our bodies, but also our magical fighting skills. Other employees are also allowed to visit the gym. For example, I often meet here an old cleaning lady walking on a treadmill. I'll introduce you to the coaches today, and starting from tomorrow you'll be visiting this place regularly."

Oh my God!

Dun was standing in the area for fights and sparrings, with his back turned to me. He was wearing spacious joggers for martial arts, tied with a black belt. There was nothing else on Professor. It was so good that he didn't know that I was there, gazing at him!

Up until today, I've always seen Dun in a white doctor's smock. In the house of my parents he appeared in a comfortable wide shirt and trousers, and this was already a considerable shock for me. But can you imagine my feelings at the moment when I saw him with his shirt off, throwing the adversary over his shoulder? My mouth simply turned dry and I licked my lips unconsciously.

If everything between us was the same as it had been before this anniversary kiss, this probably wouldn't happen to me. I would just lower my eyes as always, thinking that this man was not for me. But now, when I remembered how he kissed me, how he whispered to me about his feelings and experiences, how gently he removed the disheveled strands from my face that evening, how carefully he squeezed my fingers during the flight. . . Even if all of this wasn't true. . . Seeing him like that was more that I could handle.

I had to hide behind Paul to collect myself. Thank God, the place for fights was quite far from the entrance and was partially covered by the training machines. Professor hasn't noticed my appearance yet. I was afraid that my face would give my feelings away.

"Dun is a very good fighter," Reincarnologist told me, seeing the direction of my gaze. The guy didn't seem to notice what was happening to me, and I was very grateful to him for this. "His family is traditionally specializing in martial arts, and he has been training in this direction since his childhood. We have some guys who are learning from him when Dun has enough time for this. In my opinion, he's even better than Arthur at this."

I was so surprised that my mouth opened. Professor turned into the warrior at breakneck speed. Just one more thing was very interesting to me that moment — was Dun a professor at all or was it just a legend too?

The gym, meanwhile, was quite equipped, though not very spacious. There were simulators and a target shooting zone, sparring mats, horizontal bars and a place for exercises. And all of this fit into one room perfectly, making it possible for a couple of dozen people to train simultaneously. At the end of the hall, opposite to the entrance, I noticed an open door behind which a variety of weapons gleamed. What a big arsenal!

"Hello, Helga!" a hasty elderly woman hurried to meet me. She was wearing a black T-shirt and spacious sports breeches. These clothes accentuated her excellent physical shape. I determined that she was a martial fire magician immediately. "I'm a coach, my name is Inga. And this is my brother Arthur. I work with women, and he works with men."

On the other side of the room where the sparring took place, the same lean man hurried towards us. His hair was very gray. Nevertheless he didn't look old, although the sinewy body clearly belonged to a middle-aged person. Unlike Inga, Arthur preferred white clothes. They looked like a funny Yin and Yang in the flesh.

"We're twins," Arthur explained to me.

His change of place attracted the attention of the fighters, and Dun finally looked around. Upon seeing me, Professor smiled, and I felt a hot wave flooding my face, neck and ears. I couldn't smile back at him, so I just waved my hand.

"Come here tomorrow and we'll test you," Inga interrupted the conversation again. "Because we're already finishing our shift for today. And don't forget to bring your gym suit to future trainings."

I decided to use this excuse to leave and quickly said goodbye, because otherwise in another couple of minutes Reincarnologist would have to take me out of the gym on his shoulder. Mamma Mia! Black belt! I thought that he was just a doctor, a scientist working with the mysterious Grenons, and there I have witnessed such a 'disappointment'.

Paul meanwhile continued to inform me about the peculiarities of the local order of things, completely ignoring my condition.

"We have the opportunity to work by the Pitman fixed shift. Employees with families use it to see their children more often. For example, this is how Head of the security sector works. And there are some Department specialists who work eight hours in a way that spans both day and night shifts," Reincarnologist explained to me. "Their work begins at four p.m. and ends at midnight. Arthur and Inga are the best in their area, so it makes no sense to invite additional coaches, this is why they also have such a schedule. You have to remember that you must come to the gym no later than an hour before midnight."

"And when is Dun training?"

"Basically, he goes to the gym immediately after coming to work. He prefers to limber up before going to the wards."

Ok. So, I decided to visit the gym only an hour before midnight, otherwise I could say goodbye to all my focus during work. Oh, Dun. . .

***

I was sitting at the table, buried in safety instructions, and was chewing my early breakfast in the Department's dining room. I was already sleepy, but I had to wait for Dun who promised to accompany me home in a half an hour. Someone landed in a chair next to me. I raised my head. Lina was sitting nearby.

"Hi! You're Helga, aren't you?"

"Hi! Yes. And you're Lina?"

"Right!" she laughed. "I wish my parents had called me Helga! I would have been called Elle and I would have been making a mysterious expression with my eyes. Just like you do. What are you reading?"

"Safety instructions," who'd have ever thought that my eyes were mysterious.

"Ah, yeah! So you should read and memorize it carefully. Because we had some accidents here--- Listen, is Dun good in bed?"

"I don't know," I answered automatically and choked on a bun when the meaning of what my interlocutor has said reached me across the dry lines of instructions. "What kind of question is that?"

"Oh, sorry! I thought you've had--- And haven't you? The whole Department is sure about that."

"Why are you all suddenly so sure?" I got angry.

"Don't be mad at me, please. I'm a good girl. I just blurt out all sorts of nonsense from time to time," Lina began to look into my face imploringly.

"I'll forgive you if you answer my question."

"Well, Dun's ha-a-andsome. However he's too short to fit into my ideal of a man. But half of the female employees of the Department are into him, and even one guy, ha-ha," Lina covered her mouth with her palm. "And I've shared too much again. Dun hasn't been looking at anyone since Sophie's death six years ago. And here we can see that suddenly he is in it again."

"Sophie?" I was all ears at that moment.

"It's not my business, and I haven't witnessed that story personally, but the employees say they were in love or something similar. She was self-confident and made a huge mistake in her work," Lina nodded at the safety instructions. "And the Clevres are big. They squeezed her to death. It happened when the Department had just started working with cloning. Paul tried to resurrect her, but nothing came of it. Dun was young. They say that he doesn't want to even stand next to the Clevres. And they are very sensitive, so they will not work with a specialist who treats them poorly. Listen, haven't you really had--- that?"

"And have you and Paul had 'that'?" I thought that it was necessary to cut such conversations short. And the best way to do this was to transfer attention to another fundamentally opposite topic.

"With whom? With Paul?" Lina was sincerely surprised, and then got thoughtful. The girl possessed an ideal type of female beauty that I didn't have myself. She wasn't tall, was in wonderful shape, had a perky upturned nose and plump lips. She was wearing a doctor's smock, which flattered the shape of her legs shod in stilettos. I was envious. I've always admired the beauty of stilettos, but could never wear them myself because of my height. My Mom adored such shoes and looked very beautiful in heels. So did Lina.

The girl was so deep in her thoughts that she didn't notice Dun giving me signals from the door. I gathered my books and quietly left the dining room.

"What did she want? Did she was to get acquainted with you?" asked Dun, nodding toward pensive Lina.

"She asked me whether you're good in bed," I answered honestly.

"What?" Professor was surprised and burst out laughing. "Well, Lina's really something! And what did you answer?"

"I asked her about how good Paul is in bed."

Dun looked at me thoughtfully.

"The very fact that she's in such a state after your question says something. Apparently, this case is not hopeless. You're an expert in scheming, as I see. We need to watch this bonfire carefully. Keeping our distance."

"But don't say anything to Paul, please," I got scared.

"I won't," Professor appeased me. "It will be a secret in exchange for another secret. But I have to say 'well done!'. It's necessary to stir the swamp of their melancholy somehow. Lina likes tall guys."

"How do you know that?"

"I'm too short," Dun said with a smile and I decided to be very careful with this man. Nothing concerning him should be said out loud in the Department.

We soared up into the sky again and took the opposite direction — to the house of my parents. A thin strip of the sunrise was emerging behind the trees of the botanical garden. My first eight working hours on a new job flew completely unnoticed.

"It's five in the morning," said Professor. "Would your parents wake up so early?"

"It will be half past five by the time we arrive. My mom usually gets up at six," I looked into the sunrise thoughtfully. Dun decided not to disturb me. He knew that I was tired and that I have got more than enough information for today."

Near the door of my house Professor held my hand, which was about to insert the key into the keyhole.

"I've been dreaming about this all night," he said kissing me. Then Dun tucked a hair strand behind my ear and disappeared into the night sky, leaving me completely confused. And I've just decided that all of this was for the sake of my loyalty, and now the courtship would end. Was I wrong? Or did Professor simply decide to secure the result so that I wouldn't change my mind?

Chapter 6

"Are you ready?" Inga asked me when I got acquainted with the gym and its equipment, and then admired the arsenal in the adjacent room. "Let's check your physical fitness"

I shrugged. My physical fitness could be deemed as good without any hesitation. I still had the habit of training that I kept up with since my martial classes at school, and I haven't cheated on it for all these years, running to the stadium with magical protection every single morning. It was so cool that I could train here from now. Instead of allocating some time in the morning I could legally spend an hour of the work schedule training. I decided to leave my old tracksuit at home for the weekend exercises. I'd stopped by the sports store before its closing and purchased a new kit. This time I decided to choose clothes in blue color instead of reaching for my favorite green.

I calmly passed all the necessary martial examinations under the supervision of a coach. Inga was pleased.

"Great! How do you want to improve your physical shape?" she asked.

"I want to train in martial arts."

"Perfect! Let's check your level."

After another half an hour of a sparring, I was breathing heavily and also realized that Paul was right yesterday. Inga was good.

"You can relax for five minutes, and let's test the last thing," the trainer suggested to me.

"You mean, my firepower?"

"Yes. And your accuracy as well. Do you know how to shoot?"

"Yes, but I prefer to throw knives."

"Oh, yes?" the trainer's eyebrows raised. "What a strange choice."

"My knives are more convenient when it comes to killing spiders. Nobody gets alerted by the shootings and the house remains intact," I replied grimly.

Inga laughed and went to the arsenal to find the throwing knives for me. There were a lot of people in the gym, apparently some of the trainees preferred to come here in the middle of the shift to stretch themselves and take a break from regular work. I saw Paul practicing punches on a punching bag, sometimes replacing his fists with streams of compressed air. I thought that he was the air martial specialist. The coach brought two buckets of water while I was resting. She asked one of the water magicians to freeze a large target at the end of the gym.

"Shoot with the pulsar," Inga suggested to me. I stood in front of the target, formed a pulsar and shot. The spark spread across the ice somewhere around the eights and melted a small hollow. The coach was satisfied.

"Very well! Not a bull's eye, of course, but you don't need it. Do you throw knives with the same precision?"

"Better. With a knife I hit the spider."

"I thought you were joking."

"No, I wasn't," I shook my head. "I'm terribly afraid of them. I'm even afraid to approach a spider. The martial teacher at my school used this fear to train my knife skills. Now I prefer to stay away from spiders. I throw the knife from another corner of the room immediately."

Inga shook her head and called the same water guard.

"Freeze a spider on the bull's eye," she asked him and turned to me. "Shoot with another pulsar please. Amazing!"

The ice monster was blown away by a powerful wave of fire. I didn't see exactly where I hit, because the only thing remaining from the target was a thin bagel.

"Please, don't make me use pulsars against the spiders," I pleaded. "I don't control myself."

"How did your school survive? Awesome firepower!"

"My teacher taught me how to hit them with knives first and this served to develop my muscular reflex. Then she began to teach me how to use pulsars."

"She's definitely a wise woman. Can you make a shield?"

I nodded.

"Defend yourself!" and Inga threw an apple-sized pulsar at me. It was a big one! It can blow my head off if it hits me. I trapped the pulsar into my fire and levitated it into the water that a security guard collected in an empty bucket after I melted the target. Judging by the facial expression of the coach, she was impressed.

"How did you do that? It's impossible to catch a pulsar! You can either push it away or extinguish it with water, or direct it back at its owner, but not catch."

"I know. But a fire martial healer can do that. During medicine lessons we were taught how to catch the sources of infection in the blood of patients. In other words, to catch the aggressor. And then we had to encapsulate it in one place and then inject drugs in there. It's the same principle here. I mix two gifts — medicine and fire, catch your pulsar aggressor in my trap and, controlling my own fire, I extinguish both of them. Pulsars are even easier to stop this way. Unlike bacteria they are large and fly one at a time. My martial teacher taught me the same thing. She loves her work."

"What is her name?"

"Mrs. Elsa. I'll give you her phone number later."

"Oh, you definitely will. And is it possible to teach this to our security guards?"

I looked around. Everyone in the room, including Paul and Arthur, who came closer, looked at me with interest and listened to our conversation.

"I don't think so," I disappointed everyone. "Mrs. Elsa said that theoretically you can train a pair which is comprised of a healer and a fire magician. She believes that cooperation is the basis of any success. Doesn't matter if it's a marriage or a battle, which is the same though."

Colleagues laughed. I continued.

"My teacher devoted a lot of time to the issue of cooperation. But she wasn't allowed to experiment with catching pulsars."

"And that's understandable!" said Arthur. "Helga, but are there any additional conditions for the formation of such a healer-fire magician pair?"

"Yes, there is one. Partners must feel and trust each other unconditionally."

"A romantic couple?"

"God forbid! There will be victims," listeners laughed again. "No, it should be either huckleberry friends, or twins like you and Inga."

"Twins always have the same kind of gift. It never happens that one twin is a healer and the other is a fire magician, unfortunately. And what about the water and air magicians?"

"There's no point in it. A blow of air is the easiest to dispel, and water can be beaten off into the sky. A pulsar, even a redirected one, will do a big harm."

"Well, Helga, I'm going to visit our HR department tomorrow and sort out all the employees," Inga said. "I hope to find such a pair of friends. You'll spend another hour on their training in addition to the usual gym time."

"And what about my safety exams?"

"I'll talk to Director about it. Transferring your skill is more important. Maybe we'll begin recruiting the healer-fire magician pairs for our security team. We'll see. Now go and take a shower."

At the women's locker room exit Paul caught me.

"Listen, do you know what happened to Lina? She took the day shift suddenly."

"No, Paul, I don't know. You should call her."

"I called, but she rejects my calls. I don't want to ask colleagues about her. Everyone's already whispering without it."

"She rejects your calls--- Hmmm--- You know what, Paul? Starting from the day after tomorrow I'm going to take a couple of day shifts. I'll see what I can do."

"Thanks! I'm worried. That was an unexpected decision, you know? Suddenly something happened."

"Ask the Lonquies," I winked.

"It's pointless. Even if they know they won't tell. Their ethic is different from ours."

"So you have to be patient until the day after tomorrow. As soon as I find out what's the matter I'll call you."

"Okay," said Reincarnologist sadly. I decided to distract him a little.

"I've always been interested in one thing. What does an aura look like and how does it differ from a magic field?"

"Haven't your teachers told you?" Paul rejoiced.

"We didn't have the aura specialists on our course. Therefore our teachers only spoke about the magic field."

"The magic field is the flow within the body. And the aura is the outer shell and it's much bigger. Each person has a unique mixture of colors. They are determined by the basic qualities of the soul — kindness or hatred, gaiety or envy, integrity or venality. The combination of aura shades allows you to understand how a person will behave in particular situations. It's rather approximate because there are some other emotions that affect one's behavior. Well, in general people can be terribly unpredictable sometimes."

"Emotions are also visible, aren't they?"

"Yes. We can see them as bright flashes in the zones of the main chakras. They do not affect the overall impression, but are quite visible. The stronger the emotion, the more visible it is."

I blushed because I started to understand something.

"Helga, I remind you: not only do we take physician's oath, but we also give the non-disclosure oath. They're enforced on a magical level. For example, if you break one, you would lose the gift of seeing. Everything is very strict. There are of course some loopholes, but I won't give your secret away. Even to Dun. And I won't give him away to you, mind it too. I never interfere into other people's relationships. It's my personal taboo."

"Thank you!" so that's why Paul pretended not to see my condition yesterday. "And when have you seen Lina for the last time?"

"Yesterday at three in the night. Why?"

"I just got one assumption. But you can neither confirm nor deny it, so please be patient until the day after tomorrow. And now I have to get back to studying my safety instructions."

***

Lina came to accompany me to my first day shift. She had been tweeting with my Mom while I was getting ready for work. Mom was impressed with the girl, treated our guest with her signature coffee, adding magical decorations, which clearly improved Lina's mood. While I was putting on my favorite green jumpsuit and doing my hair, my Mother revealed her coffee recipe to the girl and taught her how to create the special magic butterflies for it. When we left the house and soared into the sky, Lina said:

"Dun called and asked me to come for you. He said that you haven't learned the way yet, and he couldn't accompany you because the Grenons were naughty and he's tired."

"He just likes to think that I haven't learned the way," I said. I was interested if he was going to come for me after work and accompany me to the day shift and then back home? As if I was a little girl. "But thanks for coming, it will be more fun flying to the Department with you."

"It's not difficult for me," the girl waved her hand. "I live three blocks East of your home. It's along the way. And it's fun for me too. Recently I didn't want to be 'face-to-face' with my thoughts."

"Do you live alone?"

"Yes, I'm renting a small apartment in the area. It's quiet, clean, comfortable and no one bothers me with questions."

"And what about your brother?"

"Well, he's married and lives with his wife and children in a slightly different block."

"If so it will be possible to fly together in the evening as well."

"Yeah. Oh, and there are rumors about you in the Department. They say that you, along with Inga and Arthur, will train the security guards."

"That's nonsense!" I brushed it off. "They are merely rumors. I'll transfer one unique skill if there is someone who is able to receive it. Lina, why did you stop working the night shifts? Paul is worried."

"Let him worry" Lina soared suddenly. We were talking calmly before this, but then there was such a surge of emotions. "I haven't slept for two nights because of him! I'm barely able to walk and fly!"

Being incredibly surprised I opened my eyes widely, and the girl continued:

"Why did you ask me about him that day?! I was imagining how good he is in---" it was a real cry from the inside. What a pity that it was cut off shortly. Lina hunched up.

"Wow! How is that my fault?"

"You think I don't know that he likes me?" Lina soared again.

That was it, I was right. She'd seen everything. She's only pretended not to notice. Now I had to find out the most important thing.

"You like him too, don't you?"

"I don't know!" moaned Lina. "He's smart, tactful, open-hearted, cheerful. He's an excellent specialist. But he's a womanizer! I try to avoid such guys!"

Paul's a womanizer? Everything became weirder.

"Why do you think that he's a womanizer?" I continued to liberate a poor girl's soul from unexpressed doubts.

"He compliments all women in the Department including the old cleaning lady! He always embarrasses everyone in the laboratory! Who knows whom else does he like? Every time I enter the dining room he sits there in the middle of a girls group, enjoying everyone's attention."

"And nobody invites you---"

"But what does this have to do with it?" flared up Lina. "They did. But I refused several times and they stopped asking me. Only Paul sometimes invites me over habitually."

Oh, yeah, habitually. . .

"Lina, can I tell you something? But don't be offended, please."

"What?!"

"Lina, Paul's a reincarnologist."

The girl stared blankly at me.

"I know, Elle!"

"What do you know, you little dummy? He's a reincarnologist. He can see an aura and a soul."

"Elle, why are you saying such obvious things?! After all, it's not me who should be called a little dummy here."

Oh, I could see. Her brain wasn't functioning properly because of her agitation.

"Okay, I'll be blunt. A reincarnologist cannot be a womanizer. A specialist who constantly touches human souls cannot be a philanderer a priori! If he likes you it means that he likes everything about you — your appearance, character, soul etc."

Lina started to hear and understand me at last. She frowned, closed her eyes for a second, rubbed her temples and objected again:

"Okay! Maybe he's not a womanizer! But why is he so skinny?"

"He's tall. You like tall guys, don't you?"

"Yes, but he's skinny! He always wears that horrible medical scrub, looking like death. And what about those yellow glasses? His eyes are almost invisible because of them."

I was surprised again.

"They're absolutely visible. Have you ever looked into his eyes?"

"No," the girl admitted, hunching up again. Oh I could see, she made her own conclusions even though she never looked. And apparently she wanted to look into his eyes. The girl clearly liked Paul as a person, so I decided to finish this conversation with the same advice that has affected me the other day.

"Lina, here's my advice: calm down. Now you have to get used to the idea that Paul is not a womanizer. I'll make a phone call and tell him that everything's fine with you. But you have to relax and to get some sleep finally. And after a couple of day shifts return to the night ones. And go to our gym. Meet Inga personally, choose a training program. You'll always be in great shape as a result of training. Paul spends a whole hour without glasses and a medical scrub there every day. He wears only special sports pants. As soon as you notice that he's getting ready to go for a training, come right away. You'll have an opportunity to look at him attentively. And then you'll think."

"Okay. Where are you going now?"

"I want to visit the documentation sector. I have to finish something. This can only be done in the daytime."

"Then, if you want, I can accompany you to visit the Clevres. I'll introduce you to my brother."

"I can't be there for now; I haven't passed the safety exam yet."

"The Clevres are the only wards whose sector is not enclosed by blank walls. There are only thick cage bars there. You can look from aside, and I'll call my brother."

***

In the documentation sector I finally made up my mind and went to the table of a legend specialist.

"Ahh, Helga!" the stylish gray-haired old woman was delighted. Rumor has it that she has been the best legend specialist in the several hundred years of the Department's work. "How can I help you?"

"Tell me, please, is it true that everyone here is being married off?"

"This practice is quite common but not compulsory. It's convenient. The marriage is fictitious, for relatives' peace of mind. We don't have a lot of female staff members who are able to work night shifts. Two dozen healers, some of them are not reporting to their relatives, then attendants, and a couple of security guards. And you. The rest of the female staff works during the day, like me or our accountants."

"I understand. And if I don't want to get married, even fictitiously?"

"Then you should think about how to protect yourself from any questions that your family may ask you."

"I was hoping you could help me."

"To do this, I need to interview you very carefully with the involvement of an aura specialist that will help to identify all the emotional points. A good legend should be almost entirely true, including the emotional and magical component. I spend a lot of time analyzing all the information about a person, comparing the relevance of certain facts. Otherwise, the legend can get exposed, especially by the relatives. Are you sure you're ready for this procedure?"

"No," I was horrified, imagining having all my secrets dug out. "And why don't the relatives expose fictitious marriages?"

"It's because they're usually trying their best to stay out of a relationship between young people, and a certain coldness between them can always be interpreted as a quarrel or a bit of resentment. Well, just think about it. If you can't find any other explanation of your night work, you can always come to me."

I said goodbye and went out. Lina was waiting for me at the door. I was thinking about the legend specialist, while my new friend was calling her brother. Apparently, the Department valued this old woman, otherwise she would have already been retired. She must love her job and execute it so well that even at that age they hold on to her.

Victor turned out to be a tall man with broad shoulders and a powerful neck. His sister seemed tiny next to him. Even I had to raise my head to have a proper look at my colleague. Now it was clear why Lina likes tall guys better and why Paul seemed skinny to her.

"This is Elle," she introduced me to her brother.

"Hi!" said Victor. "How do you prefer to be called? Do you want to be Elle or Helga?"

"It's up to you. Both Elle and Helga work for me."

"I'll choose Elle then. It will be our family nickname for you. Come here and look from afar at the Clevres."

The sector of these creatures was separated from the main pavilion of the Department by an underpass. Going up the stairs, we came to another indoor pavilion, the size of which was not smaller, but maybe even bigger than the size of the main one. The room had translucent walls and a ceiling which was penetrated by the sunlight. But at the same time, it was hardly possible to examine what was happening inside from the outside. In the pavilion there was a huge cage-like fence, which enclosed the Clevres' recreation area from the technical rooms. The entrance to the territory of the wards was located on the opposite side of the underpass. We didn't go there, stopping right in front of the underpass stairs. The local temperature was much lower than the temperature in the main building of the Department.

Such position of the sector and its temperature regime became clear almost immediately. So that's why Julie asked me how I felt about pigs. Huge pink and blue piglets were frolicking on the other side of the fence. The young ones were the size of a hippopotamus or a small elephant, and the enormity of adults was simply beyond imagination. They could be differentiated from the usual pigs not only by their body size, but also by the presence of a trunk and fur. This fur was actually blue, while the trunk and ears were pink.

"Wow! What a cutie!" I exclaimed at the sight of the young Clevres.

"They're sweet, aren't they?" Lina's brother said with some kind of tenderness, unusual for such a giant.

"Absolutely! I want to touch one!"

"You can only do it after you pass the safety exam," Victor said sternly. "Then we'll teach you how to create a contact with them. And only after that you'll be able to touch them. This is needed for the sake of not being trampled accidentally."

"Oh, sure! Victor, what do they eat?"

"They prefer grass, fruits, vegetables. Just like any other pigs. They also eat tree branches. We have some cold-resistant plants here so that the Clevres can have something to eat if they wish. In general, the Department buys food for them from trusted suppliers, because our giants eat a lot."

"Can I ask you an awkward question?" I was excited. Viktor nodded. "Who cleans their--- excrements?"

"We have several cleaners for these needs. They have to work at night to avoid scaring the Clevres. Our wards are very tidy and do not stain their sleeping place. Manure of the Clevres, unlike the pigs' one, is considered to be a very valuable fertilizer, so the Department sells one part of it to several farms, and another part is sold in exchange for the wards' food."

"And what about the secrecy?"

"Nobody tells customers what kind of fertilizer it really is. It's said that it's just a mixture of different types of organics. I have to say that no one is particularly interested. 'It works well, that's why nobody bothers to ask,' they say."

I could see beautiful clay structures inside of which, apparently, slept the wards. An artificial pond was dug nearby. Over there a couple of adult species were watering each other using their trunks. It was clear that the Clevres were really enjoying this activity. Young piglets were lying on the territory with cold-resistant grass, and some man was scratching their stomachs with a rake. The Clevres were squinting their eyes in delight and patiently waiting for their turn to be scratched. Well, pigs are pigs and there is nothing to add here.

"Are the Clevres, unlike the Grenons, inhabitants of our planet?"

"We don't know this for sure. They do not belong to the animal kingdom, they have their own laws and their magical field is very similar to ours."

"Why don't they live in a natural environment then?"

"Because they had almost been destroyed in their natural environment. Rumor has it that the Clevres' meat is very tasty and that it has even got a rejuvenating effect. However, in my opinion this is nonsense. Dead meat devoid of a magical component cannot rejuvenate. A few hundred years ago the Clevres were almost completely eaten. It's good that scientists became interested in the similarity of the magic field with ours and viewed it as a benefit for humanity."

"They were almost completely eaten?" I asked in shock. "The whole population?"

"Aha. 'All they want is just to eat'," Viktor sang the words from a song. "The Department employees had gathered all the species that they could find. There were only eight of the Clevres left — three females and five males. In view of the fact that these creatures form their pairs for life, two males were left without females and couldn't give their offspring. There was a moment when the population was on the verge of extinction due to inbreeding, but then we'd found some individuals frozen in the ice, and the blood was diluted."

I looked at the stunning lop-eared cuties, saw how they indulged in the magic of water and couldn't believe what I'd just heard. How was it possible to eat the whole population? Probably, people were making blue fur coats as well. I imagined a dead Clevr and a heartless hunter putting his foot triumphantly on its head. . .

Probably, because of this imagined picture, I suddenly felt very cold. Of course, the temperature had been lowered in the pavilion, but not so low to be able to freeze me. Fire magicians don't get as cold, if necessary we can warm ourselves up with the heat generated from the magic field. My condition couldn't be explained by environmental conditions only. I cringed.

Lina, who stood nearby silently and has already been shivering, seized the opportunity and pulled me towards the exit. We said goodbye to Victor and hastened to run away. For the rest of the day I was reading about the Clevres. The thought of a hunter frightened me. If there were no Department, these beautiful creatures could have disappeared altogether.

Chapter 7

In the evening me and Lina were returning home together as per our agreement. It wasn't dark, and the weather was just beautiful because it had stopped raining yesterday, and this evening the sky pleased us with a wonderful sunset. My companion has obviously been quite relaxed and kept telling me about a breakthrough in the life prolonging laboratory.

"And then these flies suddenly began to multiply unprecedentedly and even ceased to die. Can you imagine that? We limited their food intake, so they stopped their reproduction, but still they wouldn't die. Usually such insects live for about six hours. And here it has already been three days since their birth!" the girl was chattering excitedly.

"Listen, Lina, I wanted to ask you something in the morning, but I forgot to do it. So I think it's time to ask it now. Why on my first day all the employees were so happy and congratulated Dun along with me?" this conversation had to somehow be started because I wanted to find out the things that interested me a lot. My companion was the best person for this purpose, as she had no interest in hiding something from me. She could compare the facts and draw conclusions, of course, but fortunately Lina didn't have these facts.

"There's a tradition to congratulate the coach if the martial healer has agreed to start a job in the Department. I saw this for the first time, because such specialists come extremely rarely and you're the first one that I have witnessed."

"Do you happen to know if there were any martial healers in the history of the Department who refused to work there?"

"As far as I know, this happened a maximum of ten times throughout the whole history of its existence," my companion waved her hand carelessly. "And in the end most of them agreed anyway."

We were getting closer to the topic I was interested in.
"Why?"
"I think they had been persuaded."
"How?"

"It was different each time. Mostly with money, but they had also been tricked."

"What do you mean?"

"Elle, I don't know. It's necessary to ask the coaches who invite the newbies to start a job in the Department. What has Dun offered to you?"

"He didn't need to talk me into this. I've been dreaming of working with Grenons since my childhood."

Lina was surprised. I had to tell her about our family photography. At the same time, I strengthened her confidence, because I had yet to find out everything that worried me and was going to ask more questions.

"Have there been any cases in the history of the Department when martial healers left their jobs?" I continued.

"Yes, there were four of them. And three more were persuaded to stay."

"What kinds of arguments were used?"

"Two of them liked the Department's team. We also have other bonuses in addition to salary. We all support and protect each other just like members of one big family. The whole corporate culture is aimed at strengthening these relations. Rumor has it that one employee was even seduced in order to make him stay at work. But I don't believe in this."

"And how are these relationships formed? Are there any common goals or what?"

"Oh, no. Everything is much simpler. The Department is constantly arranging events. Either team shooting competitions, or creative evenings, or joint viewing of football matches, or races. You can choose any event and enjoy yourself there. Sometimes they even happen during our work shifts, so that the employees with families can visit it together. People enjoy socializing, having fun, and are establishing new clubs all the time."

"It's really cool! And what, hasn't Paul ever invited you there?"

"Not personally. Only when we were in a company. But I think that he was right. If he invited me personally I wouldn't go, because I'd think that he is a womanizer."

"Okay, okay. This is clear. But you mentioned two martial healers who were talked into staying. And who was the third?"

"And Dun didn't leave for another reason."

"Dun?"

"Yes. After Sophie died, he wanted to leave the Department. But Director asked him not to rush with his decision and gave Dun half a year to think about his future. Six months later Dun came back. Director did the right thing, in my opinion. It's better to lose a specialist for some time than forever. Dun had been writing a dissertation during those months."

"And what about the employees who aren't martial healers? Do they quit frequently?"

"The Department's a good place to work," Lina shrugged her shoulders. "People usually like it. Of course, it happened that employees wanted to change their occupation completely. In that case our managers made them sign a non-disclosure agreement, enforcing it on a magical level, like an oath of aura experts. And then you are free to go wherever you want. But sometimes it happened that employees came back, because swimming with the Grenons and working on new developments is really great."

"Not every employee is working with new technologies."

"Yes. The security sector is not working. But these guys also appreciate the opportunities that the Department gives. For example, security Chief had left for three years and then returned."

"Why did he leave?"

"An aggressive neighbor attacked his country, and the security guard left to defend his homeland. He doesn't really like to speak about it, but there are rumors. He has many awards and unique combat experience. Some cinema guys even shot a movie about his team, although the cast of course is made of actors, not the veterans themselves. We all respect our security Chief greatly. You'll see him yourself. You can always recognize such people, because veterans really cherish and treasure life."

Lina stopped talking. What she was thinking about that moment was unknown to me. Perhaps she was remembering something about the war. I didn't know anything either about the country of the girl, or about security Chief's homeland. Who knew if they were from the same territory?

"Well, have you calmed down?" I asked my companion, as we have already flown up to my house.

"A little bit," Lina yawned. "One cannot be nervous all the time."

"That's for sure! Will you sleep tonight?"

"I hope so. I can take sleeping pills if I need to. Would you like me to accompany you tomorrow?"

"Yes, of course."

"Okay. See you tomorrow than."

"See you tomorrow."

I was glad for her. She would sleep. Well, that's good. And I would not apparently. I was wondering what kind of methods the coaches use to persuade martial healers to take a job in the Department. And how much truth was in Dun's courtship? What if all of it was just so that I would come to work and stay in the Department?

I quietly opened the door with my key, trying to make as little noise as possible. Slowly and smoothly I took off my cloak and hung it on the hanger, then I carefully took off my shoes and tried to sneak into the room unnoticed. But Mom caught me. How could she feel my state of mind? The point was that sometimes I was more upset, but my Mother hasn't intervened until Ш asked. And this time she grabbed me by the hand.

"Helga? What's happening?"

"Nothing, mom," I said tiredly, realizing that this conversation couldn't be avoided. It was possible, of course, to keep silent, but there was no reason to run away. Firstly, I didn't want to offend my Mother, and secondly, it was the right time to vent in order to decide how to act. And my Mom was the best person for this purpose. I was sure that the conversation would remain between us and she wouldn't mention it to my Father. Dad shouldn't know anything about (Может, можно как-то перефразировать, чтобы избежать повторения? Всё-таки about — это не the и не should) what was happening, because this could create some additional problems.

"Dad is late at work and you need to be fed. So, go, change, wash your hands and come here immediately. And don't even try to argue! You'll work off your extra millimeters in the gym."

I burst out laughing. I haven't complained about the extra millimeters since I was nineteen, but my Mother recalled them periodically anyway, which amused me incredibly. I took off my strict green jumpsuit, which flattered the shape of my body and was perfectly suitable for flying. Then I came into our kitchen, drove the cat from my favorite chair and started eating. Frankly speaking, I was ravenous. Mom seemed to know what her adult daughter needed at the moment. After dinner somehow I felt better and my mood has slightly improved.

"Well, I'm all ears," said my Mother, after I moved the empty plate away from me and sat back. My cat was waiting for this too because it jumped in my lap immediately, curling up under my hand. Feeling his support and protection I decided to express what had tormented me all this time aloud.

"I don't want this wedding."

Mom dropped a spoon with which she was stirring her flower tea.

"Did he offend you?"

"No, mom. Dun's attentive, caring, intelligent. He's terrific. But I don't know how much sincerity there is behind this.

"That's fine!" Mom said confidently. "Every woman goes through this. We always have qualms. We often assume the worst and see bad things where there're none."

"You don't understand. There are some, shall we say, circumstances," I was collecting my thoughts and sorting out all my doubts. I had to lie to explain my feelings to my Mother without giving out confidential information. On top of that the topic of fictitious marriage had to be circumvented. "I was offered another job. And he is persuading me to stay at the old one. He says that I'm a very talented healer, almost unique. And so I cannot understand his motives in our relationship. What if all of this is just for the sake of work?"

"It's very easy to check," my Mother laughed. "You just need to accept the new job. And you'll see if his attitude to you changes after that. If it changes then you'll stay away from him and it will be easier for you to forget him. And if not then all your doubts will disappear."

Hmm, I thought that it was better to tell her the truth. Anyway, then I would have to obliterate my Mom's memory.

"I can't accept it for now, and Dun is aware of it," I had to continue lying.

"Why not?"

"Well, firstly, I initiated the procedure for obtaining a license for carrying throwing knives," in fact, I've had such a license for a long time, but I hadn't told it to my parents for their peace of mind. "To do this, you need to go through a full examination and get a bunch of permissions. I can do this in our medical institution. Just imagine how much time I'll lose if I quit now. I'll have to either start all over again in a new place, or wait for the transfer of the documents which is the same, given our bureaucracy."

"Apparently, this is not the main reason."

"I just don't know if I want this job," it was too hard for me to keep lying but I had to.

Mom thought for a moment. She stirred the lukewarm tea mechanically and looked somewhere deep into herself. Finally she said:

"Then just tell him that you want to postpone the wedding. You can blame everything on me and your father. And then, either you deal with your fiancé or you make a decision about a new job."

"I probably will do as you said," the idea was really great. Telling Professor that my parents have insisted on postponing the wedding was a perfect option. However, there was another issue that I wanted to discuss with my Mother. This thought was prompted by the morning conversation with Lina. "Mom, one more thing. I want to move out."

"But why?" Mom was distraught. This topic clearly took her by surprise, although there was nothing illogical about it.

"I'm twenty five years old. I graduated, took an internship, and I've been working for two years. How long can I live with my parents? It's not normal."

"Well, okay!" strongly declared my Mother. "I don't want to let my girl go anywhere, of course, and your father will be upset. However, a young woman needs to live in her own place. But, please remember that we're always glad to see you home!"

Chapter 8

Dun met a request to postpone the wedding with an absolutely impenetrable expression. I was unable to understand what he was thinking about. Over the years of our relationship and collaboration I generally noticed that it has been almost impossible to put him out of temper. Professor laughed with pleasure, but I've never seen him angry or upset. Most likely, this was due to the strict discipline which has been imposed on everyone engaged in martial arts.

"What did you tell parents about your night schedule?" he asked me in response.

"I said that so far I was transferred to night shifts at the hospital. I'm going to move out of my parents' house and start living separately."

"Do you want your space?" Professor was amused.

"First of all, I'm an adult. For how long can I tire mom and dad with my presence? I want to let them finally enjoy themselves. Ma has been saying for many years that she wants to change their house in the city to a suburban cottage. But because of me, parents couldn't do this so far. Secondly and most importantly, it will immediately solve all the problems with their questions. I'll visit them on weekends."

We were flying through the night streets. Cool April days gradually gave way to warm May. The suffocating heat hadn't come yet, everything around was blooming, and these trips to the Department and back have brought me sincere joy. Dun asked me what kind of apartment I would like to rent. For the first time I have managed to formulate my unclear desires on this subject in words and was extremely grateful to my companion for supporting this idea. I thought: 'Oh my God! He's so terrific! He's perfect! Why is it always so complicated with me, huh?'

In the Department we walked into the meeting of computer specialists at one of the workstations. The deputy director, the head of the Department during night shifts, was standing nearby and frowning.

"What happened?" asked Professor.

"Someone started a rumor that the healers of maternity hospitals conduct prohibited scientific experiments on newborns. The tabloids have hyped it up immediately. The information has quickly leaked into the global network and began to spread like a wildfire. Most of discussions are taking place in the communities of young parents. I've already received the first reports that women-in-labor began to renounce the presence of healers at childbirth."

"Such discussions never last long, everything will calm down soon," said one of the young network specialists.

"The problem of this situation is that if something goes wrong and there is no healer, there may be children with deviations," Dun told him. Neither of us needed any explanations about all the terrible consequences of this incident.

"Frightened women don't listen to any warnings and sign statements that they take full responsibility of all the consequences," Deputy added.

"This is the price of secrecy," I muttered under my breath.

"What, Helga?"

"I'm sorry," I said, embarrassed. "I just think that the strictest secrecy the Department lives in is terribly wrong."

"Helga, I told you why this decision was made," Dun said.

"Yes, I understand the reasons. But I still think this is wrong from an ethical point of view. People should have the right to choose whether they want their children to have new abilities or not."

"And how do you think this can be implemented?" asked Deputy director gently. "Even if we gave parents the opportunity to make a decision in the case of each specific child, this would not change anything for humanity as a whole. Anyway, after a couple of generations everyone will have new magic knowledge and skills. But we'll have problems with the safety of the Department's staff again. We live and work in relative stability for now. And the inhabitants of the planet consider the appearance of more gifted kids as a consequence of natural evolutionary processes."

"I think that it would be better to make the activities of the Department completely transparent and public. We have to report to people about the ongoing research. We have to hold public discussions about new technologies and give people the right to choose whether they want their children and grandchildren to have new knowledge. This would save the Department from encroachments of greedy individuals. It's difficult to appropriate something that is on public display."

"Unfortunately, this is impossible," Deputy director shook his head. "We possess technologies that humanity simply shouldn't know about. I would agree with you if we were really able to make our work one hundred percent public. But with partial secrecy, the system simply will not work."

As for me, I thought that all of this was just an excuse. It was easier for the Department to keep secrecy, and for some reason the management didn't care about the ethical side of the issue. As always everything was covered with beautiful words about the common good for humanity.

Sitting with a cup of coffee in the dining room, I couldn't understand why I got so angry. After all, the Department has been doing nothing wrong, only improving the population. It's great to be able to fly, to feel your loved ones, to be able to treat many diseases that were previously considered incurable. Orphan homes have disappeared on the planet, mortality at a young age has been greatly decreased, and some types of crimes have been forgotten like a nightmare. And no negative consequences have appeared during all this time.

In addition to complete transparency, the exact opposite problem could arise, of which Deputy director said nothing. There have only been a few martial healers who could pass on new magic skills to babies. Therefore, the children on this list can be considered a chosen few to some extent. If parents know everything about the transfer of new skills, disputes and even fights can begin over what skill exactly their child is going to obtain. How to explain to loving parents why their baby was not included in these lists of the chosen ones while the neighbor's kid was?

I'd go to Deputy director and talk to him about this. I met this person on the second day of my work in the Department. Unlike Director, Deputy was phlegmatic and calm, never annoyed or in a rush. I wanted to talk to him because I was sure that I would get some kind of a friendly advice. Now that I had a couple of thoughts about the situation I wanted to check if someone else had the same ideas.

I came to Deputy director with questions.

"I'm sorry to disturb you. May I ask you something?"

"Of course, Helga!" Deputy pointed at a comfortable chair which was standing opposite of his desk. "You're a martial healer. This is one of the highest positions in the hierarchy of the Department. Or rather, it's the position outside of the hierarchy. You can ask about anything. Except for the confidential data of the employees, of course. You have to get used to the fact that you have the right to access any work-related information. And after a while you'll become in charge of it in some sectors."

"What has been done to dispel this latest rumor?"

"The Ministry of Public Health has released a series of information materials refuting the experimentation on babies. But judging by social surveys and discussions in the global network few people believed in this. Citizens are generally not inclined to trust the authorities."

"I feel bad for the children."

"Yes, Helga. I understand what you're talking about. My youngest daughter is alive and healthy only thanks to the intervention of a healer during labor. I dread to think what would have happened had my wife written such a statement."

"In my opinion, it's necessary to give as much public attention as possible to the cases when such statements had led to problems during labor. I used to work in the maternity hospital and I know what patients think of us. People believe that healers do nothing during labor. Our actions, unlike the bustle of obstetricians, are not visible to anyone."

"That's a great idea, Helga! I'll give an order to our legend specialists to write a couple of particularly horrifying stories."

"But they will not be true again."

"Helga, it would be better to spread the news about the sorrow of unreal people than to cry about the real tragedy of a real person."

With this in mind, I went to the gym to find Inga. Four pairs of potential students were already waiting for me there. I was wondering how Inga had managed to find so many friendly couples with an appropriate gift. Taking into account the number of the Department's employees, this was a sheer luck. Probably, the organization had its corporate culture on top and people, united by a common secret, have made really close friendships. Or the employees have invited friends to a well-paid job, maybe just to have someone to talk about it. Three pairs consisted of people of the same gender. I could see strong male friendships as well as a strong female one. The fourth pair consisted of a healer woman and a fire magician security guy.

"I don't believe that they can work something out," I said quietly to Inga.

"Why?" she asked her question just as quietly. "You don't believe in friendship between a man and a woman?"

"Only if they grew up together. In other situations friendship is possible, but there still cannot be the level of trust I spoke about the other day. If this kind of trust arises between a man and a woman, then they're no longer friends. You'll see that this pair will be fighting all the time. Perhaps after a while we'll see them in a completely different role."

Inga shrugged and looked thoughtfully at the pair.

"Listen to me carefully, please," I said loudly to the participants of our experiment. "Today we'll try something completely new and there's no guarantee that we'll succeed. I am capable of this only thanks to the unique combination of my magical gifts. I only have a theoretical idea about how two different people can do this. This idea has not yet been applied. I promise that there will be no danger for you, but you can leave the experiment any time you want."

One female pair left the gym, the other three didn't budge. Inga was extremely indignant at my headstrongness. She believed that it was necessary to work with everyone available, but I thought that she was wrong. If something works out for us, then we can try to persuade that pair to come back. But in order to have at least the slightest chance of success, I needed the full feedback from the participants. Why should I spend my energy and attention on those who aren't interested in the experiment?

Then I checked the reaction rate of each of the participants. Only one healer inspired some doubts — his abilities might simply not be enough to catch a pulsar. The physician's reactions have played a decisive role here, so my doubts were well founded. But the speed of the pulsar's flight could be slightly adjusted and we decided to start at the lowest one. I was hoping something would work out even with this healer.

"You'll have to combine two magical gifts at the very start. The fire magician must be the first one to release his fire, which will enclose the pulsar in a shell. And the healer must catch it in time to give it another direction, as if attaching medical magic to the magic of fire in order to catch the pulsar subsequently. Healers have to remember how we were taught to catch bacterias and viruses in the patient's body. As soon as you catch the pulsar, a fire magician must step in again to levitate a double fire into the water and extinguish it there."

"It's difficult to understand," one of security guards complained.

"This is more difficult to explain in words than to actually perform. You'll start now, and everything will become much simpler."

"I understood and I'll explain it to you now," the healer comforted her friend. Then she turned to me. "And how will our safety be ensured?"

"We invited a water magician to make shields and targets for you," Inga intervened. "I'm going to throw pulsars at the target, not at you. You'll stand by the flight line and attempt to catch the pulsar from there. If you fail, my pulsar will hit the target, and your fire will hit the ice wall in front of it. Let's start."

At the beginning Inga and I demonstrated what the process and its result should be. At the same time, I asked healers to follow my actions on a magical level. Then the participants of the experiment began their attempts as well, and I walked alongside and adjusted their actions.

I was right. The man and the woman in the pair were constantly arguing and couldn't concentrate. Water magician didn't have the time to update their target and shield. Even for me it was difficult to catch those pulsars, so the participants of the experiment had to coordinate their actions and at that point the pair in question was in a major fight. The healer accused the security guard instead of monitoring the change in her partner's magic field and attacking herself. Security guard tried to justify himself and blamed his friend instead of controlling the flight of his own fire. I tried to focus their attention on a common goal, on cooperation, but there was no sense in it.

Everything would be much simpler if people could just share their gift with a friend. Unfortunately, the magic that we give each other loses its features immediately after leaving the donor's body and acquires the features of a person who is going to receive it. A fire magician can give his fire to a healer, but in a physician's body this energy will immediately acquire the features of healing magic. Therefore, it's necessary to mix gifts at the very end, trying to take up the magical features of the partner. A pair of girls got the hang of it almost immediately, and it was clear to me that they have more than one successful joint project. A couple of boys suffered a little longer, and this was only due to the slow reaction of the healer. But they also quickly agreed on the coordination of actions. And the pair of disputants couldn't catch even one pulsar during our hour-long experiment.

After the training I thanked all the participants and asked those who succeeded to come again tomorrow. At the gym exit everyone was in good spirits. Everyone except for the arguing pair. I suspected that by the next evening they would either have a row because of mutual accusations, or become a couple, uniting against me and their own frustration.

Chapter 9

"Elle, I'll get my revenge on you for this!" Lina exclaimed the next evening in the locker room after the training.

"What are you talking about?" I was confused.

"He has such biceps! O-o-oh! And such shoulders!" the girl whispered. "And his eyes are incredible!"

Yeah, I saw that. All the gym visitors had been watching stealthily as Paul had been flaunting in front of Lina for the whole training hour. The girl tried her best to turn away, but it was futile. It seemed to me that the flashes on her aura transferred on her face. I couldn't see the aura, but Paul definitely could. And all of us were looking at him. Besides, Lina blushed very eloquently. Even Inga became interested and pushed the girl to work on the simulators which were placed next to the punching bag. It was exactly the place where Reincarnologist was working. The training became even funnier. Two pairs of "healer-fire magician" were constantly missing pulsars because they couldn't focus. For the first time in ten years I missed a target while throwing a knife, and got painfully hit by Inga during our sparring. In general, it was a show, not training.

"So, he's not skinny," I delivered the verdict. Lina moaned.

"Elle, what should I do now?"

"Don't give up so easily!"

"I haven't given up for a year! Maybe it's time to do it already, huh?"

"Oh, you will! But you have to do it by the book. Otherwise, you'll be the first who'll lose the interest."

"Is that why you're running from Dun?"

"Lina, stay away from my relationship with Dun, please! Otherwise I won't help you!"

"Okay, okay, I'll hold my tongue," the girl raised her hands in a conciliatory manner. I doubted it, but I decided to take her word.

"So, listen to me now. Try to keep looking independent. Same as before."

"How!?" the girl moaned again. "He's a reincarnologist! Every single emotion of mine is always written all over my face. Is there anything to say about the aura?"

"Lina, emotions are written on many faces, and we all have to live with it somehow. Do you think it's easy for me? I'm almost drenched a hot wave from my feet to the tips of my ears. In my opinion, it's Dun only who can be cool as a cucumber. So you have to learn how to handle this. You can start with familiar actions, avoiding the 'womanizer', not looking into his eyes. If he speaks, you answer. If you blush, you have to explain it with something believable. Think. You're talkative and smart, you can always find the answers easily. Any emotion that you show in relation to Paul has to be explained for safety reasons."

"So how can I give up then, if everything will be as it was earlier?"

"It's not necessary to do everything as you did earlier. If he invites you to join a company in the dining room, you agree. If he calls you to work together, you go. But do it all with an independent look. And one more thing. Do you and your brother have affectionate nicknames for each other?"

"Well, yes," Lina was embarrassed and started to giggle. "Victor is a tigerboy."

"Wow, who could imagine!" I remembered sturdy Victor who was ten years older than his sister. A Teddy Bear — that's what you could say about him. "But this is not my business and it's good for us. Call your brother a couple of times in the presence of Paul and drop this nickname at least once in a conversation."

"What for?" scared Lina.

"If you're lucky, after that the object will turn insolent, and will start doing stupid things. I can't believe that Paul is so--- Hasn't invited a girl anywhere except to join a company of other girls in the dining room for the whole year! How is it possible to wait for an opportunity for so long?" I suspected that these words came from my own dissatisfaction with Dun, but I said nothing about it.

"Okay! And what's next?"

"You'll find a new way. And now you have to go take a quick cold shower, because all your emotions have to be washed away. Otherwise, you won't be able to work, I know this from my own experience."

"Did this happen to you too?"

"Oh, yeah! On my first day in the Department."

Lina became interested.

"Listen, tell me, please. I'm dying of curiosity. You owe me!"

"What makes you think so?"

"Because you see what's going on with me and I've trusted you with this."

I sighed.

"Lina, I'd been working with Dun for four years. And for all these four years I'd been forbidding myself to even look at him. Well, yeah, he's young, attractive, smart. But he used to be my boss! He walked around in his white smock, carefully observing my work, supervising me as a young healer. I had to respect the hierarchy. And three days before I came to the Department he'd kissed me."

Lina's eyes lit up after my story. She seemed to have forgotten about Paul. I continued to talk.

"Just imagine: all this time I was used to seeing him only in the medical scrub. And on my first day here I was on a tour to the gym, and there he was sparring---"

"Oh, yeah, I can imagine," Lina widened her eyes. "So that's why you have dragged me here. Okay. So, what's happening between you guys?"

"I don't know, Lina," I sighed. "Do you understand how valuable a martial healer is for the Department?"

"So you think all of this is just for the sake of your loyalty, right? But that's nonsense!" the girl waved her hand.

"Lina, I'll figure it out sooner or later. Now the main thing is not to mess this all up. And you should better take your cold shower quickly, because it's time to work."

After the shower Lina was trembling like a leaf.

"I overdid it," she explained to me, her teeth chattering.

"You'll warm up during the walk. Let's go."

We left the locker room and took the security sector's direction.

"Hey, girls, where are you going?" Paul caught up with us.

"Julie called and asked me to come," I said. "Lina received the same call right after me. Something happened there."

"I see," Paul turned sulky. "Why are you shaking, Lina? Are you afraid? I thought you're brave."

"The water in her shower was too cold somehow," I explained without telling him that cold water was pouring at the behest of the girl herself. You can't lie to a reincarnologist. You have to tell the truth or it's half. "So now she's a frozen heart."

"Just a frozen body," Lina said quietly, but Paul heard her.

"Here you are," he took a towel off his neck and wrapped the girl with it. "It's dry and clean. I usually get dry without a towel. I wear it habitually. You can return it later."

Lina blushed.

"Oh, I can imagine what the girls in the laboratory will think after I return you the towel," she got angry.

"You can just put it on my table when there will be no colleagues," Reincarnologist shrugged. "Well, I have to run, there's a lot of work."

"Hey, you're good!" I praised Lina.

"He's wearing a hoodie and glasses again. So now it's easier to control myself," the girl said shortly. "I'll never go to the gym when Paul is there anymore."

I was amused.

"Lina, it's not so easy to do. He'll track your training time from now on and will start following you."

"Elle!" the girl groaned again.

"Be strong!"

We went through Julie's white door, but no one was there. In the corridor we saw some healers who were going to the conference room. A whole crowd of people, including Inga and Arthur, had already gathered there. But there were no martial healers there except for me. In the center of the conference room there was a table with some kind of a round device laying on it.

The conference room was not very large. All the staff would not have fit here. But now there were still quite a lot of empty seats there. The crowd buzzed like a disturbed hive.

"I would like to ask you to sit down and listen carefully to what I have to say," Deputy director said loudly. He waited until everyone sat down, and silence reigned in the hall, and then continued: "Keep calm, please. This is a bomb."

The crowd became noisy, and some of the healers jumped up, but they were pulled back by the security guards sitting nearby. Apparently, the guys already knew all the details, and therefore were not worried. I tried to be as calm as they were, but Lina was shaking again. She wrapped Paul's towel around herself even tighter.

"It's not dangerous because it has been demilitarized. The charge is there, but the magical component was disconnected, thereby rendering it harmless. It will not explode. Please, listen to me."

The employees slowly calmed down.

"This explosive device was discovered accidentally under the walls of the Department's pavilion by a late visitor to the botanical garden. He called the guards, and they informed us immediately. It took several hours for the bomb to be demilitarized. The explosive device was located directly under the outer wall of the Lonques' sector. If it had exploded, the entire population of mentalists would have perished."

Now I was the one shaking. I felt bad, thinking about the scale of the potential disaster. The people around me were grumbling again. Deputy director raised his hand.

"Fortunately, the tragedy didn't happen this time. But we must strengthen our security measures and set up additional protection to the walls of the pavilions that enclose the sectors of the wards, so that nothing could damage these walls, even a bomb."

I imagined the Clevres' sector and thought about the upcoming workload and financial costs. I wouldn't like to be in the authorities' shoes now.

"And what about us? What if this bomb was not for wards, but for the employees?" came a female voice. Probably it was some frightened physician.

"I gathered you here to give you instructions. It's not possible to make a full reinforcement of the Department's walls. This will draw attention. Therefore, we'll only strengthen the sectors of the wards from the outside, and then do the same to your workspaces from the inside. Healers and other non-martial employees shouldn't walk alone. Martials should also cooperate. You have to at least go to work and back home in pairs and only by public transport. Preferably in a big crowd. And no flights, please! Ask your relatives to meet you at the stops. If someone has any problems with this, contact the documentation sector, you'll be temporarily provided with a hostel. Inform your colleagues who're not here, please. And we'll also arrange additional corporate mailing to staff's devices. You can form the groups at your own discretion."

"So, it's too early to move out from my parent's house," I wasn't pleased with this thought. And I didn't want to give up on my flights. Spring will end quickly and it would take a whole year of waiting until the next blooming period. Not all people travel by air, such trips take time and strength. Therefore, public transport and taxi are popular. But I'm neither an old lady, nor a mother with a bunch of kids. I love to fly.

"I'll move to my brother's place," Lina muttered under her breath at the same time. "He's a martial magician and his wife has been inviting me for a long time."

"Lina, are you in love?"

The girl looked at me blankly. I nodded at the towel, one edge of which she pressed to her cheek. Lina dropped it and got angry.

"Elle, what are you thinking about? Who will accompany you?"

"Dun, who else? It looks like I won't be able to avoid this."

Lina's mood improved immediately. She nudged me with her elbow and giggled. I suspected that she's received the same joy from watching me and Dun as I did from watching her and Paul. And Lina would have even more fun after what I told her today. But everything was clear in their relationship, all she had to do was surrender in the right way. As for me and Professor it seemed like I have already surrendered, but everything was still so unsteady and incomprehensible! My friend was having fun, but it wasn't fun for me at all.

When everyone started to leave, Deputy director asked me to stay.

"Helga, I'm transferring you under the temporary leadership of security guards. I want you to try your best to understand the bomb mechanism and to look for ways to organize the immobile fire traps."

I was surprised.

"What makes you think that we'll succeed? Nobody has done this before. There's no such technology."

"Two days ago Dun said that the Grenons also know how to catch fire clusters. They don't do this the way that you do because their magic is not about fire. Our martial healers are now trying to find out how the Grenons do this. Previously, we were not interested in these skills because the Department is not a military organization; our field of concern is different. But recently we have heard about your unique ability, and your colleagues working with the Grenons decided to conduct an experiment. And now we need to put the new skill into practice quickly. Honestly, we didn't want to rush you because until today we took interest in this direction purely out of curiosity. But now it needs to be mastered as soon as possible. You'd pass a safety exam on working with the Grenons tomorrow and then you will begin to study this new technology. And after that security officers will help you to look for a way to build this system into the walls."

"Yes, sir!"

I turned and left the conference room. I spent the rest of my shift time studying the instructions and preparing for tomorrow's exam. As I told Lina, Dun accompanied me home. He tried to joke, but I asked him to test my knowledge to prepare me for tomorrow. The night shift was full of events and strong emotions. I was already falling asleep when we approached my home.

***

"Do you know where Lina is?" I asked Paul the next evening. Reincarnologist was sitting alone in the dining room, stirring his coffee with a spoon. He was looking thoughtful, one might even say that he was upset with something. It was a completely unexpected picture. Lina was right — usually Paul was surrounded by laboratory ladies and was joking all the time.

"One-day internship. She'll come back tomorrow," he waved his hand lazily and suddenly perked up. "Listen, by the way, do you know who's that tigerboy?"

I got interested.

"What's the problem?"

"There's no problem. Yesterday after these conversations about security she called some 'tigerboy' and asked if she could stay at his place for some time. It seems to me that you two are friends now, you even flew to work together. Who's this tigerboy, Helga?"

Wow, Lina just didn't waste an opportunity! I was in awe. And more importantly, how skillfully she used the situation! But Paul was waiting for an answer and it was impossible to lie to him.

"I can say for sure that he's neither her husband, nor her fiance. But I can say nothing about the depth of their relationship," and that was true. How could I say something about the depth of their relationship? Who knows, maybe she hit her brother with her potty when they were little.

"Thanks, Helga," Paul became even more thoughtful. Are you going to visit security guards?"

"Yes. It's time to take the exam. I'll finally see the Grenons live!"

"You're going to like them," Reincarnologist forced a smile. "They're funny, strong and really beautiful. It's a pity that they almost never get out of the water. But maybe they will come out to you? You're the great-granddaughter of one of their favorites."

Wow, I got some new information! Why hadn't Dun told me this?

"My great-grandfather was their favorite?"

"Didn't you know that?" Paul was surprised.

"Who could have told me?" I moaned. "I have to force the information out of you. If I don't ask no one will inform me. As if I already knew everything."

"Well, the Grenons love having fun and fooling around. They treat people as their younger brothers. Just like we perceive dogs. That's why they have their favorites among us."

"What a terrible comparison!"

"That's why I prefer to work with the Lonquies. They treat us like children. But don't worry. The Grenons are also cool! Come on, let me walk you there because my coffee has completely cooled down, and I don't like to drink cold coffee."

The next five minutes we were silent. I was trying to recall the instructions, and the guy became even more thoughtful. We approached the door of the security sector and I had to go in. The laboratory has been located further and my interlocutor went there, wishing me good luck on a test.

Chapter 10

"What's going on with Paul?" Inga asked me in the gym when we were sparring. I looked at Reincarnologist, who was pounding a punching bag with frenzy five minutes ago. Now the guy was sitting on a bench and treating the cuts on his knuckles. The blood has already stopped, and new skin was growing on the wound under the influence of the healer's magic, but Paul didn't seem to feel any better.

"Lina," I whispered to Inga and she nodded knowingly.

"I see. Let's finish the sparring. You fire at the target. I'll go talk to Arthur."

A minute later, Arthur approached Reincarnologist and took him to a group of guys working on martial arts. Out of the corner of my eye I saw that the trainer made everyone concentrate and do the breathing exercises. Poor Paul!

When I left the gym, Arthur was still training Reincarnologist in concentration techniques. That was good! Maybe this will help Paul clean his head, and he'll begin to think hard at last. And maybe then he'll begin to act, finally.

But it was time for me to focus on my own breath, because I was going to visit the Grenons' sector! I have been dreaming about this meeting for so many years! My heart was pounding like crazy, I was walking on air!

In the vestibule in front of the entrance to the wards I was firstly sent to the women's locker room, where an older female healer helped me change into a diving suit.

"We're always on duty, ready to help," she said. "The management ordered a wetsuit for you a few days ago, it arrived this morning. Here's your smartwatch. Put it on, please, and watch the time. You can see the sensors in addition to the dial. Pay attention to the oxygen level in the cylinders, as well as to pressure and to your own parameters like the heart rate and external body temperature. I think there's no chance for you to get cold, and our men will stand by you, but for the first time everyone is so excited that they might forget to follow the safety instructions, even though they have to pass the exam right before the submersion."

"Is there anybody else there besides martial healers?"

"Not now, but sometimes various employees visit this sector. The Grenons treat everyone well and other colleagues come to relax with them from time to time. The managers allow everyone to do this because the Grenons need to be entertained. If they don't have fun constantly, their magic disappears and they fall ill. And the employees always work more efficiently after those sessions. Okay, it's done!"

I turned to the mirror and dropped the watch. I was almost naked. The fact that my body was completely covered by the wetsuit changed nothing. Instead of hiding my body the wetsuit was emphasizing it! Mama Mia! Dun was waiting for me in the Grenons' sector! How could I stand in front of him in this?

The assistant helped me to hide my hair under the swimming cap and put the watch on my hand which was hanging limply.

"Oh my God! I'm naked!"

"Your body is excellent!" the healer reinforced my anguish. "The guys will put the air tanks on your back and give you a mask inside the sector because we don't carry such things here. Well, why did you stop? Go!"

I took a deep breath and stepped outside. There was one bright side to it. I'll have an opportunity to see someone in such a suit as well. That is why I should put on my usual proud look, straighten my shoulders and chase my dream! I mean the Grenons, of course.

There was a huge artificial pond behind the main door. It was fenced off with a special wide wall, which however was not high. A middle-aged bearded man in a wetsuit was sitting on the wall half-turned to me and talking to someone who was in water. When I entered the man turned to me and behind his back I saw Dun protruding from the water. I recognized him only by his smile. Professor's eyes were hidden behind a pair of special swimming goggles. Also there was a cap on his head. It was impossible to examine the expression of his eyes because of goggles, and I wanted to know what he was thinking about my appearance in the Grenon's sector.

"Welcome, Helga! I'm Alex," the bearded man hurried to meet me. "How are you feeling?"

"I'm excited!" I admitted honestly, waving to Dun behind Alex' back. Professor smiled again and went underwater, covering his mouth with a breathing tube.

"Oh, I can totally understand you!" the bearded man grinned. "But it will pass soon, you'll see. Look over there."

He pointed at something far off with his hand, where two large water bubbles swelled near a tree that was growing over the pond. The roof of the pavilion was also translucent here. And although it was night outside, during the day it was clear that they used natural sunlight. But now specialized lamps provided light. Water began to move and five seconds later Dun soared over the wall, holding the heads (or backs) of two wonderful creatures with his hands. Oh, God, what a poseur!

Paul didn't exaggerate at all, the Grenons were surprisingly beautiful. The bluish-gray skin with a slight admixture of warmth seemed to glow from the inside with pearly light. I'd already seen their outlines on the black-and-white photo of my great-grandfather, but it couldn't convey this beauty. Each Grenon had only four tentacles, but otherwise they looked very octopus-like. The large head was dotted with lines that shone with bright blue light and formed a unique ornament, the central point of which ended with the mind's eye on the forehead. Under the mind's eye the Grenons had ordinary eyes, in which I saw considerable interest in me and some kind of childish joy. The creatures were taller than Dun, but very graceful.

And the most amazing thing was their magical field, which swayed like the thinnest cobweb, covering the entire body of the Grenon and stretching far beyond it. It was an incredible sight!

I stepped forward as if spellbound, but Alex held my hand.

"Where are you going?"

"I want to touch them!"

"Mask. Glasses. Air tanks," the bearded man said sternly and gave me glasses. Dun picked up the air tanks and began to place them on my back, not forgetting to grope my butt with his palm. I knew it!

"Do I need flippers?" I asked Alex, pretending to have lost the sense of touch. At least as if my butt did.

"No," Dun answered from behind. "It's more convenient to swim without them here. You'll see. Put on your mask when you jump into water. Can you breathe with it?"

"Yes. I have received a thirty minute training on how to do this before coming here."

"And what about equalizing your ears?"

"Well, I know this theoretically. I'll practice it under water."

"Okay. So, you can start diving now. We're following you."

The first thing I felt was a touch of a magic field. At the same time it seemed like the Grenons were touching not me, but something inside me. I looked at my own body and realized that the Grenons were studying my magic gift, weaving together the healer and martial directions. The sensations were very pleasant. It was like a loved person stroking my hair and touching my fur, which I actually did not have. Perhaps, this was exactly how the dog feels when it's caressed by its beloved owner. I understood where association with pets came from. The Grenons put some special meaning in each physical contact. It was kindness and at the same time condescension. People don't know how to touch someone's magic field in such a way.

I froze a step away from the magical creatures, and the next movement was made by the Grenons. They touched me with their tentacles, letting me do the same in response. The skin of the magical creatures was pleasantly warm and was drying up on air instantly. I knew that I wasn't allowed to touch the luminous blue lines, because the Grenons would be hurt by this, so I tried to stroke their backs as carefully as possible. On the heads of my new friends there were areas without the blue pattern. Also, there were small protrusions that could be grabbed by hands. Apparently, this was exactly what Dun was holding onto when he jumped out of water.

The magical "octopuses" harmoniously moved towards the pond, urging me to go with them. I put on my mask and stepped over the edge into water. Out of the corner of my eye I noted that Dun was diving nearby.

I didn't expect that depth would begin beyond the edge immediately, and therefore sank three meters down. The Grenons went to the bottom after me, grabbed me by my arms and jumped out to the surface. What a delight! Well, I didn't blame Dun anymore. If there were no mouthpiece in my teeth, I would probably scream from joy. Diving back, I saw that the new magical creatures were rushing towards us. Everyone wanted to meet me, to play with me, to pat my magic "fur". Being in a whirlwind of joy, I didn't want to keep track of time and sensors, but my colleagues were looming nearby, reminding me of safety measures with their silhouettes.

An hour later I was sitting on the wall, dangling my bare feet in water and watching Alex playing a ball with the Grenons.

"And on top of that the Department pays us money for such bliss!" I wondered aloud.

"Well, you also have to work," Dun grinned, sitting next to me with a notebook and a pen in his hands. "Look, right now Alex is studying the way the Grenons catch the ball."

This sight was really interesting. Magical creatures seemed to capture the ball with magic and levitate it back. Sometimes they were naughty and threw the ball without using their tentacles. Alex, as an air magician, returned the ball with a shield, which led to the blinking of blue patterns on the Grenons' bodies.

"They're showing their joy this way," Professor explained.

"How do you know that?"

"Paul understood it from their auras. And they can catch pulsars the same way they catch the ball. It looks like the Grenons kind of freeze it in time. The pulsar seems to be both on fire and not on burning at the same time. Do you want to try it?"

Oh, hell, yes, I wanted to! I came next to Alex and took his place. The Grenons blinked, welcoming this change of a game participant and anticipating a new round of entertainment. I formed a pulsar and threw it at the magical creatures. They caught it into some strange capsule indeed. I could see the frozen flames of fire. It looked as if the fire clot was cast out of translucent glass with bright light shining inside of it. The usual color play of fire was not visible at all. If you did not know what it was inside the capsule, you'd never guess.

The Grenons cheered up and threw the pulsar back at me. I caught it in my own way, which has definitely pleased them.

After having played with them for a while I returned to Professor, who hadn't taken his eyes off of us during all this time. I was hoping this was not because of my wetsuit.

"Well, they take a pulsar in some cocoon, encapsulating it. What do they know about time?"

"They don't feel it," Dun said thoughtfully. "Listen, you're smart!"

"Yeah," I agreed. "But this means that security guards are waiting for the trap devices for bombs to no avail."

"Why?"

"Because time is a relative concept that has been invented by human beings. That is why we won't be able to synthesize such a magic component for those devices. Encapsulation with time is possible only in conjunction with a living magic creature that would be aware of this variable, as well as able to accept its evanescence. Also, it should be able to overcome it, believing that it's really easy to control the relative and illusory concept of time."

"Umm... Helga, you're kind of freaking me out. I'm joking. Listen, what if we try to encapsulate time with time?"

"To make such traps effective there must be a trigger that would react to fire. However, fire is not animate, it is not alive. Without a conscious living creature the encapsulation of time won't work," I regained consciousness. Where did my words come from?

Dun was looking at me with interest and strange thoughtfulness.

"Helga, don't be alarmed," he reassured me. "This is one of the side effects of spending time with the Grenons. We have so many people who like to come here just because of this effect. I wrote your words down. Alex and I will work on this. But I'd like you to come here every day, okay? Maybe we'll hear something interesting from you again?"

'Of course, I'll come!' I thought. 'Where else can I see you in a wetsuit? At least I'll have a plausible reason to look at you.'

"Okay, Dun! I'll never miss such fun anymore," I said aloud.

"And what if you start to like the Clevres or the Lonquies more than Grenons?" Professor smiled.

"By the way, is it necessary to choose one species or it's possible to work with all three of them?"

"You can choose either one or all of them."

"In that case you have nothing to worry about."

Chapter 11

The next day, I was sitting in the dining room with instructions about the Clevres when my phone rang.

"Where are you?" Lina asked shortly. There was a panic in her voice.

"I'm in the dining room."

"Don't go anywhere."

Two minutes later the girl burst into the room.

"Elle, I seem to have overdone it!"

"Sit down!" I shouted at her because Lina, in my opinion, was out of control. And then I added more gently: "Pour yourself a cup of coffee, have a sip."

I waited until the girl did what I have told her and calmed down a little, and then asked:

"So, what's up?"

"I was sitting in the life extension lab," she said. "I heard Paul was talking to someone outside the door. Then it was about to be opened. I understood that he would enter now, and when I see him I would get overwhelmed by emotions, so I decided to launch a preemptive strike. So, I imagined him at the gym and dialed my brother at the same time. Paul came in with a bottle in his hand the moment when I was saying something about the tigerboy---"

"So?" I rushed the storyteller.

"So now Paul is sitting in the lab, and our girls are dancing around him, pulling fragments of glass out of his hand!"

"Wow!"

"Elle, what should I do?" Lina got scared again.

"You're repeating yourself. You have to calm down. Oh, hell, I'm repeating myself as well! Once you calm down, you can rejoice — I think the object has matured. Now it's important not to give him time to dive into his insecurities and impotent jealousy. You should talk to him."

"About what?"

"About anything. About work, about colleagues, you can even try to discuss Dun and me. Oh," I perked up. "Have you returned the towel?"

"Not yet," Lina was embarrassed. "There was no convenient moment and I didn't want to give it back, to be honest."

"Great! So you can give it back now. But with a hint, with a bottomless gratitude in your eyes, you know? Tell him how it was protecting you during those terrible discussions of the bomb. I don't think I need to teach you, because you understand and use this kind of situations much better than I do. Just don't overdo it again! All gratitude is exclusively in your words, eyes and aura. And no touches!"

"Elle, you're just a geisha! Now I'm not surprised why Dun has fallen for you!"

"Lina, if I were a geisha everything would have been much simpler there," I said sadly. "I've lost a lot of time, and now I'm suffering."

"And why are you suffering?" my interlocutor was surprised. "Enjoy yourself!"

"Okay! You should go now! Think about your towel-returning strategy! I need to learn, you have to work."

It's easy to say, 'Enjoy yourself!' Suspicions about Dun's motives had continued to torment me, and I just couldn't relax. On the other hand, if Professor was sincere, then any hint, coldness or detachment on my behalf can ruin everything. I had to constantly balance the fine line of favor and interest, risking either losing the remnants of my mind and analytical abilities because I fell in love, or pushing a dear person away from me and thereby destroying with my own hands the relationship that has just started to improve. I preferred to salvage myself from these fruitless thoughts by eating delicacies that the local cooks have been serving to the employees of the Department. Oh, and now I needed to go to the gym, otherwise the missing "millimeters" threatened to return at an alarming rate.

After the training I sat down in the dining room again, gathering strength before visiting the Grenons. Sports take a lot of energy, and I always tried to eat something starting the work with the wards. Otherwise it would have been very hard to dive.

Lina came in.

"I did it! I returned the towel!" she reported to me in a conspiratorial whisper, because there were people around us.

"So?"

"He was very glad!"

"Cool!"

"I also said that I didn't want to part with the towel."

"And you're saying that it's me who's geisha here," I was amused.

Paul entered the dining room.

"Oh, girls, I was looking for you. It's good that both of you are here. Do you want me to show you something interesting?"

"Of course!" I answered for the two of us.

"Let's go then!" Reincarnologist winked at Lina. The girl turned pink, but didn't look away. What a strong little thing she was! I couldn't act the way she did. I suspected that she was also able to win a staring contest.

I have to say that Lina has been amazingly beautiful these days. According to the order of our management we all had stopped flying for a while, so female part of the Department gladly used this opportunity to put on skirts and dresses. Pants and overalls stayed at home, along with their convenience and egalitarianism. Lina put on a beautiful dress with a fluffy skirt and her cool stilettos, which made her taller and even more elegant.

We hurried after Paul to the laboratory sector at the very end of the long corridor. I suddenly noticed an inconspicuous door. During the tour of the Department on my first day I didn't pay any attention to it for some reason. Looking at Lina, I realized that the contents hidden behind this door had been a secret for her as well. The girl's eyes were full of interest and excitement, and it was pleasant even to me to look at her. What could I say about Paul?

There was another laboratory for growing magical plants, but all the boxes were filled with only one kind of a plant — bright lilac grass with a bunch of yellowish pods. Containers stood on the floor, tables and tiers of racks by the walls. There was a drip irrigation system there, nourishing the plants with the necessary moisture and nutrients.

"Wow!" Lina opened her mouth in surprise.

"Do you know what it is, Helga?" Paul asked me.

"Alturis Kontis," I answered. "Or simply, Lilac Fun."

"That's correct! Did you study that at school?"

"Yes, I'm a healer, so I had to take a course on painkillers."

"Paul, how? Why?" Lina flung her hands up.

"We make a sedative for the Clevres out of this plant," Reincarnologist explained. "It has a different effect on them than it does on people. Girls, did you know that you can actually eat the Lilac Fun?"

I was surprised.

"And not smoke?"

Lina laughed and Paul explained with a smile:

"We smoke or drink medical extracts from leaves for the sake of pain relief. And we're eating pods in creamy sauce for gastronomic pleasure."

"I wonder why I didn't know that. Our teachers didn't tell us about it at school."

"Perhaps it's because the cultivation of Lilac Fun is allowed only to those producers who have a license. And in order not to provoke gourmets to violate the law, they try not to disseminate information about the pods."

"And what, there will be no euphoria if you eat the pods?"

"There will be, but it'll be very weak. It may slightly improve your mood. It can only be detected with special devices, and for patients it is imperceptible. You have to eat about a kilogram of raw pods to feel the effect, but this is not realistic. The raw pods are tasteless."

"Oh, yeah! But you should cook it with yoghurt instead of cream," Lina objected, and they started to argue about the taste of Lilac Fun with different types of sauces. I thought that it must have been Victor who told his sister about the nutritional value of herbal painkillers. Lina and Paul were such a great couple, arguing so avidly!

"Why are you hiding Lilac Fun from employees?" I interrupted the lovey-dovey sweethearts.

"Otherwise they'll smoke it!" giggled Lina.

"Or eat it all up!" added Reincarnologist and they laughed together.

I imagined a ragged clearing of Lilac Fun and laughed too.

"So, girls, I would like to invite you to a friendly dinner tomorrow. Helga, I've called Dun already. If you agree, he'll pick you up and we'll hang out at my place."

"Oh, do you cook?" Lina opened her eyes wide.

"As a hobby," Reincarnologist was embarrassed.

"I'm delighted!" the girl added fuel to the fire.

"We'll come, Paul," I replied for both of us, because it seemed like the guy was blushing to the top of his ears.

"Hooray! It will be an informal dinner, just a meeting of friends. But don't be late!"

Leaving the laboratory, I whispered to Paul quietly:

"Don't wear your glasses! And you shouldn't take on anything that looks like the top of your medical scrub!"

My phone rang when I was on my way to the Grenons' sector. The head of the security guard asked me to approach him. I turned around and went there.

"We want to take the bomb to the shooting range and detonate it there. Do you want to come with us and try to catch this explosion?"

"I'm afraid that I don't have enough strength for that."

"We'll take several healers with us, they have great potential, so they'll provide the recharge if need be. But you can refuse."

"No, I'll go," who'd refuse to test one's abilities in such conditions? "But can we ask Dun to go with us?"

"Why?" security guard was surprised.

"We have known each other for a long time. I've worked with him from the very beginning of my career. He's always been there for me, helping to handle all the difficult situations. I just feel more comfortable and safe in his presence," I looked straight into security Chief's eyes and tried my best not to blush.

"No problem! I'll call Dun now and invite him to join us. If he agrees, then we'll take him instead of one of our healers.

It will even be better — as a water magician, he can provide additional protection to our group."

Dun came into our security sector ten minutes after the call. The ends of Professor's hair were wet. Apparently, we pulled him out of the Grenons' basin in the midst of his work.

"Are you ready?" asked security Chief. Dun nodded.

"Let's go then," we left the office and headed towards the documentation sector. I saw a massive door behind it. The door was closed with the same lock that was hanging on the doors of the laboratory and other important premises of the Department. Behind the door there were the down bound steps and a long underground tunnel which led us to a large covered hangar, where I saw a helicopter, a couple of modern aircrafts and some specialized vehicles. I was wondering how many of the pavilions of the botanical garden actually belonged to the Department.

"It's our transportation base," security Chief explained. "We have airplanes of the latest design here. Only the army has even better ones in its possession. These airplanes can start up straight from the spot thanks to the air magic. They are able to land in the same way too. The base adjoins to the wall of the botanical garden, and we are moving underground right now — it's more convenient this way."

"What is all of this for?" still dumbfounded, I asked when we were boarding the nearest plane. "We're a secret organization that almost no one knows about, and we specialize in science. "What do you do this for?"

"Firstly, sometimes we receive reports about the Clevres and the Grenons, which are located in deep-water basins or in glaciers," Professor said. "Every year on the planet there are less and less unexplored places, and after some time we will not be able to find any more wards. However, the messages keep on coming periodically. A big boom took place seventy years ago after the invention of scuba gear. We always have to react very quickly so that the information does not have time to leak outside. With the advent of the global network, this has become even more relevant. The high ranking officials have allowed us to rent any military aircraft, boat, ship, not to mention smaller transport. But the Department is trying to get by with its own transport to avoid answering additional questions and obliterating the memory of random witnesses."

"And secondly?"

"Secondly, we are obliged to help other services during the most urgent cases," security Chief answered. "For example, when a tsunami hit the Yellow Archipelago, all of our water and air magicians rushed there to stop a disaster. Every state that finances us is entitled to our assistance in such circumstances."

"Have you been there too?" I asked Dun.

"No, I was a student those days. My mom had been there though. She's retired now, but during that tsunami she was working at the Department."

Yeah! Who would have thought? I found myself liking the Department more and more. It was an ideal workplace for someone who loves helping people. At the same time, security Chief sat me into a chair, put a helmet and a mask on me, and then pressed a special button that activated a cocoon of compressed air around my body.

"The nearest shooting range for explosive devices is in two hours by air transport from here. Since these planes take off strictly vertically, we protect our bodies from overload with such a cocoon," I heard his voice in the helmet's headphones. "You can turn it off when we're airborne."

The sensations were not pleasant at all. I seemed to have been squeezed from all sides with something elastic. If oxygen was not supplied into the mask, I would probably suffocate. For now, it was barely possible to endure this. It was good that I didn't suffer from claustrophobia. Despite the fact that everything was clearly visible through the cocoon, it seemed that the cramped walls were confining me from all sides.

The roof of the hangar opened, and the plane made a sharp leap upwards, but I didn't feel any transition. Suddenly, just a blurry streak of light rushed down the window and after about a minute we were already flying somewhere towards the huge moon. Security Chief showed how to turn off the protective cocoon. I took off my mask and breathed a sigh of relief. Dun, two healers and two security guards were freeing themselves from captivity nearby. After a brief acquaintance, I decided to spend some time trying to recall the instructions regarding the Clevres, which I studied today in the first half of the night. Professor helped me fill in the gaps; he also had nothing to do during these two hours of flight.

"The bomb is not very big, so even if you fail nothing bad will happen," security Chief told me two hours later. We were walking from the plane to the shooting range. One of the security guards was carrying the bomb. "We'll set it off with an additional special detonator, which will commence the process. It's not dangerous for us at this moment."

"If it's not very big, then how can it destroy the entire population of the Lonquies?"

"Such devices are dangerous due to the fragments that spread around and hit everything that comes in the way. An additional magical component provokes the appearance of new fragments from the destroyed structures. Often a roof or its pieces will fall as a result of an explosion of such devices, crushing and hitting those victims who were not killed by the fragments. Therefore, it will not be dangerous to detonate the bomb at the shooting range, taking into account protective measures. But its explosion in the building or near it ---" the security guard shook his head. "The creator of the bomb knew very well how to arrange a big disaster with very little means. Have you visited the Lonquies' sector?"

"No, I haven't yet. Yesterday I passed the Grenons exam. A visit to the Lonquies will happen another day."

"When you look at them, you'll see that they're very fragile creatures. Fragments are certain death for their soft bodies."

I've listened to him and at the same time thought that it would be better if I had put on trousers and comfortable sneakers for today's shift. Walking in pumps was very difficult for me here. I was leaning on Dun's arm so as not to tuck my foot on the bump and fall. If it was summertime I could just take off my shoes and stomp barefoot, but so far the ground was still too cold. Especially in the middle of the night.

When all preparations with the placement of the bomb were completed, we were asked to take on a special protection. A minute before the explosion, an ice shield had appeared in front of us, which was clearly made by Dun. There was only a narrow gap to look through. I glanced at Professor and saw that he was in full readiness to close it off too if there would be at least a little threat. It seemed to me that Dun had an attack of paranoia, because the fragments couldn't reach us there. Having received a confirmation nod from each member of our group, security Chief pressed the push switch.

Oh, God! I didn't have enough time! A bomb is not a pulsar. How come I didn't think about this before? Have I felt proud because of my unique abilities, or what? Pulsar is a plasma clot that is stable in its size. Despite the fact that it's very fast, at least it's predictable and at a certain reaction rate it's quite perceptible. The bomb, however, transforms from a small ball into a huge clot of flame instantaneously. I was struggling to envelop this clot with my fire, but it seemed my power and speed were not enough. I couldn't work ahead of the curve.

Talking about this would take a long time. In fact, both the explosion and my attempts to stop it took a split second. And I lost, spending almost all of myself.

But from aside it looked like a victory. I managed to collect fragments and release the might of the bomb into my fire cocoon. However, if this had happened next to the Lonquies, it would have been hardly possible to save everyone. The fragments would certainly not have scattered, but the very force of the explosion would kill a lot of creatures. I just couldn't stop the growth of the flame at the level of the small bomb device. Throwing a huge ball of fire onto a specially prepared place, I fell into Dun's arms. Healers rushed to us and started to pump me up with their magical power immediately. Professor wrapped me in his jacket over my cloak, but it didn't help much.

"Helga, drink it!" security Chief handed me a mug with a protein-vitamin shake used by athletes to restore their strength. He was gloomy and depressed.

My teeth were clattering on the edge of the mug, so I made my first sips heavily. Dun was helping me hold the mug, because I was too weak even for such a simple effort. As soon as the first drops reached my stomach, the heat went through my body and I started to warm up.

"We're definitely missing something," security Chief said grimly.

"W-what are you t-talking about?" no, my strength hasn't returned yet.

"The explosion was too powerful for this type of bomb. Perhaps we misjudged the potential of the magical component in this device. Too bad. I have to report this to Director urgently, because we have to strengthen the outside walls of the wards' sectors even better."

Dun carried me all the way back to the plane. I tried to argue, but my legs didn't work well yet — other people's magic had overwhelmed me, but the body needed some time to recover. Professor didn't even listen to my objections. Security Chief supported him, saying briefly: 'We have no time!'. I had to stop protesting. Dun was gloomy and silent during the entire flight back to the Department. However, all of us were in the same mood. Security Chief was frowning while the healers were drinking a restorative drink. By the time I got off the plane at our base, I was completely fine and even managed to think about my arrogance, promising myself never to overestimate my own abilities again.

Chapter 12

On the way home, Professor was still silent and frowning.
"Dun, what's up with you?"
"Promise me to never put yourself at such risk again!"
"I can't. I took the doctor's oath".
"I know, damn it! Then promise me that you'll call me to be nearby at any similar situation, so that I can protect and recharge you!"
"Isn't that what I did today?"

Dun couldn't find an answer. Because I was right! I decided to change the topic in order to distract Professor from his gloomy thoughts. So I asked my companion to bring Lina to me an hour and a half before the time appointed by Paul. We all had a weekend ahead, that's why Reincarnologist decided to organize this dinner.

"Helga, what did I miss?" Dun became interested.
"Everything!" I snapped. "By the way, why aren't you going to the gym?"
"I am," Professor finally smiled. "Straight after I take you to work, I head to Arthur for breathing and concentration exercises."

What a rascal! Why was he confusing me? Actually, it was my fault. Paul told me about the time Dun visited the gym. Why did I ask this question to Professor at all? However, my companion didn't expect me to know this, so. . .

"Maybe if you went to the gym with Paul, you'd have known. Dun, I'm a confidant, I won't tell you a word. You'll see everything with your own eyes soon."
"I seem to be also a confidant, but for some reason I know nothing."
"So have patience, please. Will you fulfill my request?"
"Of course!"

The next day, Dun brought Lina exactly at the time that I had appointed. We tried to get Professor out for a walk, but my Dad came to the rescue of the guest and led him away to play Weigi. My cat strolled to their room too. As if he understood at least something in Weigi. Apparently, the feline mustachioed muzzle finally made a choice in favor of Dun. However, we decided to let them have fun so they wouldn't bother us. Lina came dressed in shorts, a T-shirt and white sneakers. I shook my head.

"That's not good."

"Paul said that it would be an informal dinner!"

"This doesn't mean that you shouldn't put any thought into your outfit at all, although your legs are beautiful even without stilletes. Mom, come here, please."

Parents also had a day off today, so the whole family was at home. Except for my brother who has long been married and lived separately. Our family owned a private house in one of the sleeping quarters of the city. I had my own comfortable room, where there was enough space not only for me, but also for dressing my girlfriends in front of the mirror.

"We need an outfit," I told my Mother when she came in. "You and Lina are of the same height and complexion, help me choose a dress for her, please. The dinner is informal, but we have to find the outfit so that one guy gets crazy about Lina."

Mom livened up.

"One moment, please," she said and slipped out of the room, shouting from the corridor: "You can make her a ponytail while I am busy."

"Ma, you're a genius!" I said a little bit later, when Lina was standing in front of us almost ready. The snow-white fluffy skirt-shorts didn't constrain movement, but looked very feminine. The outfit of a naive athlete was complemented by a tight pink sports top. Its vertical white stripes were quite slimming and made Lina's waist appear even thinner. A ponytail revealed her graceful neck, and her legs looked even more appealing in white socks. I even imagined a racket in her hands. Who would argue that she doesn't look informal?

"This outfit is thirty years old," Mom admitted. "I tried to impress your dad in it. When I hid it away in a chest, I thought that maybe I could pass it on to you someday. I refreshed it periodically to prevent the skirt from turning yellow. But you grew so tall that it simply wouldn't fit you now. It's good that I didn't throw it in the garbage."

Yes, I wouldn't mind having such a skirt too! It would be necessary to buy something similar in my size after receiving the first salary.

We didn't put makeup on Lina because we knew that Paul wouldn't appreciate it. The girl has just freshened her face with herbal ice cubes. I put on comfortable wide breeches and a tunic, my Mother braided my hair into a french braid, and then we entered the room where the Weigi players were sitting.

Dad smiled and winked at Mom. She was embarrassed.

"You remember, don't you?"

"Of course, I do! I'd dreamed about you in this outfit for a month after that picnic."

Dun was silent, keeping his promise not to question or interfere. But he looked at Lina attentively, smiled and suggested that we two should take his arms.

"You both are charming, girls. Well, let's go?"

We stopped by the store on our way, and Dun bought four bottles of beer. Following the safety instructions for movement, we reached Paul's apartment by taxi. Reincarnologist met us barefoot, in jeans, a tight-fitting short-sleeved shirt and a funny kitchen apron.

"Suit yourself," he waved at us and sped off into the kitchen. "I'm almost done."

Lina moaned behind me.

"Elle, I can't stand this!"

"What happened?" Dun was alarmed, but I glanced at him, asking not to interfere.

"Shoulders! Eyes!! Apron!!! My Goodness!"

"Hold on! He hasn't had enough time to look at you properly yet. Dun, teach her how to concentrate on breathing, please. What are you laughing at, you, heartless?"

"I'm sorry, Lina!" Professor winked. "I didn't know that everything was so serious here. Helga didn't sell you to me yesterday. So, let's try: inhale-exhale, inhale-pause-exhale. You can't even imagine how much I understand you! One more time: inhale-pause-exhale. Now again, but quietly, so that it can't be heard. You should breathe through parted lips. Don't clench your teeth in any case, otherwise you'll get a whistle. Think about flies. Oh no, don't think about flies! Think about the sea. It's so calm, and the quiet rustle of the waves brings peace and puts your soul in balance. Do you feel better now?"

"A little bit. Thanks, Dun!"

"Not at all! You can use meditation in the moments of crisis. I've done it a lot lately."

I pretended that I didn't hear his words.

"Why are you still stuck in the hallway?" Paul leaned out of the kitchen and suddenly loudly sucked in the air through his clenched teeth, clearly demonstrating the whistle which comes out because of this. Lina was standing on her left foot, taking off a white sneaker from the right one. Dun was supporting her under her elbow for balance and because of the narrow room, the girl bent over as a beautiful figurine. Oh, I could see. Someone has still not learned how to concentrate on breathing, despite all Arthur's efforts.

"We're ready, Paul," I said. "Something's boiling over."

Reincarnologist finally exhaled and rushed to the kitchen again, and we went into the living room. It turned out that Paul's apartment didn't have a wall between the kitchen and the living room. These two rooms were separated only by a massive bar counter. We saw how the owner was doing his cooking magic. Lina started her breathing meditation again.

I understood her very well. A guy who's keen on something interesting always looks special, and Paul obviously liked to cook. This fact was indicated by a chic shelf for spices with a bunch of jars and a whole set of various cooking tools. Even my Mother didn't have so many of them in our kitchen. The future food smelled very tasty, by the way.

I was examining the decoration of the kitchen and the set of dishes attentively, making notes in my mind. Why? I was going to move to my own place and so I would have no one to cook for me because Mom with her goodies would stay at home. It was necessary to take a closer look and to consult with someone on this question. For example, that little pan was quite an interesting option for sauces in my opinion. And the other one was the best for making pancakes.

"Paul, give me a bucket or a big pan, please" Dun asked. "Big enough to put four bottles of beer. I'll freeze up some ice to cool our drinks."

"Come and get it. I'm already finishing."

Dun went to the kitchen, and from that moment on both Lina and I were admiring the busy guys. Without any doubt, she liked to look at Reincarnologist, who was cooking, and I was intently watching Professor's magic flows, which allowed him to work with water. I tried to distract both Lina and myself simultaneously, whispering in her ear:

"Listen to me carefully, please. It's not necessary to hide your emotions anymore, and you won't succeed. But try not to look so often, otherwise you'll get the oxygen shock because of your attempts to stabilize your breath and heart. When Dun brings ice in a few minutes, put your hand on the bucket, it will become easier to distract yourself. Just don't freeze your fingers, please. And remember! You can't touch the object first! No touching until he takes a step. We've done everything possible to make this happen. Moreover, he's on his territory now, so this is encouraging."

An hour later, we were sitting at the table with empty plates and slowly drinking our ice beer. A magical marine illusion picture was rustling above the bar, where the missing wall was supposed to be, and covering the bedlam in the kitchen. Paul didn't waste his time cleaning after cooking and simply turned on the projector, unknowingly helping Lina to focus on her breathing. However, I suspected that it wasn't just her, because absolutely all the participants of the party periodically looked at the illusion of the sea. Lilac Fun turned out to be really delicious. It was like a brackish hybrid of fish and mushrooms, stewed in yogurt. I hope Lina appreciated the "curtsy" that Paul did by choosing yogurt instead of cream for the sauce. Beer was a perfect choice of drink for this food. Reincarnologist entertained us with funny stories from his medical practice:

"She asked him: 'Are you tormented by erotic dreams?' By the way, she was asking a regular question in that situation. And he, apparently, remembered a bad old joke, and replied: 'No, I'm not. They are not tormenting me. On the contrary, I enjoy them!'"

We laughed.

"Paul, you had psychiatry practice, hadn't you?"

"Yes, Helga. Partially. A reincarnologist studies to become an aura specialist at first. Psychiatry constitutes a big chunk of it."

"And who was your mentor before you came to work at the Department?"

"Alex. Both of us are air magicians."

I remembered bearded Alex, who met me the day before yesterday at the Grenons, and asked:

"So you didn't hesitate to take up a job at the Department?"

"Of course, I didn't! Just like you. I would never miss such an opportunity!"

"And what about you, Lina?"

"My brother invited me here. When the healer position had opened, he called me. I used to miss Victor a lot, and my job was not very interesting anyway. So I agreed immediately. He was my mentor."

Lina's phone rang.

"Oh, here he is, by the way, speak of the devil. Yes, tigerboy."

It was funny to look at Paul at that moment. I burst into a fist, and Reincarnologist hissed:

"Helga! I'll remember it!"

Lina continued to twitter into the phone, explaining to Victor that Dun would accompany her on her way home. And that her brother should tell his wife that there was no need to leave a dinner for Lina, because she had already been fed. I couldn't calm down and continued to laugh, burying my face into Professor's shoulder. Dun was looking at me with a silent question in his eyes. That wasn't a big deal, I'd tell him everything later.

"Well, okay!" Reincarnologist said resentfully, glancing at Lina. "I'm going to wash the plates. Then, if you want, we can play a magic twister."

"Wait, Paul, I'll help you!" the girl had finished her phone conversation. Paul perked up.

"Great! Take this large plate from Fun, it's not heavy, and bring it to the kitchen sink. I'll take care of the rest of the dishes."

"You have no dishwasher?" Dun asked, hugging the laughing me.

"There's no need for it," Reincarnologist was embarrassed. "I live alone. How long does it take to wash one plate?"

"A magic twister?" I asked Dun when our friends left the living room. I haven't played this game before.

"Yes. It's the same as the usual twister, the only difference being that after arms and legs you can also use your magic gift for additional support. What shall we do while they are washing the plates?" Professor asked me, and at that moment something broke down in the kitchen with a loud sound of crushed dishes.

"Quiet," I whispered, holding Dun by his sleeve to stop him from rushing from the sofa. We got up, tiptoed to the kitchen and peered through an open door.

Lina was sitting on the bar, which was hidden from view from the living room by a voluminous magical illusion. Paul was standing right in front of her, and the girl's arms and legs were around him. Fragments of a large plate were lying on tiles. The guys were so into each other that they wouldn't have noticed our appearance even if we had burst into the kitchen screaming and shooting. Dun grunted under his breath and quietly pulled me back onto the sofa in the living room.

"Helga, I'm delighted! This longing had been lasting for the whole year, and then you came and made everything right during the course of one week!"

"Oh, finally! I can do my work at last, otherwise this matchmaking has taken a lot of my time and energy. Why are you so happy?"

"Paul's a good guy. And Lina's a good girl. It's bad when good people are wasting time."

Our friends appeared in the living room at the moment when I was telling Professor about a memorable training in the gym, having finished my story about the tigerboy, the towel and glass fragments in Paul's hand. I was on fire. Apparently, Lilac Fun and beer took their toll on me. Dun was laughing and trying to stroke me or hug me at every piquant moment. I was fending him off jokingly in an attempt to finish the story.

"On top of that, she thought that Paul's a womanizer," I wanted Professor to see the humor of the situation.

"Did you really think so?" Reincarnologist asked Lina. "Why?"

"You've always been surrounded by girls, and you're complimenting everyone all the time," my friend said, looking down.

"I told you that you've been making a huge mistake with your behavior," Dun blamed Paul, clearly continuing some old argument.

"But guys, why are you always forgetting about my specialization?" said offended Reincarnologist. "I come to work and see that one girl is having some troubles at home, she's sad; the other one is angry either at her husband or some of her colleagues; the third one is annoyed by a stain on her cloak that some careless driver had gotten on her clothes. I make some compliments and then it's easier to work with them. I joke a couple of times and everyone becomes relaxed, the atmosphere gets better. Helga, remember, for example, what you were thinking about when Dun introduced me to you."

I smiled. My mood was really down after the meeting between my fictitious fiance and my parents. And then Paul managed to distract me. Dun looked at me with interest, but didn't dare to ask.

"Does it mean that you compliment me only when I'm sad?" Lina put her hands on her hips.

"I always compliment you," Paul assured the girl, hugging her more tightly.

"So I said to Lina that she had been very mistaken. Then she started talking about your working hoodie and glasses, which make your eyes barely visible. That's why I advised her to come to the gym. That day, everyone's focus on training had been disrupted."

"Oh, I can imagine that!" Professor was amused, and Reincarnologist grunted, glancing conspiratorially at me.

"Heh, you're having fun now! And I couldn't believe my luck. Especially after that incident, Helga. Such a chance to show off! I thought, maybe she'll finally notice me. Did I overdo it?"

Dun stopped laughing and looked at me again, and then looked at Reincarnologist.

"After what incident, Paul?"

"The day when I pulled Lina out of the cold shower," I hastened to intervene. "It would be wrong to just say 'noticed'. The poor thing had her teeth chattering because of your efforts."

"You look so skinny in your medical scrub!" Lina poked Reincarnologist in his chest with her elbow. By the way, she wasn't embarrassed because of her own feelings and reactions at all.

"And what about me without a medical scrub?" Paul asked with a smile, stroking his girlfriend on the back with his palm.

"And without it you're not skinny!" Dun and I said in chorus, looked at each other and fell into a fit of unbridled laughter. Seriously, laughing together is, in my opinion, as great as kissing. Lina looked at us and then rolled her eyes.

"Listen, guys, stop joking, please! We should call it a night. Paul will walk me home, his apartment is not so far from Victor's house. And you should take a taxi. To hell this bomb."

We all became serious at once.

"I don't think that something is threatening us outside the Department," I said thoughtfully.

"Why?" Lina was surprised. The girl was sitting in Paul's lap and clinging to him, with Reincarnologist's arm around her, as if he was covering her from danger. I wouldn't be surprised if there was a thin air shield around them, which air magicians sometimes put out unconsciously when there is even a hint of danger.

"Just think about it. We had a bomb. A powerful explosive device, which would be enough to destroy the entire sector of the Lonquies. We detonated it yesterday on the shooting range, and it took every bit of my double magic power to catch the fire in my trap. Then healers had to pump me up with their energy to prevent me from fainting. I warmed up with difficulty. It was a very unpleasant surprise for Chief of security, because initially he underestimated the might of the bomb. He thought attackers would be mainly counting on the damage due to fragmentation. Therefore, this device is not ordinary, either a very competent fire magician or a group of people did it. It's unlikely that such people would hunt for employees one by one. Given the spread of the myth of scientific experiments on newborns, I think that the goal is to discredit or even to stop the activities of the entire Department."

"If you're right, then martial healers are under attack," Dun said. "Bombers would only need to kill us to freeze the work of the Department."

Now Lina hugged Paul, the guy pressed her to his body, and I replied:

"Yes, it will be suspended, but its activity will not be stopped forever. Too many people know about our work, including the governments of most countries. Sooner or later new martial healers will be born, and the Department will be reborn with them. To achieve the goal, it's wiser to destroy the wards," said I, and immediately became horrified by the resulting scenario.

"What should we do?" asked Reincarnologist.

"I think that it's not so good to leave the sectors of the Grenons, the Lonquies and the Clevres unattended, either during the day or the night. At least one martial healer should be there all the time, but preferably there should be two. And after that, we should wait for what will happen next. Judging by what I heard from security guards, they have no leads."

"Yes," said Paul. "The Lonquies said that there was a shielding helmet on the bomber, so they couldn't recognize his identity or understand the intentions. And programmers say that they didn't succeed in tracking the source of rumors about the experiments on newborns."

"We simply don't have enough martial healers for round-the-clock duty in pairs," Dun said pensively.

"There's an opportunity to make such a pair from a martial healer and a security guard for the Grenons' sector. We just need to choose those who're crazy about the wards," I said. "It's also desirable to temporarily pull out all specialists from maternity hospitals."

"Helga, you've worked with security last week, haven't you?" clarified Professor. I nodded. "Great! So you have to present all your ideas to security Chief on Monday. As for me, I'll communicate with Director. He'll control the selection of employees for this duty. We can't withdraw anyone from the maternity hospitals without his permission. But still, let's move around the city according to security recommendations, so that we wouldn't worry about each other."

I didn't argue. Lina and Paul didn't mind as well.

Chapter 13

On Monday, at the end of my shift Director called me to his office. I was working during the day, preparing to take exams about the Clevres and get to know them in more detail. Lina had also decided to take the day shift a couple of times so that she and Paul would be seen together less. Therefore, in the morning we went to work together.

"Helga, we got a report that a group of divers saw a strange creature in the ocean. It had a third eye in its forehead and four tentacles. Selfies have already appeared on the Internet and you can say for sure that this is a young Grenon, still a child. You'll have to work on such cases in the future, so I ask you to stay and join the tracking team to gain experience in this sphere. We'll pay for the overtime. Are you tired?" – said Director.

"No sir. I was with the Clevres and basically watched Victor's actions."

"Great! I called Dun here a little earlier before the start of his shift. He's one of the employees who are constantly dealing with this type of wards. Alex is an air magician, and it would be nice to have him too, but someone has to be with the wards, and it's better to choose a water magician for diving. Therefore, Alex will stay here. There will also be an aura specialist in your group to make it easier to detect an object, as well as a security guard who possesses an element of air and is also a mentalist just a bit. She will help if you suddenly have any problems with the breathing mixture or sharks. Pay attention to everything, please, but be careful and don't interfere with your group mates. And watch your back. In the ocean there can be a variety of troubles apart from sharks."

I nodded.

"Okay, you can take your wetsuit now. Our guys will load your plane with the rest of equipment. And ask for flippers of the appropriate size in the warehouse. Call your parents and eat something before you leave."

What a caring boss! Instructions say that you shouldn't dive tired or hungry. They also warn about the need for full equipment for deep-sea work and about the right behavior in dangerous situations. I'd learned it all by heart, so I didn't waste my time now and simply went to the dining room, calling my parents on the way.

In our women's locker room I received not only my wetsuit, but also a sealed bag with some pills.

"What is it?" I pointed at pills.

"These are the magic cucumbers. You don't have to chew bitterness anymore. You'll need a lot of magic energy, as far as I understood the task," answered the employee, who usually helped me to put on my wetsuit.

"I thought they could only be eaten raw," I wondered.

"The laboratories have figured out how to work with the most necessary properties and to compress them into pills. This form of magic cucumbers has not become widespread yet, but it will enter the market soon. Many people will want to get these pills."

"Yeah," I remembered what range of feelings I had experienced every time before the shift, biting this bitter squiggle. Why hadn't they told me about the pills before? Truly, the employees of the Department were so afraid of blabbering that they didn't even share the information with their own colleagues. I thought that it would be necessary to ask Lina about some other hidden utilities of the Department.

We flew to the ocean coast. The nearest military base, which could take our plane, was not quite close to the diving site. Therefore, we had to travel to the shore by car, and then sailed to the coast on a guard boat. And during all this time Dun was lecturing me.

"Helga, we'll dive in pairs in a bunch. I'll be watching you, and Natalie will be watching Ron. In our group, you two are new to diving, so you obey us implicitly. Military said that the place where divers saw the Grenon, is not very deep — it's only fifteen meters. This is just fine for the first serious dive. You should look at your diving computer every five minutes. If the air in your tank runs out earlier than in any of ours, you should pull the tench. In the worst case scenario Natalie will help you with breathing. Immerse at the same speed as we'll do. Don't forget to blow out so that your ears do not be hurt. Don't touch anything under water; there may be poisonous fish and plants. We'll float together. We'll deal with buoyancy on a boat, and then on the bottom if needed. And most importantly, don't be afraid. I'll be with you."

A partner who'll be there for you at a dangerous moment — isn't this what every loving woman dreams of? After such words, even my annoyance has disappeared, which had accumulated due to this excessive custody. No, I understood that immersion is not a children's fun, you really need to observe absolutely all the nuances of the instructions, and additional repetition is really appreciated. But still, this repetition was a little annoying. Until I heard the warm and confident 'I'll be with you'.

Stop! Did I just understand that I love Dun? I experienced a strange feeling of both fear and delight, tenderness and bitterness. I couldn't just afford to give free rein to my feelings in that situation with the bomber.

"Why are you trying to scare her, Dun?!" meanwhile, security guard Natalie was indignant, apparently misinterpreting the expression on my face. "Helga, an amazing adventure awaits us! The ocean is incredibly beautiful in this place, we were diving not far from here last year. There are so many colorful fish, beautifully swaying algae, incredible stones, which you'll never see on the ground. And I hope we'll find the baby Grenon."

An aura specialist winked at me from another seat, and for some reason I clearly understood that this guy saw everything correctly, and his sign had something to do with my last emotions. But I somehow stopped even being embarrassed about that. Let it be. I couldn't hide what was happening to me from aura specialists, but they wouldn't tell Dun. So I winked back.

However, I definitely had to do something with my feelings. Otherwise, emotions could block my mind, which could potentially cause quite serious troubles in the current circumstances. And it was not about my doubts, but about the events taking place in the Department. If I relax I could find myself without an arm or a leg. Therefore, I had to be alert and think about the situation permanently. And this meant that I needed to hide my love and tenderness somewhere deep in my soul and to turn on my brain again.

Natalie helped me to put on a gear. A wetsuit was just the foundation of all the equipment. There was also a compensation vest with specialized automation, making manual blowing unnecessary. I had to take on flippers, a mask, a scuba gear, a helmet with a powerful flashlight to search for the Grenon. It was great that in our wetsuits there was a special magical heating system. Information about water temperature, external pressure, state of a body, remainder of air — everything was fed to a diving computer. An automation of heating temperature and an amount of air in a vest also came from there. If necessary, it was possible to switch manual control, but so far this has not been discussed. I was hoping Dun would help me if I need it suddenly.

"The biggest problem of all beginners when it comes to diving is their fears associated with breathing under water. But you already swam with the Grenons, which means that there's no need to think about it," the security guard told me. "The main task for you is to watch your sensors. And keep an eye on Dun, please. Although he's an experienced diver, everyone needs to be looked after underwater. Most often, experienced divers got into trouble because of their arrogance, and also because there was no one to notice the problem in time. So watch out. Just for your own peace of mind. We have only an hour for the first dive, then we'll need to go to the surface and to make a pause. However, we all hope that Ron will find the baby Grenon quickly."

Security guard and I repeated divers' conditional gestures and went out on deck. Military put heavy scuba gear on us there, after which Dun and I as Natalie and Ron were sealed with a special cord in pairs. Sailors helped us get down into water. The dive has begun.

We went down very slowly. Dun held my hand. In Professor's second hand there was a powerful lamp in addition to a flashlight on his helmet, which my companion had turned off so that it would not drain the batteries. Natalie and Ron also descended by the hand. I tried not to waste time on emotions that arose as a result of this proximity, and turned my head around, staring at everything that came my way.

The feeling was just awesome! I always loved great water, and in front of the ocean I felt some kind of sacred awe. It was like a deity to me. A deity, who can be a good and loving father today, and then turn into a formidable and terrible beast the next day. And now, plunging into its depths, I thought that I was condescendingly allowed into some kind of eternal secret. So it seemed that in a second I would see a flooded pirate ship full of chests of gold. Or that Poseidon would come up to meet me, waving his amazing trident in greeting. And this anticipation of a miracle evoked a lot of joyful emotions in me.

According to Natalie, we were very lucky with the weather — the excitement was weak and due to this, excellent visibility was provided. Flocks of colorful fish circled around us, a small slope swam nearby. We saw several jellyfish and noticed moray eels. I didn't know most of the inhabitants of the depths, so they remained nameless to me, but they were no less beautiful or bewitching. Apparently, tourists really dive here often, because the inhabitants of the deep sea were not afraid of us at all. I wanted to touch a fish, but I remembered Dun's warnings and safety instructions. So I was just watching around and enjoying diving.

Wonderful octopuses and crabs were crawling on the bottom of the ocean. There were huge blocks of stones that formed picturesque groups. Dun showed Ron a sign that it was time to start our search. We went down to the bottom not far from the place where the Grenon was seen. On the plane Professor said that the cub couldn't swim far from here. All of us were tormented by only one question: where did the baby come from, and were its parents nearby?

The first half an hour the search didn't bring any results. But we found the remains of a sunken ship, and I fell into children's delight. Unfortunately, it wasn't possible to levitate in water. Apparently, this magical technique could only be applied in the air. I had to use my flippers and swim around the ship in order to consider everything. Dun had to follow me, since we were tied with one cord, and Professor didn't want to let me take an underwater trip completely on my own. Ron waved his hands joyfully nearby. Natalie had to yank him constantly to remind the aura specialist why we were here in the first place.

But Ron finally felt a familiar glimpse of an aura, which, according to Paul, is slightly different from the glow of human auras and even more different from the glow of those of the animals and fish. We rushed in the indicated direction and saw a small Grenon hunting the inhabitants of the depths. Noticing us, the cub ran for cover. Was he really scared so much by divers that he was now running away from masked people? Dun tried to approach the Grenon with his Gift, hoping to show the cub that he wasn't an enemy. The Grenon stopped near a group of huge stones, but he didn't let us get closer — he rushed away in the opposite direction as soon as Professor made the slightest movement towards him.

Then I showed Dun signs that I want to try. I held out my Gift to the magical field surrounding the Grenon, and stroked it. The cub stopped on one of the boulders towering above us. I made a movement towards him, fearing that the Grenon would swim away again, but he didn't. I slowly began to approach the cub, holding out my hand. I waged my foot, shod in a fleaper, trying to raise myself above the boulders, leaned my left hand on the stone closest to the Grenon and stretched my right palm to his tentacles. And then my left hand slipped, I made an awkward motion and hit my foot in the gap between two stones, cutting the wetsuit on my ankle with one of them. Sharp pain burned my leg and, pulling my limb out of the crevice, I saw a small, colorful fish that was biting my ankle with its teeth. I got goosebumps all over my back — this fish was deadly poisonous.

Panicked, I waved my arms and legs. A whole flock of bubbles rose instantly from my mouth — I was wasting too much air. The fish let go of my leg and rushed back somewhere into the stones. My companions were already hurrying up to me, making signs about an urgent need to emerge.

I blinked and suddenly found myself in a laboratory of the Department. Water splashed around me. My ankle was terribly hurt, and the tanks with respiratory mixture pulled me down. In the corner there was a huge barrel of water, which an adult Grenon protruded from. It seemed that he was gazing at me with curiosity. Someone was helping me to hold the tanks while removing them from me. Dun, dressed in a white coat, rushed up to me. He was wearing a mask with a pipe leading to an air tank behind him. In his hands Professor held a sheet of paper. What happened? Where did an episode of my life go? How did this even become possible!?

"Helga, don't worry," was written on a sheet that Dun put into my hands. He began to take off my helmet quickly. The mask was still on my face, and I continued to breathe through it. "As soon as I take off your helmet, lie down on the couch, on your back. Alex created pressure in the laboratory, which is similar to the one which was at the deep sea so that you won't have problems. He'll now reduce this pressure with the safest possible speed, to make it feel as if you're rising up from the bottom. Just breathe. It would be better to wait until the pressure is normalized, but it will take time, and we don't have it. Be patient, baby, it will hurt."

Now it was clear who helped me with the air tanks and why Dun was in the mask. At this pressure, breathing on your own was impossible. And this explained the sheet of paper with the text — it was also impossible to speak in this situation. I hastened to lie down, because it was extremely difficult to stand and move. My leg was gradually losing its sensitivity.

Dun, meanwhile, was attentively looking at his diving computer, apparently waiting for a change in pressure readings. Alex carefully took the flippers off of me. Then Professor put his fingers on my bitten and cut leg on both sides of the tearing suit and I felt the flow of his healer's strength, and then a wave of burning pain swept over me. I flinched. Dun grabbed my leg in double iron grip and Alex pulled my shoulders to the couch. But I perfectly understood that everything was being done for my own sake, so I decided not to bother them anymore, and soon the grip loosened a bit.

I seemed to have tears running down my face and accumulating inside my mask. I tried not to make a sound. I just squeezed the mouthpiece with my teeth even tighter without stopping to breathe. My hands grabbed the edge of the couch, it was easier to endure the pain in such a way. In particularly difficult moments, I squeezed my fingers so hard that I ceased to feel them. At the same time, concentrating on breathing for surfacing turned out to be the best tactic for dealing with pain that went from my hip to the wound on my ankle. I don't know how much time has passed. First, the pain began to leave my thigh, then — my knee, then — my shin. My foot was the last to surrender. Dun pulled a tiny milky white drop out of the wound.

"It's poison," he explained, removing his mask and picking up the drop with a special tool. "I'll put it into the test tube and that's it. Hold on a little more, please. Alex must remove nitrogen from your blood. It won't hurt anymore. You can take off your mask now."

A bearded man took Dun's place at my foot. I understood that nitrogen would also be removed through a cut. Perhaps, this might have been much easier than through the lungs. I merely felt sleepy, as it always happens in those moments when the pain finally subsides. While Alex was removing nitrogen, Dun took off a hat from my head, carefully wiped away my tears and helped me to untie my hair that had been tied up in a ponytail before. 'Baby', well! This was the first affectionate word that Professor called me. Until now, I had always been only Helga for him. And only my dad called me 'baby', as my height did not prevent him from thinking that I had been a little girl. It turned out that for Dun this was not a big deal too. I relaxed even more because of his touches and almost fell asleep right on the same couch.

Two hours later, I was sitting in a laboratory near a regeneration box. An episode of my life has just disappeared and now it was already late morning. After the operation of extracting poison and nitrogen, they put me into this box for recovery. Thank goodness, at least Natalie was called to help me change from the wetsuit into my clothes. I slept a little while my wound was healing and the residual effects of poisoning and immersion were being eliminated. At that moment I was blinking sleepily and chewing that breakfast that Dun had brought me. Professor was sitting nearby and wearily talking about what had happened.

"When I saw the fish clutching at you, I panicked. This was the first panic in my life, because I have been taught to keep everything under control since my childhood. But then panic came to me like a flood for a second. I know how menace this fish is and in that moment I clearly understood that we might not have time to emerge. I already thought that I would have to do the surgery right in the deep sea. This was fraught with its own consequences. And then I saw that you didn't move and the cord between us wasn't whole anymore, as if someone had cut it with a knife. I turned around and saw that an adult Grenon was coming up to us out of a pile of stones. I showed Ron and Natalie with signs not to move. The Grenon had sensed us with his magic field, called his baby and they began to rise up together. And you were swimming after them, being in the same stationary state."

"So, what do you think, was it a time capsule again?"

"It looks like that, because when we ascended to the surface, the Grenon levitated you over a boat side directly in a certain amount of water and didn't put you on a deck. I think that he was afraid to destroy the capsule from touching anything. I don't know why ocean water didn't ruin it. Maybe the Grenons have evolved and learned some new things, or maybe we just don't understand the whole principle of this technology."

"I can imagine the surprised faces of the coast guards!"

"Yeah. The good thing is that they all are under an oath. We'll call them here later and obliterate their memory. Anyway, they found a barrel for the Grenons and we went to the Department."

"Did the Grenons fly quietly?"

"Imagine that! Both of them were absolutely calm, traveling themselves and carrying you. A few hours of work on your transportation and at the same time no stress on their part. However, if they were to make a journey among planets in these capsules, then such transportation is a joke in comparison with space travel. We had to demand a larger plane from the military and transported you in it to the airport nearest to the Department, and from there we secretly carried you in a huge helicopter. You do understand that such a barrel cannot be transported in our plane, don't you? There's simply nowhere to land a larger plane on the Department base. Thanks to the military and our Deputy director, everything was organized as secretly as possible and without witnesses. You were delivered to a laboratory quite promptly, but then another problem arose — how to let you out of the capsule without harming your body? The pressure in the lab differs from the one at the bottom, and with the sudden destruction of the temporary capsule you would simply die with a quick and painful death."

I cringed. My death could be faster and more agonizing than from poison? However, I read about decompression sickness, and understood what Dun was talking about.

"Without going into details, we arranged a consultation with a specialist who works with such cases. It was necessary to wait until morning and the beginning of the next business day. The consultant told us how to create an air chamber with the necessary pressure. We had to spend some more time to organize a gradual increase in pressure, because Alex and I needed to get used to the changes in the external environment as well. I have written a text for you. The most interesting thing is that it wasn't necessary to give the Grenon any signs, he waited for the right pressure and did everything himself. Alex has barely managed to catch a scuba gear so that you wouldn't fall because of its weight. And then you saw everything yourself."

"How are the Grenons doing now?"

"Paul said that they enjoy reuniting with their friends."

"Given the fact that they breed by budding, there's no need to look for a second parent."

"Thank God! I feel that I need rest from such extreme dives."

My excited Mother met me at home. Dad was still at work, and Mom had apparently already returned from her shift in the children's clinic and was now waiting for me.

"Helga, what happened to you tonight?"

It's good when parents sense how their little kids feel, but it's bad when they sense problems of their adult children. I had to make something up again, invent a plausible story.

"There was nothing special, mom. Why are you asking?"

"I woke up in the middle of the night feeling that something bad is going to happen. But after a few minutes it all went away and my peace came back. But there was something, I'm sure!"

That was interesting. It looked like my Mother felt immediately that nothing threatened me anymore. Was it a foresight? Or maybe that were new jokes with time?

"And what about dad? Did he feel anything?"

"He said that he had nightmares about many huge fish with sharp teeth that were chasing you. And then an octopus appeared and dispersed them all."

I thought that maybe my early suspicions were not so groundless, and my Father has had the gift of a mentalist, even though it wasn't found at his first initiation when he was twelve years old. I should question him carefully on this subject. Perhaps the gift has been too weak, and Dad didn't see the point of even mentioning it? The gift could superimpose on family sensitivity and manifest only in relation to children. In this case Father's silence was understandable. But Mother looked at me expectantly, and it was necessary to answer her question.

"At night, one of the women in labor got flowers, and our team was presented with a bouquet either," I sighed doomedly, inventing a believable story. "The midwife went to take a vase, washed it, filled with water and brought it to the doctors' lounge, but a wet, heavy vessel slipped out of her hands and crashed on the floor. One of the fragments pierced my leg right into a vein. There was a lot of blood, but Dun was nearby and helped me quickly. As you can see, my leg is completely fine, only the new skin is slightly different in color."

"Dun was nearby," my Mother emphasized. "Everything will be fine while he's nearby."

I wish I could have her confidence! However, in that moment, there were enough facts to support this statement. In any case, it turned out that I've been valuable enough to the Department and, as far as possible, everyone who is involved in our work would protect me. Although that day I was alive in the first place thanks to the Grenons and only in the second — to Dun.

Chapter 14

After the dive, managers gave me a day to recover, and I spent Tuesday at home, preparing to take the upcoming test. Before the evening shift, Professor came and took me for a walk to the nearest park, checking how much my leg had healed. I enjoyed May's green and flowering trees, confirming the mobility of my ankle. Wednesday went quietly. I passed the Clevres exam and was preparing to get acquainted with the giant pigs.

Victor rejoiced at my appearance.

"We need someone who should distract the kids from adults while we work with them. If cubs are with their parents, magic fields get mixed up, and we can't distinguish who is where," he told me, giving a special warm jacket. "Come with me, I'll teach you how to build connection with them."

We went inside the enclosed cage and took the direction to clay houses, in which the Clevres usually slept. A black martial healer of Dun's age came to meet us. It was he who scratched the youngsters with a rake on my first visit here.

"This is Martin," Lina's brother introduced me to a colleague. Martin gently shook my hand.

"Hello Helga! Nice to meet you. Today you'll work with the kids. This is the best option for the first time. If anything goes wrong just fly into the air immediately. They get excited because of it and freeze on the spot. And they will not hurt you."

"What should I do?"

"Don't let them get closer to adults, just restrict them with your magic gift. Use it like a leash."

"All of them?"

"Yes. It's not difficult, you'll see now."

"Oh, can I touch them?"

"Yep!" laughed Martin. "But only after you establish connection."

We stood in the meadow with cold-resistant grass. Victor already led one 'kid' the size of a cow to us. Judging by dimensions of the others, this one was still a baby. The cub confidently followed the martial healer and tried to reach into his pocket with its trunk. Probably it was looking for a treat. I thought that I should have taken an apple with me, or at least picked up a bunch of juicy May grass from the lawns of the botanical garden. Well, next time I'll grab it.

"So, Elle, evoke both of your magic gifts at the same time. Then form an arrow with a two-color tip in front of the inner eye. In your imagination shoot it directly into the magic field of the Clevre. As soon as connection is established, I'll let it go."

"And how can I understand that it's done?"

"You'll understand, don't worry," Martin grinned. "This moment cannot be missed."

I followed Victor's instructions. Everything was described in textbooks, but in fact, dry words turned out to be completely untrue. It seemed to me that I have simultaneously plunged into a feeling of my own adult strength and children's curiosity, when everything around is so new, so interesting, so tasty.

The cub has finally paid attention to me and came closer. It stopped three steps away from me, waiting for my reaction, and grunted. It grunted, really! But because of the trunk, the sound turned out to be something like a trumpet, and because of the cub's size it was considerably loud. I jumped in surprise, my colleagues laughed, the Clevre was joyfully running nearby, shaking ground. It seemed that it liked my reaction very much.

"You can touch it now," Martin pushed me towards the 'piglet' with the trunk. "Victor will bring the next one in two minutes, and I'll get the headphones for you. Because when these hoots begin to grunt in a crowd, you can go deaf. Hang the headphones on your neck and put them on immediately if necessary."

We stayed alone with the baby Clevre. I slowly moved towards the cub, but it wasn't afraid at all, and I almost jumped on it in the end. Piggy wool was pleasant to the touch, even though it wasn't as soft as it seemed to me from afar. But ears could be twisted into a tube. The Clevre loved my touch, touching me back with its trunk and constantly muttering my magic field. The sensations it gave me were quite funny.

When the second youngster appeared, the first baby became tense and hid behind my back. I suspect that it looked quite funny from the outside, as I was obviously not able to cover it with my body. Apparently, the 'pig' felt more confident behind my back, because in its mind I was an adult and strong person. Victor stopped and advised:

"Separate a new two-color arrow from your connection with the first cub and make a second connection. We can hold up to ten individuals this way. You'll have to keep control of only six today though."

"How can they be controlled? This connection is stretchable as far as I can see."

"Imagine a two-tone loop of a lasso that you throw on the neck of a naughty youngster. Then rest on the ground with your feet and stop it. They don't run fast, even despite making giant leaps. That is why when they try to separate from you, the speed will still be considerable. But you have good reaction."

"Are you sure I can handle it?" I was still a bit scared.

"Elle, I see no reason why they would start running away from you," Victor told me. "There are no frightening factors, no strangers. If they see adults or some goodies sniffing out aside, they can try to move away. You'll have enough time to throw a loop and to pull the runner back. Don't worry."

Martin brought me headphones and went to adults. Victor went for the next Clevre and then the older cub decided to attack the younger.

It rushed to the victim, who stood right behind me. The baby screeched in such a way that my ears popped. I bounced to the side so as not to fall under the feet of the aggressor. Pulling headphones over my head, I realized that the eldest cub had already leaned on the younger one with all its weight and was biting the baby everywhere. Oh, you, brat! I'll kick your ass now!

I got red with rage, formed a loop instantly and pulled the wretch to the side, simultaneously whipping it with a part of the connecting thread along the magical field somewhere in the area of its furry blue buttocks. I hate it when someone offends the helpless!

Oddly enough, it helped. I had no idea that such a magical blow could be somehow felt. My actions were purely intuitive, designed to let go of my fury rather than punish the offender. However, the aggressor lowered its ears and trudged to make peace with me. It would have been better to make it reconcile with the younger cub, but I didn't know how to crank it up. It was enough that the fight stopped quickly without any casualties. I heard claps on the side. Victor came to us with the third Clevre.

"I had no doubt that you could handle it, Elle," he said. "There's some kind of power in you that such creatures do respect."

"Victor, I hate you!" my hands were trembling. "You have to warn about such things!"

"Elle, nothing terrible would have happened. The Clevres observe the hierarchical structure of society, and the education of their youngsters is included in their relationship. It's about hazing. The bigger cub would have bitten the smaller and let it go."

"And if I were trampled?"

"You've passed the safety exam to exclude such trouble. I should nonetheless remind you to fly into the air. And you can beat them, of course. You're doing great in it. Probably it's because you're a fire magician. I can't do that."

"Okay, I think I can handle it," I calmed down a little. My rage could really scare pets so they usually were afraid to become impudent after its first manifestation. Apparently, the Clevres are arranged in much the same way. "But, please, Victor, don't tell Dun about this."

The next time I imagined a magic broom, and after that no 'piggy' undertook any further attempts to fight. That's it!

Chapter 15

"Elle, we have an emergency!" Victor ran into the dining room to drag me away from studying the next guide on Thursday morning. I was done with instructions, and now I was studying the unique memory technique that Dun talked about on my first day at a new job. Information was very interesting, and I couldn't wait to try to test the new knowledge in practice, but there was no such opportunity for it right now. "Leave your printouts here, nobody needs them anyway. Except you, of course. We have to hurry up!"

"An emergency? Again?! What happened?" I asked on the way. Such unpleasant events in the Department have happened too often lately! However, I hadn't worked here in calm times yet, there was nothing to compare with, and this pressure seemed to be becoming normal for me. But there were no longer those parties that Lina had told me about before. Apparently, the management decided to postpone additional activities until everything calms down. Ensuring the safety of fun and taking care and control of the tipsy employees was an extra worry as well. Meanwhile, Victor answered my question, interrupting my thoughts:

"The Clevres ran away. We have to catch them all and obliterate the memory of botanical garden visitors. At the same time, you'll master this method in practice, so to speak."

"How could they run away?" so my dream about the full development of new skills was becoming true. Dreams always come true in the most unforeseen way and often it's not too pleasant.

"I don't know! But we'll find it out. Now we urgently need to catch everyone and take them back, while no one was hurt, and there are not too many witnesses."

We rushed through the entire Department and ran out into the street. Remembering the inconvenience that I had to experience at the shooting range, I had stopped putting on my pumps, instead opting for white sneakers, the same kind as Lina's was. They fit my sports style yellow dress. And now I was easily running in them across the Department and rejoicing at my own choice of shoes. A huge hole gaped in the wall of the Clevres' pavilion. A clear trail loomed in the implantation. The nearest flower bed was completely destroyed.

"I've already called everyone, the rest of the martial healers will come here now. It's only us, who can catch the Clevres. They will not let other people get close. It's really good that there are a few of them."

"Did every one of them run away?"

"No, only the young individuals did. Six of them. Only the ones you were working with yesterday."

"It's more than enough with their size. Is that my fault?" the question was quite reasonable.

"Of course not! Something seemed to scare them."

We understood the approximate direction of search by screams, coming from the right side and along the clearing. Sleepy Paul joined us while we were running, then the others came as well. Only those three healers who were on duty near the wards on the order of Director were absent. Dun appeared nearby.

"Helga, don't get under their feet, please. It's necessary to calm them down first."

"Dun, I remember that! I have passed the exam just recently," I snapped and felt ashamed of myself. He was just worrying, and I was annoyed. What a shame!

"Don't be angry," Professor asked me and then turned to Victor. "Do we have darts?"

"Of course, we do. Here are some."

"Uh! What about me?" I was indignant.

"No, Elle. Your job is to bring them to the Department after we calm them down."

"Is that a kind of sexism, Victor?"

"You tell this to the Clevres, they follow women as if attached," Dun said with amusement. "And they resist men even after sedatives."

"Females too?" why wasn't this information included in the instructions?

"Yep. I think that's because of female solidarity," Professor continued to joke. The rest of the healers around us smiled. Well, yes, they all were men. "It's good that we have you in our team. Otherwise, it would be impossible to catch the runners. We'd have to sedate them all and organize their transportation. And this is much worse. And much longer."

"Women are an amazing rarity among martial healers," Victor explained to me. "So, Dun is telling the truth, we're very lucky that you came to the Department."

"Dun, how did you and Paul come here so quickly? You should have been home after the night shift," I decided to change the topic of our conversation.

"We live here nearby. All employees of the Department try to choose the apartments close to work. Haven't you noticed when we were at Paul's?"

"No, I didn't. Apparently, we came from the other side," it was also necessary to leave this dangerous topic, because there were too many witnesses around. We could accidentally blurt something out. And it was okay about the Lilac Fun, but the relationship of our friends so far was not possible to share. The guys must decide for themselves when to stop hiding.

I saw the security guards and several of our ordinary healers on the left. Lina was there too.

"Why are they here, I thought that it's only us who have to catch the Clevres?"

"And they are catching the second flock," no, apparently there was something wrong with Dun that day. Why was he laughing? "The eyewitnesses."

Everyone was laughing now. Terrible tension began to let go of us, although we continued to run.

"Yes, Elle," Victor smiled. "Everyone needs to be gathered in the conference room. Our healers will check whether somebody needs medical care and we'll obliterate all the dangerous memories."

"And Julie is there too."

"She's an aura reader. Paul is with us, Ron is sleeping after the night shift, so she should catch everyone with fear in their aura. If she fails, Director will call Ron to help her, but I think that she'll handle this."

"How playfully the oldie runs," Dun continued to have fun.

"Dun!" Paul yelled at him.

"He's so angry with Julie because she hadn't told him something," I explained to Reincarnologist. He coughed and apparently understood my hint, and Professor laughed out loud.

"Dun, why are you so happy? Did you scratch yourself with a dart of the Lilac Fun? Calm down, The Clevres are ahead!" Victor shouted, and Professor's gaiety disappeared at once. The others immediately became serious as well. We stopped and peered out from behind the trees.

Enormous size of the Clevres was clearly invented by nature to protect them, because the brains of these animals were not too developed. They were somewhat similar in behavior to cows — they run if they are scared, and they stop if they notice that they are not in danger anymore, and there's a tasty bush nearby. The same thing happened now — almost all the individuals who have escaped were scattered across the clearing with fountains. Spring greens appealed to our 'piglets', and the Clevres were not going to leave the gracious pasture until they didn't feel hot on a sunny day. One creature was cutting flowers from a nearby flowerbed, another one was biting a lush bush, and the youngest individual was bathing with enthusiasm right in the fountain. It was the baby cub that I protected yesterday from an older one. Only one Clevre was missing, the rest were there. On the side I saw a group of young people taking selfies with the strange animals. Dun ran to them. I watched how he showed the guys his ID and took away their phones and camera. After that, Professor led the guys to our healers.

"Victor, they're so calm. Maybe there's no need for darts?"

"There is a need, Elle. They can be scared immediately. If they were in their aviary, then it would be unnecessary. But strangers can appear here at any moment, God forbid, and these bib beauties will run again. They can still trample somebody so we have to avoid this situation. Don't worry, they'll not be hurt. They won't even feel darts."

Lina's brother went towards the baby cub in the fountain, tuning into a common magical wave with it so as not to frighten the animal. The rest of the martial healers were already heading towards the Clevres. One cub, who was indulging in the magic of water, was creating small and large rainbows in the air. A dart went exactly into the center of its forehead. The second one got stuck in its ear. The Clevre wasn't even bothered and kept having fun. Five minutes later, its rainbows began to appear less often, after ten minutes they were completely gone. The cub became lethargic and stared at one point. I felt terribly sorry for it, but I understood that it was impossible to do it in a different way.

"Elle, now it's your turn to work. Come here. Tune in."

I experienced that strange feeling of simultaneous appeal to two gifts again. Gathering my medical and martial magic in an arrow which consisted of two halves, I sent it into the Clevre. It felt a connection and moved towards me, as an adult who protected it yesterday from the attack of the elder cub.

"Well done! Lead it into the aviary," Victor commanded.

"How?"

"Just go."

I turned and went towards the hole in the pavilion wall. Ground was shaking behind my back — the baby cub was following me, as if on a leash. I led the Clevre into the pavilion, then through the open doors of the aviary. I gently turned there at last and released the cub, breaking the thread of magic. The Clevre saw adult 'pigs' and trudged to them slowly. I went back.

Establishing and then eventually breaking up the communication was becoming easier and faster with each next individual. Forty minutes later, there were already five escaping Clevres in the aviary. Only one was still absent — the largest and oldest cub, which we couldn't find in the clearing.

By the time I returned, having brought the fifth individual into the aviary (this one, by the way, was the female) only Victor was waiting for me outside. We went further along the trail left by the last Clevre. Five minutes later we saw our colleagues crowding around a 'piglet' lying on the ground.

"Is it dead?" I shrieked, immediately feeling the lack of life in the body of the individual. "How did this happen?"

"Someone shot it with a poisonous dart," Paul said sadly.

"Do we have any?"

"No," said Victor. "Militants have. And also our security guards, of course. I don't even know what for. Who found the cub?"

"I did," Dun's voice sounded from behind. I turned around.

"Did you shoot it?" Victor was trying to hide his anger.

"No."

"Sophie died because of this Clevre! Everyone knows that you have a special relationship with it!"

"Victor, what kind of relationship can there be with the Clevres?" Dun calmly asked. "There has to be some intelligence from both sides to have a relationship. And the Clevres are just stupid clumsy animals with certain valuable magical qualities. To take revenge against them is the same as to take revenge against a tornado or a brick."

"Look into Paul's eyes and say that you didn't kill it."

"I. Didn't. Kill. It." Dun said clearly and separately, looking for some reason into my eyes. I exhaled and noticed that I was holding my hands behind my back. Paul's voice sounded right over my ear.

"He's telling the truth. But let him repeat this to Julie so that no one can doubt his words. Let's decide what to do with the body, while we're still lucky and there are no more onlookers."

I wasn't involved in dragging gravities. I didn't like doing it at all. My colleagues could figure it out without me, coming up with a transportation method. In the end, they had more experience in this regard, and I was a little tired of bringing the Clevres into their pavilion. I wanted to rest a bit, and therefore I didn't participate in the general discussion, going to go around the clearing perimeter. And so I heard strange clicks behind the bushes. Without betraying my excitement, I returned to my colleagues in the arc and touched Dun's hand.

"What?" he turned around.

"I've heard clicks of the camera shutter in the bushes."

"That's what would happen next! Where?"

"Just don't look there, please, I'll describe the place now. It's the bushes near a flower bed with roses, directly opposite from the head of the Clevre."

"Okay. Tell Victor about it, please, and I'm going to hunt the photographer," Dun went towards the Department, which was located in the opposite direction from the suspicious bushes.

"Where's he going?" Victor became interested, and I quietly explained the situation to him. The rest of martial healers were not curious, but Victor was considered the head of the Clevres compartment, so he tried to keep everything under control. We returned to the fuss with the carcass, but were still all ears.

Five minutes later someone screamed in the bushes, and Dun revealed a stubborn man with a professional camera on his neck. Professor wrung the photographer's hand behind his back and pushed him forward. The man tried to resist, but he didn't have a single chance against the martial healer with a black belt.

"A reporter," Dun explained to us, "who knows how many photos he managed to take. It's good that Helga heard him, and he didn't have enough time to escape. It's urgent to sweep the territory, because we are in danger of suddenly founding that he wasn't alone here. Victor, call Director, tell him to call everyone who isn't here now, including Ron. I'll take this one to the Department."

"Take Elle with you either. Let her attend the interrogation. And check the camera, please, maybe there's a photo of the Clevre's murderer."

We were sitting in Julie's white room, trying to extract information from the journalist. Unfortunately, there were no pictures of the ward poisoning on his camera. Dun went back to his colleagues to help with the transportation of the body. The reporter refused to answer the questions of an aura specialist and has only said that he had accidentally found himself at the clearing — he had shot rare trees in the botanical garden and was at the epicenter of events.

"He's lying and enjoying it," said Julie to Director, who was also present at the interrogation. "I can see the superiority and contempt that he feels for us now. And he won't tell the truth. Bullish stubbornness comes up when I'm asking about the source of information."

"Send him to the Lonquies," I advised thoughtfully. "I think they'll quickly draw the truth out of this fool."

"Great idea, Helga!" Director was delighted. "We have to obliterate his memory anyway, so let them do everything right away."

"Why am I a fool?" the journalist tried to be indignant. "I'm a famous photographer! A lot of magazines are paying big money for my photos!"

"You didn't cooperate with us, that's why you're a real fool," Julie explained gently to him. "You don't know who you're messing with, do you? Oh, that's not a big deal, honey, we'll try to save at least the grain of your brain."

A trembling struck me because of her voice.

Outside the white room, Director ordered two security guards to escort the photographer to the Lonquies, and sent me to the conference room.

"The martial healers have already removed the dead Clevre from the meadow and are now busy with memory obliteration. Go there to practice."

In the conference room, regular healers assisted everyone who was injured. I saw Lina and waved at her with my hand.

"Imagine, a couple of people have even had to be placed in regeneration boxes. One Clevre overwhelmed several trees and hit some visitors. It will take too long to heal them without boxing, and it's advisable for us to let everyone go home today. Otherwise, there will be too many gaps in their memories."

"And where does the work with memories take place?"

"There's a large room for such 'whole' processing."

I took the direction that my friend had waved at. The room was divided into eight parts. There was a passage in the center, and the rest of the place was occupied with booths. I went into one of them and saw Martin in a white coat sitting at the table. A young woman was sitting opposite him back to the entrance and to me. She was telling something, and the healer was holding her hand and listening carefully, looking into her eyes. Noticing my appearance, Martin interrupted the woman.

"Is Dun here?" I asked.

"Yes. You can find him in the third booth on the right."

I thanked him and left. Booths were definitely soundproof. As far as I was able to understand, they were also constructed of some special material that shielded the mental impact. The healer and his "patient" were alone. I think that this was done so that nothing would interfere with the process of memory obliteration."

When I left Martin's working area, one of the guys who was taking pictures against the background of the fleeing Clevres went out of Dun's booth. His eyes looked empty, as if he was trying to remember something. At the same time the guy was moving heavily. One of the medical girls led an arm to the "patient". I decided that it was the right time to come in.

Dun was delighted at my appearance and tried to seat me in his lap, but I dodged and sat down on the table.

"You decided to come to me? Have you been looking for me for a long time?"

"I went into the first booth that came across, and there Martin told me where you are."

"Why didn't you stay at Martin's?"

"You're my supervisor, and you have been teaching me medicine for so long. So go on, teach me again," in a white coat Dun looked exactly the same as he used to look during my work in the hospital. I plunged into that very mood and was embarrassed.

"Are there any news about the journalist?" asked Professor.

"Julie couldn't crack him. He shirked and didn't want to tell the truth."

"It was only necessary to ask him the right question and then track his emotions. Julie is a good specialist, but she's a mediocre psychologist."

"That's not a big problem, we sent him to the Lonquies. I think that everything will be quickly found out there."

A medical girl peered through the door.

"Wait a minute, please. I'll show Helga some nuances of the technique, and we'll be ready to work with the next visitor," Dun said to her and then began to instruct me. "So, Helga, I'll bring a second chair, and you can sit on mine for now. And I'll get you a white coat."

"By the way, why is it necessary to be in a white coat?"

"People trust doctors and it's easier to work with them if you're in the medical scrub. Watch and listen carefully to what I'll be doing. Put your hand on my back discreetly to the patient, and track the magical currents and technology. It's possible to do without physical contact, but it will be better seen in touch. Don't talk, don't touch the patient and don't pull his gaze on yourself. Any questions?"

"No."

"Sit down!" Professor stood up and grabbed me in his arms, put me into his chair, and then went out quickly. I was surprised again at the ease with which he carried me. I'm not Lina, I'm heavy enough because of my height.

"Wait a moment, please," Dun told the people at the door. "We need one more chair here."

The memory obliteration procedure was very interesting. A medical girl brought an elderly gray-haired woman. Professor smiled warmly and offered her to sit down. I didn't put my hand on his back, because both of us would feel uncomfortable in this position. Instead, I simply touched his leg with my knee under the table.

"How are you feeling?" Dun asked a woman.

"Thank you, I'm fine now," she answered with dignity. "You have good doctors here. They're friendly and very attentive. And believe me, I know a lot about this!"

"We believe you. We select them from all over the world. Especially the attentive ones. I'm attentive too," Professor winked at the patient. "Tell us what happened to you in the botanical garden today and I'll listen to you. Just try not to miss anything."

The woman became a little flushed. No, look at him! Is Dun a hypnotist? When young women of my age are crazy about him it's normal. But that elderly lady! I saw this for the first time. And this ladies' man covered the patient's hand with his palm. And she suddenly rumbled, looking right in the eyes of her interlocutor in a white coat.

She talked about how she was going to visit the botanical garden for her morning yoga class, how she got there by public transport, how she laid out her gymnastic mat and did the first asana. When the Clevre appeared in the woman's story, I caught the movement of magic and tried to concentrate on Professor's actions. The stream went from the patient's head through her hand to the martial healer.

The words ran out. Dun was still looking into the woman's eyes.

"Where am I?" she suddenly said and pulled her hand from under Professor's palm.

"You're at the first-aid post of the botanical garden," Dun said gently.

"What happened to me?" she began to look around.

"You have lost consciousness during your yoga classes. We helped you and have just checked your brain function."

"Why don't I remember anything after the start of classes?" it seemed that she would jump up and run somewhere now.

"You have been lying unconscious under the supervision of our doctors for a long time. Don't worry, everything is fine with you, and after a while your memory will return. Now our doctor will conduct you and the botanical garden's employees will help you to take a taxi to your house," Dun got up, opened the door and called the medical girl, who was waiting for the end of the process outside the booth.

"We'll take a pause for five minutes," Professor told our colleague. "You can go and make yourself tea. And we'll be very thankful for coffee for us either. I've slept for only three hours today."

The girl was delighted, nodded, and led the elderly lady out of our booth.

"Have you considered the process?" Dun asked me.

"Yes. I just didn't understand it fully. You're not a mentalist, so how is it that you are able to do it?"

"That's why we ask eyewitnesses to tell us about the events in detail. The memory rises up to the surface, and from there it can be caught and pulled out by our healer gift. It's even easier for water magicians, because we direct the second gift to go through blood and lymph vessels. But you'll succeed too. Let's look again, and then you'll try it yourself."

"Wait a minute, but is it necessary to look into the patient's eyes? As far as I could see, the look doesn't participate in the process of memory obliteration."

"It's easier to establish trust this way, and also help a person tell everything without interruption. If it works without visual contact, then you can even obliterate the memory with your eyes closed. But this usually happens only in the case of a high level trust."

At that moment the girl brought us coffee and said that in five minutes she would bring the next witness. We didn't spend more time talking, and quickly drank the roasting drink. As soon as the mugs were set aside, a teenager of about seventeen years old came into the booth. I looked closely and recognized the second of the guys who took selfies in the meadow.

"I won't talk to you! You're not a doctor at all, but an employee of some intelligence agency! I saw your ID! All the pictures on the phone were deleted," he said from the entrance. "Where are my friends?"

"We'll ask you a couple of questions and you can go to them."

"I won't tell you anything," he rang out. I knew this age. The most nasty and stubborn one, with many hormones, courage over the edge, and the brain hanging out modestly somewhere in the background. I was wondering what Dun would do?

Professor looked at me calmly.

"I have a cool girlfriend, huh?" he asked the guy a question that I didn't expect from him at all, and suddenly grabbed my thigh with his right hand. I can't even imagine what my face expressed at that moment, but the teenager completely forgot about his stubbornness and said in a different tone:

"Yeah, she's a pretty chick," and he examined me from head to toe with a shameless appraising gaze. "She has a sexy white coat!"

I think I blushed. Dun bent over to an eyewitness, put his left palm on guy's shoulder, continuing to hug me with his right hand, and said in confidence:

"She thinks that you're scared to be in that clearing again in your mind, and to tell us everything."

"What is there to be scared of? These hefty furry pigs with trunks came out there. We were thinking about how to ride them---"

Dun's strategy turned out to be absolutely correct. The teenager rushed to prove us that he wasn't a coward, but a hero. I was afraid to move so as not to cut his "heroic" story off, and carefully watched the flow of magic again. This time I was really able to catch some thin scales that Professor's magical gift removed from the guy's memory and carried over his shoulder and arm to the healer. At the end of the story Dun took his hand off the teenager's shoulder and told him:

"You and your friends climbed onto the slippery fence of the fountain. You slipped, they tried to hold you and you all fell down. You hit your head, and your friends drank water. All three lost consciousness. Our doctors have barely dragged you out. You've been unconscious for a long time, but everything is fine now. Even the bumps are gone, we have good specialists here. Try to behave a bit more carefully in the future. The real strength of a man is not in rage, but in the ability to assess circumstances correctly and use his brain."

The teenager nodded, and Dun stood up to call the medical girl. When the door closed behind them, Professor said:

"I'm sorry, Helga. You saw him, he's in the age of obstinacy. I remembered myself in his years and thought of what I'd been worrying about then. It was beautiful girls and their opinion of me. If you hadn't played along with me, we would have to tinker a lot to crack him. And this way it went quickly and easily."

Oh, yeah. If he had been ashamed even a little! Frankly, I didn't play along with him, I was just shocked by what Dun has revealed to me. But I didn't admit it out loud. I must pay tribute to Professor, the guy really gave out all the events in detail.

"A sexy white coat!" I had to express the emotions that overwhelmed me. I thought I should begin to wear trousers and overalls at work again. "A young squirt!"

Professor laughed and winked at me. I was ready to hit him if he would say something about my white coat. And there was no more shyness inside me in front of him, so that the proverbial black eye could appear at last. It was not a serious wish, of course, but I still was angry.

"Well, so, are you ready to work with the next eyewitness?"

Chapter 16

"Helga, come to us quickly!" Paul's voice over the phone was terribly excited.

"But where are you?"

"In the laboratory with the box for human cloning!" and Reincarnologist disconnected.

I raced through the entire pavilion without feeling my legs. Did something terrible happen? Who would be resurrected? Lord, if everything was okay with Lina!

The laboratory was not too big and almost all of it was occupied. Paul was standing near the box control panel, pale young men and women were sitting on the chairs next to him. Everything was fine with Lina, she was kneeling near the box and holding in her hands the bloodied head of a four-year-old child. She clearly did a quick diagnosis. The boy in the box didn't breathe and was so pale that he seemed blue.

"Helga, please, make a complete picture of the magic field pattern, very quickly," Reincarnologist ordered, and I started the procedure. It was good that I rushed in full steam, because I wouldn't have time if I came a little bit later. The field disappeared and seemed to dissolve right in front of our eyes. The child was in a state of clinical death.

"Hold the thread!" Paul ordered the man and woman, who apparently were the boy's parents. "Hold it and don't dare to let it go. You can't close your eyes, just blink. You'll hold it in turn — one works, the second sleeps or eats. Lina, are you done?"

"Yes," the girl was scared, but took hold of herself.

"Move."

The box lid has been closed.

"Your son's brain is badly damaged. Most of it will have to be removed, and we'll build up a new one. We have data, DNA and material for this. But we're not able to give you any guarantees. I can only promise that I'll do everything in my power and even more. And you must hold the thread of the soul."

Parents nodded.

"Girls, come to me!" Paul commanded, and I marveled at the changes that occurred in him. It was an iron man, assembled, knowing his work and appreciating the value of every second, every moment. Lina, it seemed, also saw the guy being like this for the first time. "Upload the data to the box quickly. The one who'll upload it first will run to call the surgeons."

Lina was the first and so she rushed off somewhere immediately. She came back when I was downloading the information about the unique pattern of the child's magical field. Dun and one of the medical guys were accompanying her. Apparently, colleagues were already aware of the problem. Paul opened the box and put the device on the boy's head. This device allowed us to conduct the ultra-precise brain surgeries. I was surprised at the variety of technical equipment of the Department again. I couldn't even imagine that there was such equipment here. The medic began to manage the device, and Dun provided timely cleaning of the areas under surgery from the remnants of dead tissue. In such situations, magic recharge is usually performed too, and apparently it was supposed to be done by Professor. But the child's body was already devoid of magic, so Dun merely assisted our colleague.

At the end of the operation, Paul closed the box again immediately. The kid's body had been connected to all the necessary life support systems before the surgery, and now, as I understood it, the cloning procedure was launched. Lina and I stayed in the laboratory until the end of the surgery in case the healers suddenly needed additional help or just quick legs to run if Reincarnologist was to give such order.

"Sixteen hours," said Paul. "The cloning and building up the lost brain lobes will end in sixteen hours. Girls, you should go home. I'll wait for you here tomorrow morning."

"And what about you?" Lina was worried.

"I need to be on duty with the parents to hold the thread."

"Won't you sleep at all? You've been at work for twenty-four hours!"

"I'll sit here for another four hours, then I'll ask the changer to hold it up. We have a second reincarnologist, he can handle it. In general, everything depends on parents now. We're only here for some additional support. When a specialist is nearby, people somehow feel more confident. And I'll make sure that they will not close their eyes."

"So then, Paul, I'll bring you all something to eat---" I began.

"Don't even think about it!" the guy interrupted me. "It's forbidden for the parents, because they can fall asleep after eating. And I don't want to embarrass them. We'll eat in shifts, when it is possible. Go home, girls. And take Dun with you out of here, because he's after a night shift –either, and I don't think he has rested yet."

On the way home Professor and I attacked Lina with questions.

"Have you been there? What happened?"

"Elle, why are you making such a fuss? I'll tell you everything, don't yell. When the Clevres ran they burst out into the botanical garden. When they broke the wall of the sector along with the protection against explosions, panic arose. We ran there to gather everyone, who was looking scared, wounded, or just curious. There were these two — the boy's parents. The woman cried and claimed that something bad had happened to her child. Her husband held on only because it was necessary to console his wife."

"Wasn't the boy with them?" asked Dun.

"No, he wasn't. They had been resting on the platform near the fountain, the son had been dabbling, tried to climb the trees and ran away from his mother all the time. She said that the last time she had seen her son, she took him out of the fountain, hoping that he would be there, and sat on the bench with her husband. But the kid ran off into the bushes again. And that's where the Clevre had been."

"Children of this age usually run to their parents immediately in case of danger," I said incredulously.

"I don't know what really happened there, Elle! Maybe she spanked him for disobeying, maybe something else. I only know what parents told us. We couldn't find him for a very long time, because his aura practically didn't respond. Mother said that the boy was somewhere nearby, but we'd looked everywhere. Actually, we spent a lot of time searching, until I thought of trying to look for a trace of the magic field in relation to the mother. Only after that I barely caught a glimpse in the bushes under the rubble of a bench. He was lying with almost no life in his body. His head was on a large stone and everything under it was in blood. A terrible sight itself, and it seemed like the Clevre had stepped on the kid, u-m-h-h. You, Elle, have already seen him washed up."

Lina paused for a moment.

"Why did Paul call me?" I asked.

"There were few free healers. And those who know how to make the pattern of the magic field, were even less. There were a bunch of wounded people, and all the medical employees were working with them. When I saw the boy in the bushes, I called Paul immediately. He ordered the child to be carried to the laboratory and then ran there himself. And from there he has called you."

The girl was frowning. I stroked her shoulder. Professor listened carefully, but didn't intervene.

"Dun, how do you rate the injury?" I felt like returning to the hospital. Two healers will always understand each other.

"It's grievous. It's strange that he was still alive the moment when you found him. Nothing has remained of the zones that control life supporting systems. Perhaps the boy is from those newborns to whom I passed the ability to regenerate quickly. He's just the right age. Only this explains the oddity. He'd held on until the magic ran out."

"Well, now his condition is under control," I spoke exactly as I used to do in the hospital. But this was calmer somehow — as if we were just discussing a difficult but not dangerous case in childbirth. "And we all need to recharge and regain our strength. Tomorrow is the decisive moment. Lord, if only we could bring him back to life!"

We took Lina to her brother's house and then Dun went to accompany me.

"Where did the Department get this equipment?" I asked my companion.

"We have a lot of things there. You never know what you'll need in your work, that's why the Department equips laboratories with all the novelties that appear on the medical market. Moreover, there are some of our own inventions, of course."

I was dumbfounded and silent.

"I don't really believe in the success of this process," meanwhile Professor continued, referring to the cloning and resurrection of the boy.

"Why?" I looked at him in surprise again. Did he really think so because they hadn't succeeded with Sophie?

"Helga, I have assisted in this surgery. There is only a tiny part left of the boy's brain."

I've just understood his message. Somehow, this thought didn't come to my mind at the moment when Dun was talking about the child's condition last time. Apparently, both shock and at the same time hope blew everything out of my head. I began to believe in the advancement of the Department and its miraculous technologies too much. But now the hint has become quite clear. All of this was not about Sophie at all.

A human is not only a body and a soul, combined with flows of the magic field. We are also determined by memories and the experience gained during our lifetime. And first of all, it is the experience of breathing, controlling a heart and other vital organs and systems of a body. A child's brain begins to receive these skills in a mother's uterus and gradually builds up, and develops. Every experience is replenished with a new one. You can grow a second brain or parts of it, but it will be clean, like a white sheet of paper, and there will no longer be the most important thing — knowledge about how to survive. And without it, body systems are unlikely to start their work.

"Why did the managers give Paul permission to do a resurrection?" I asked Professor after a long dull silence.

"Well, what else could they do? This is our fault. We didn't look after the Clevres well enough, we didn't provide sufficiently reliable walls for their sector, we're hiding them from people, and now the mankind doesn't even know how to behave if they appear. The opportunity to try to advance a little further in the direction of human cloning and resurrection has also played a role."

Near the house of my parents Dun hugged me tightly and asked to always be out of the Clevres' way. I joked that I couldn't be so irresponsible and leave the Department without such a valuable employee. Professor was sad and smiled very tiredly. He wished me good night and sat back in a taxi. I saw that he was trying not to fall asleep right in the car.

***

"A bad day?" Mom asked me.

No, I had to think something about my moving out. Constantly lying to parents or even just keeping silent about the details became harder and harder. I decided to distract my Mom from this tricky topic. Moreover, the photo of my great-grandfather still needed to be taken off the family archive.

"Ma, where is the album that you showed me on the day of my twelfth birthday?"

"In the bedroom. Why?"

"I want to look at the photo of my great-grandfather with the Grenons again. It seems to me that the job that I was offered to take relates to it somehow."

Mom looked at me with interest, forgetting both about her question and about my difficult day. We went to my parents' bedroom, she took the album out of the safe and we sat down on the bed side by side, touching with shoulders and bowing our heads over the photo. Opposite the bed there was my Mother's dressing table, and our reflection was visible in the mirror. I thought that, still, I'm similar to her, although it sometimes seemed to me that I'm not. I have the same oval of the face, the same eyes that Lina once called mysterious, the very same lower lip. I looked at my Mother's reflection, then looked at my face and realized for the first time that I'm really beautiful. I was wondering why I hadn't seen this before. Was it necessary that the seventeen-year-old kid appreciated me? Was it about the fact that I didn't receive a portion of attention from teenagers, or what? Mom's reflection smiled at me in the mirror. I returned my thoughts to the album.

"Does Dad know about this?"

"I don't think so. As you can see, the album has a lock, and I keep the key separately. But you can ask him yourself. I didn't tell him. This is a huge secret."

At these words, Mom made her eyes big, as if the same twelve-year-old girl was sitting next to her. It was funny to see her like that. It was funny and sad, because I realized that soon she wouldn't have this huge secret.

"Ma, please, tell me again everything you know about this. Close your eyes and try to remember all the details."

Mom really closed her eyes and started to tell me about my grand-grandfather. In this situation we didn't need a visual contact, so everything went easily. I caught the flakes of her memories, not forgetting to carefully remove the album from our lap at this moment and then hide it under the bed. I'll take it out of here too at the right moment. I felt disgusted as if I robbed my own Mother, depriving her of her dearest thing — memories of family secrets that made the image of my great-grandfather heroic and romantic. When my Mother stopped talking, I made a pause and asked her again:

"Ma, what did my great-grandfather do?"

"I've already told you. He worked at the King Palace as a healer."

"Was that all?"

"Yes. Why? And what are we doing here?"

"You've asked me about my work, remember?"

"Oh yes. I've been a little dizzy."

"You should lie down and rest. Probably, it's because of your work at the kitchen. I love you very much!"

Mom hugged me, then lied down and turned to the wall. I took the moment to pull the album out from under the bed. Leaving the room, I felt like a traitor. It turns out that my wonderful work at the Department comes at a price.

Chapter 17

The next morning I rushed to work ahead of schedule. But I was in a hurry in vain — Paul wasn't there yet. His colleague, although tired, was fine, and the boy's mother was sitting on a chair with her eyes wide open. Everything indicated that the process was ongoing, and the thread wasn't cut.

"Where's the father of the child?" I asked the second reincarnologist in a whisper.

"He's sleeping in a regeneration box," he answered me quietly. "We made the six-hour shifts for them. It's better to recover, especially inside the box."

Lina burst into the laboratory right after me. She had the same questions and obviously same thoughts. But she was sent out to her workplace by the reincarnologist. I thought that I should probably leave for now, so as not to loom in front of the people in the laboratory and not to interfere with the process. God forbid to distract them and to cut the thread. And nobody has canceled my own tasks. I still needed to learn and understand new information.

But the business day has not begun yet, so I decided to go into the dining room, drink a cup of coffee and take a bun. I didn't even have time to have breakfast before coming here. Mom tried to drag me into the kitchen, but I quickly went around her, rushing into the taxi, where Dun was already waiting to take me to the Department. In the dining room, a group of Lina's colleagues were having a heated discussion, sitting at one large table.

"Helga, come to us," one girl called me from there. I recognized the same laboratory assistant who advised me not to remember the names of the employees on my first day. "We have a free chair here."

I poured myself coffee, took a bun and joined that mysterious meeting with pleasure.

"What are you discussing so fiercely?" I asked.

"It turns out that someone let the Clevres escape from the cage!" a chubby girl with black hair informed me in a conspiratorial whisper.

"We don't know that for sure!" the other participant of the conversation said to her. "It's just that the door of the cage was open."

"How could that be possible?" I was surprised.

"The lock wasn't broken, the door wasn't broken either. It was open. Or maybe it wasn't closed because of someone's negligence."

"And Martin said that just before the Clevres ran and broke the wall, there was a bright flash and a loud pop. It scared the wards."

"Yes, Victor also mentioned yesterday that the Clevres seemed to be frightened by something," I said pensively.

"Maybe that was a new bomb?" the black-haired girl was scared.

"No, I think it was some kind of cracker, but powerful. The entire population would run if there was a bomb, not only young individuals. The security guard, who was inspecting the scene, didn't find any traces. Nothing at all. The working version of guards is that there was a short circuit, which gave such an effect. Something really caught on fire there, next to the Clevres sector, on the switchboard. Even a part of the sector was left without electricity. But why was the door open?"

"And what about the cameras?"

"There's nothing special, everything is completely standard. The security guards were the last who entered the sector. When they went out, one of them had even jerked the door, checking whether it had closed."

"That's weird."

"Don't tell us about it," answered the medical girl, who yesterday brought eyewitnesses to Dun's booth. "Somehow it becomes uncomfortable to work here. First there was a bomb, then the Clevres. But we have to go now, otherwise the management will punish us."

Girls went to their workplaces, and I stayed in the dining room to think. Oddities have been accumulating. First, it was a bomb near the sector of the Lonquies, then there were the frightened Clevres, who accidentally hit the door open. Then it was a strange reporter, who was in the right place at the right moment. Yes, and there was this rumor about experiments on newborns still. My theory about someone, who was trying to discredit or even make the Department shut down, seemed more and more plausible to me. If so, then the attacker will not stop here. And I was afraid to think about what his next step would be.

Paul called me just before the end of the shift. During this day I had managed to let myself out in anticipation, trained in the gym till the sweat ran, read the same page of the manual ten times and understood nothing from it. It was impossible to go to the Lonquies or the Grenons — they were simply sleeping. And I didn't want to see the Clevres. In my nervous state I even went to Lina's laboratory and watched the insects that I hated. But I'd been staying there for a short time, because my equally worn-up girlfriend was there too. Such a concentration of exhausted girls with magic was too big of a loan for the lab lighting — one of the bulbs died, accompanying its own death with a loud bang. Both Lina and I jumped up, and I rushed back to the dining room. I thought that I'd better try to understand at least something from the manual, instead of blowing up the laboratory bulbs.

"Helga, do you want to attend?" Paul asked me.

"I do!"

"I have to warn you. Everything may end not quite as rosy as we hope here. Are you sure you want to see this? Maybe you'd better wait in the dining room?"

"Paul, I'll come."

"In that case we're waiting for you."

Only the boy's parents, Reincarnologist and Lina were present in the laboratory. Paul had an extremely focused look.

"Girls, get ready, please. If there are any problems, you will pick up the vital systems. If something doesn't work right, you can gently nourish it, then try to start again. I ask you to demonstrate maximum concentration and attention," then Reincarnologist turned to the parents. "At the count three, we pull the soul. You don't need to do much — just imagine your child alive, cheerful. You should try to see how you hug him, how he laughs, looking at you. You can imagine joy, love, tenderness, expectation of a miracle. Try not to let doubt get through it. I'll do the rest for you when I'll understand that you're immersed in the necessary state."

The man and the woman nodded. I looked at the box and felt that there was still a soulless body there, albeit supported by vital systems. There was no magic field. Apparently, there was no aura still. My suspicions were confirmed by a picture on the computer screen, where the boy's body, lying in the box without movement, was visible.

And then Paul tensed up. And I suddenly saw how a unique pattern of the child's field began to glow. To say that I was delighted is to say nothing. I was in a state of euphoria! Lina shared my emotions.

We saw on the screen that the boy opened his eyes. Paul pushed the shutdown support button. The tube for artificial lungs ventilation came out of the throat and went into a special niche of the box. Magic stopped pumping blood to the vessels. And then a terrible thing began to happen. The child couldn't breathe. It seems that he simply didn't know how to do that. Lina supported his breathing system and began to ventilate his lungs with magic. But after this, the devices reported cardiac arrest. I supported the circulatory system. However, this didn't help much, since the boy suddenly began vomiting bile, and then blood. Dun's terrible prediction came true — the boy's new brain simply didn't know what to do with this body. I tried to stop the bleeding by reducing the pressure, but then the child's heart stopped again. Paul tried to fix problems with internal organs. Everything in the box was covered with blood, and Lina didn't have time to clear the boy's lungs. Another heart beat and the child died. Looking confused at Reincarnologist, I realized that the soul thread has also been cut.

After half an hour, we were sitting in the dining room, griefing for the child. Paul was in the worst mood, he was holding Lina in his lap and silently clinging to her with all his might. I saw that the girl was uncomfortable, but she hugged the guy and stroked his hair. The shift was coming to its end, employees periodically came into the room and looked at us with curiosity. There was no more secrecy around my friends' relationship anymore, but the guys didn't care about it. To be honest, I was also missing a person to whom I could cuddle up and try to forget the terrible vision of a blood-drenched box that stood in front of my eyes. Therefore, I was even slightly jealous of my friends. Probably, if Dun was at work, I wouldn't give a damn about all my doubts and simply go to his side. But Professor would have a night shift, and so he hasn't arrived to the Department yet.

Paul raised his head, grabbing Lina in such a way so that she was more comfortable to sit in his lap, and looked at me over the girl's head.

"Call him," Reincarnologist whispered to me.

"Would it be easier for you?" I answered him in the same way, referring to the futility of a telephone conversation.

Paul shook his head and said much louder:

"Go home, girls."

"And what about you?" his girlfriend was worried.

"I have to wash the box and disinfect it. Go, girls," he kissed Lina in front of the dumbfounded laboratory staff who drank coffee at the next table, and my proud friend got up and headed for the exit. I followed her.

I tried not to think about the parents of the deceased child. The procedure of their memory obliteration and sharing new memories has been undertaken by Alex. He had his own children so the bearded healer understood all the experiences of the parents much better than we did. Personally, I wouldn't have been able to handle this task. I just couldn't imagine how it was possible to remove the cause of death of the child from his parents' memory, how to find the right words so that the father and the mother continued to live on.

That evening, Lina and I got drunk for the first time together.

***

"And Paul asked me to marry him, hik, oh!" Lina was holding a bottle of wine in her hands and drinking straight out of it.

We were sitting in my room right on the floor. Glasses were lost somewhere, in the center between us there was a large plate with chopped cheese and apples. There was about a third of its contents left for now. I must say that part of the cheese was eaten by the impudent moustached shout of my cat. I won't be surprised if it was him who also licked some of the wine from my glass. My parents didn't intervene. I told my Mother that in the afternoon we lost a baby in the hospital, and she took away my Father, who was trying to stop our drinking party. Dun called a couple of times, but when I was still sober, I asked him to stay with Paul if he was still at work. Dun was trying to figure out our plans. I said that we would drink, and Lina would spend this night in my guest bedroom. Then I just turned off my phone. My drinking companion did the same, hoping that Dun would retell everything to Paul if necessary, so that Reincarno;ogist wouldn't worry about her.

"I hope you said 'yes'. Just keep your future children away from the botanical garden and the Clevres."

"Y-yeah," Lina began to frown again. The girl was sitting in an unbuttoned blouse, because of the wine she suddenly felt hot. Shaggy hair and one squinting eye complemented the image. I suspect that I didn't look better, because my tunic was skewed, and my skirt has almost pulled up to my waist. But we didn't care, and the guys, thank God, were not around. "The second tr-r-ragedy with these Clevres, which I've seen."

"Why does the Department need them?" alcohol didn't produce the same effect on me as it did on my friend, I was getting drunk more slowly. Apparently, the difference in height and complexion played its role too. My consciousness, of course, was very blurry, but my speech was still relatively under my control.

"Victor sa-a-ys that the Clevres have that, he-, ge-, re-ge-ne-ra-tion, oh!" Lina hardly pronounced the right word. "And a relationship within the couple. A re-pro-duc-tive system is important in something."

"They're dumb, unwieldy hulks!" I hit the floor with the bottom of my bottle.

"You're talking like Dun," Lina giggled.

"Because this is true! How could they get on a par with the Grenons and the Lonquies?"

"Easily!" my friend waved a bottle in the air. Wine splashed inside. "People are the same animals as the Clevres. We chew, mate, and b-r-r-r-breed. That's why the phi-si-o-logy in relation to the m-magical field is being studied on them."

I got sad. Lina was absolutely right. Humanity was somewhere on the same level with the Clevres indeed. We were very far away from the Grenons, and even more so from the Lonquies. The girl, meanwhile, continued.

"A-a-and they're not so stupid! They have their own hi-e-rar-chy, oh! They are forming their pairs for life. Their cubs are born strictly if they decide to. P-p-people learned to co-o-o-ontrol m-magic streams from the Clevres. S-s-so now there are no unwanted pregnancies. They are just b-big," Lina significantly raised her finger up, and because of that move she almost dropped her bottle. It seemed that my friend forgot that she had a second hand, which she used to rest on the floor.

"They're big, so what?"

"We're like ants for them. Or like mice. D-do you think about ants when you go your way?"

I thought about it. No, I don't think about ants nor about what kind of mouse I would crush by accident. If it didn't get out of the way on time, it's its fault. Though it would be a pity for me.

"I wonder who had poisoned the Clevre? Dun says it wasn't him and I believe him."

"O-of course it wasn't him!" Lina said with the absolute certainty which is so common for drunk people. "W-why would he do this?"

"Your brother thinks that's because of Sophie."

"What a n-nonsnse!" swallowing sounds, sneezed Lina. "M-my brother sits with his Clevres and doesn't see that the situation has changed."

"What do you mean?"

But Lina, it seemed, had already forgotten what she was just thinking about and returned to the topic that she was worrying about.

"So, do you think I have to say 'yes' to Paul?"

"It's your call," I laughed.

"T-too-o-o fast," the girl snapped, propping her cheek with her hand, with which she had previously rested on the floor. From such a movement Lina has almost fallen over on her side, but she changed her trajectory in time and leaned on her back against the wall behind.

"It's too fast for you, but he has been waiting for a whole year."

"What if I'm a bad hostess-s-s-s? What if I can't cook?"

"That's not a big deal because Paul can."

It was very funny for me. Without realizing it, Lina was afraid to disappoint Paul herself, and not to be disappointed in him. The diagnosis was clear and it was sweet like a peer.

"What are you laughing at?" Lina got angry immediately. "Why d-don't you get married?"

"Nobody has ever proposed to me," I fell into a fit of fun at the sight of my girlfriend. She looked really comical — small, disheveled, drunk and angry.

"That's not t-true!" my drinking companion was surprised and distrustful. Her mood changes came so abruptly that I didn't have time to react adequately. Wine has also slowed down my reaction. "Dun proposed to you, didn't he? I know that he did! Your mom told me."

"Lina, it wasn't Dun who proposed to me, but the Department. They insisted on this fictitious marriage for the peace of my family's minds," I wiped the tears that came out because of laughter.

"What a bastard!"

"Who? The Department?" I just couldn't laugh anymore.

"No! Dun!"

"Lina, leave Dun alone. I'll deal with him myself."

"And if he proposes, would you agree?"

"I would, but not right away."

"I don't want to agree right away either."

"So don't say yet!" to be honest, this marriage conversation has already made me exasperated.

"Paul is waiting for my answer! How can I refuse?"

"Well, Lina, say that you agree, but you want to have a long engagement. And now it's time to go to bed. You have to sleep on this decision," there was one positive point in this matrimonial theme. Both of us have completely forgotten and became distracted from the horrible events of the recent past.

Chapter 18

The next week, on Monday, all the night shift martial healers were gathered in the office of the Department's director. After the establishment of round-the-clock duty, at that time there were only four of us: Dun, Paul, Martin, who worked with the Clevres, and me. But now the day shift was delayed by the time that Director needed to talk to us. Apparently, something strange has happened again.

"One of your colleagues, an aura specialist Anthony, died," Director said. I was surprised and saddened. Last weekend was calm. Professor even managed to get Lina and me out for a walk on Sunday evening. Paul, unfortunately, was on duty that day, so the four of us couldn't meet up together. However, everything went well that evening, we relaxed and had fun. This Sunday rest gave us the feeling that everything would finally get better soon. And now we had a new accident.

"What happened?" asked Paul, who was on last night duty at the Lonquies with the deceased man.

"Those doctors who made the post-mortem diagnosis said that he had a heart attack."

It was very strange. I met Anthony about a week ago when we were training in the gym. He wasn't young for sure, but not old enough to die like that, instantly, from a heart attack. Weird events continued, and they were frightening. Apparently everyone else thought the same thing.

"When did it happen?" asked Paul in a muffled voice.

"Early in the morning today, after the end of your shift. You have already gone home, and your colleagues have found him. He lay in the nook where helmets are hanging. Surveillance cameras do not show this place, and it is not visible to the Lonquies **too**. Paul, just try not to blame yourself! You have got nothing to do with it."

"If only I had stayed for ten more minutes, I would have had time to help!" Reincarnologist's voice was choking, as if the guy was barely able to push the words through a lump in his throat. It was such a blow after the unsuccessful resurrection of the child on Friday!

Director shook his head.

"There could be too many scenarios, Paul. The heart attack could happen at the moment when you would go out for a snack or something else. Anthony could have left earlier and died in a taxi. Or he could have moved away for some reason and fallen in an empty corridor. No one is protected from this and there's no one to put the blame on."

I stroked Paul's arm. Dun squeezed Reincarnologist's shoulder with encouragement. Both of us didn't know any other way to show support to our friend. Director went on.

"I have to transfer a martial healer from the day shift to the night one to provide the security needs of the wards. And for day shifts I have to pick up a security guard. There will be some changes in your schedule. Be prepared. Well, I'm letting you go, wards cannot be left without attention, and your colleagues — without rest."

We moved toward the exit, but Director asked Dun and me to stay.

"As far as I know, you two have a fairly close relationship with Paul."

"We do," replied Professor.

"The fact is, his colleague has found Anthony on the floor without a shielding helmet. Maybe he just took it off before leaving the Department, or maybe this has been a tragic coincidence, but we must be attentive to every detail. In addition, the Lonquies are worried. They are saying that something bad is happening. But they can't explain it further. So I ask you two to keep an eye on Paul. And I'll say the same to the colleague on his shift. Helga, I insist that you pass your safety exam on working with the Lonquies as soon as possible, so I could call you to be with the wards for short moments in case the person on duty is absent. We can't leave martial healers alone now. In the afternoon, the Lonquies are asleep, and being next to them without a helmet for a long time is not so dangerous. During night shifts, extra precautions must be taken. And be careful yourself as well."

I didn't like it all!

"Why didn't you tell Paul about this?" asked Dun.

"I was afraid that he would surely feel guilty then, because he hadn't supervised his partner. And now he just needs to be as focused as possible. Now is not the time to feel guilty. He'll receive instructions in the newsletter, without indicating the reasons that prompted us to compile them."

After my training I stumbled upon Lina in the women's locker room. She was getting ready to practice.

"I ran away from the girls in the laboratory," my friend smiled shyly at me.

"Were they bothering you?"

"No one dared to while Paul was not far away, but as soon as he went to the Lonquies, they started to bombard me with questions immediately. And some girls have even started to congratulate me, can you imagine that? Oh, I can understand your feelings now! I'm sorry I was so indiscreet the day we met."

I waved my hand, and Lina continued:

"'Are you together now?', 'What happened?', 'Why now?', 'When is the wedding?'. Anthony is the one who has to be spoken about. Why did they choose us?"

"I'm sorry, Lina, but that's a stupid idea to think that you two are less interesting than Anthony. Their curiosity has obviously tormented them since Friday. You were sitting there, hugging in front of everybody, and then there was this kiss in the presence of your colleagues. Imagine everything that your girls have managed to conjure up over the weekend. No, you and Paul are closer and more interesting than Anthony."

"That's not true! Anthony used to work with us as much as Paul. At the same time, we're alive and will be everybody's eyesore for a long time, and Anthony's gone."

"You're right," I had to admit that.

"His death is wrong and suspicious," said my friend thoughtfully.

"Yes. He wasn't old enough to die from a heart attack. And we all undergo a medical examination periodically, as far as I was instructed."

"Anthony had some problems with his cardiovascular system, but there was nothing serious. He was practically healthy because he was following the gentle sports along with regular maintenance therapy. But there's one more thing."

"What kind of thing?"

Lina leaned toward me and whispered:

"Our girls say that the doctors who made the post-mortem diagnosis found a high titre of tsikus in the blood of the deceased."

"So you still managed to discuss Anthony's death, huh?"

"We did that while Paul was somewhere around," Lina was embarrassed. "We could only whisper about the high concentration of tsikus."

"But it's not dangerous."

Tsikus was accepted by all employees of the Department who worked in the laboratory for reading and transmitting thoughts. This plant increased susceptibility to mental magic and has no side effects. It was forbidden only for those who showed individual intolerance. As far as I knew, Anthony wasn't allergic to it. Tsikus grew in a special compartment with other magical herbs, which were actively used in work by the Department' staff. Its extract was sweet and sometimes colleagues have even used it as a sweetener. It was also good for women on diet.

"It's not dangerous until you enter the Lonquies' sector without a helmet due to its influence. And also it is recommended not to combine tsikus with regular sugar. This can lead to increased heart beat. It's not a big deal for a person with a healthy heart, but it may threaten the patient with heart problems. Anthony was well aware of these warnings, but somehow his blood was saturated with tsikus. Did he decide to commit suicide? Everything is extremely strange here."

"Yeah."

"I'm starting to catch myself having paranoid suspicion. The bomb was the first straw, the Clevres were the next, now this strange death has happened. I'm worried about Paul."

It was difficult to see Lina, who has usually been light-hearted and funny, in such a depressed condition.

"I wonder why the management doesn't have a normal investigator?" I said, expecting Lina to remind me of the Department's secrecy.

"The Department has nothing to deal with for now. The investigator is unlikely to find something suspicious and the case will be closed. There's no evidence, no motive, no corpus delicti."

"Does the Department work with such specialists?"

"They say that usually our security guards cope on their own. But a couple of times in especially difficult situations the outside investigators had been invited."

"Do such situations happen frequently?"

"As far as I know, no."

"Then how can you be aware of them?"

"Elle, I'm working in a women's team! One older colleague had been telling us for an hour about the measures that the Department introduces during all sorts of troubles."

"Okay, I have to go pass my exam."

"So, you'll finally visit the Lonquies, won't you?"

"Yes. I can't wait till I see them."

"Good luck!"

Chapter 19

"Paul, is this some kind of joke?"

"No, Helga. These are the Lonquies," Reincarnologist looked like he was feeling incredible pride.

We were surrounded by small, well-fed, multi-colored... dragons. So that's why Julie asked me about my attitude to the lizards the other day. Each individual was the size of a heavily fed cat. Dragons were stomping underfoot, flying around us and looking at me curiously. They were flashing in my eyes because of the overflow of their bodies — each of the Lonquies had an unique skin pattern. It was like sand, constantly pouring on the dragons' bodies. The pattern breathed and changed, attracting and bewitching the eye. It was beautiful, but there were a lot of them around, so I quickly started to feel dizzy.

"What pigment gives such a skin color?"

"This is not a pigment. This is a unique magical feature of the Lonquies. Don't look at all of them at once. If you want to study the modulations more closely, then choose one of them. Otherwise, you will faint," Paul advised.

"Do they have scales?"

"No, it's just a kind of skin. They're soft and poorly protected from external damage. Just like us."

The colleague of Reincarnologist went to work to the laboratory, and I came to replace him. I put on a helmet of mental protection, equipped with an electronic bracelet with a clock, an alarm clock and a timer, and then came into a huge hall behind a special protective glass. Even being behind it, I heard an unclear mental "noise" — a stream of a wide variety of muffled emotions and images. After the helmet was put on my head, the "noise" disappeared.

Behind the glass there was a large area with artificial rocks, a small pond, specially planted vegetation and even some kind of a hill. The Lonquies' houses were everywhere — in the hollows of trees, in rocky caves, in burrows of a hill and under bushes. Now they all gathered around us, looking at me and waiting for an opportunity to get acquainted even closer.

"I thought that fairy tales about dragons had no foundation."

"As you see, they have."

"They're such crumbs. How do they fly?" dragons' wings were clearly not suitable for lifting their bodies into air.

"And how do you fly?" Paul posed a question to my question.

"So it was them, who we have got the flying skill from," I made a logical conclusion.

"Yeah. And be careful, Helga, they can hear and understand you."

I shut up. The Lonquies were the first and only wards who understood human language. They didn't talk among themselves. As was written in the instructions, the dragons communicate exclusively in their minds. In general, real sounds, at least somewhat similar to trying to talk out loud, were made only by the Clevres. The martial healers have even compiled a small handbook of symbols. But the language of "piggies" was primitive and could hardly count as the conversation.

"So, you're saying that the Lonquies live for several hundred years. Such crumbs?"

"Helga, some species of turtles that are not very different in size from the Lonquies also live hundreds of years," Reincarnologist said with a grin.

"How do they manage to live for so long?"

"We've been looking for the answer to this question for a long time. One thing I can say is that in many respects the lifespan depends on their attitude to what is happening around. The Lonquies enjoy every moment. They never rush. Instead, they look for hidden joy in everything."

"In everything, absolutely?"

"Yeah. In food and training, in sleep and creativity, in pain and flight. Every moment, every experience and emotion — everything for them is a reason for joy. I try my best to learn from them. It used to work out pretty well."

"And what happened?" I became interested.

"Lina happened," Paul smiled warmly and at the same time with a bit of sadness.

I was surprised to see these emotions.

"In my opinion, Lina is the first and biggest reason for joy."

"She is!" laughed Reincarnologist. "But, unfortunately, her love is not only about joy for now. First, this tigerboy destabilized me. Then there are the thoughts about the bomb and the intentions of the bomber. You can add the unsuccessful resurrection to his as well. The death of Anthony is a new matter of concern. I'm concerned about Lina, wards, you, Dun, and the girls in the laboratory."

"But the Lonquies are not worried?"

"They know how to find joy even in fear," said Reincarnologist with some awe. "It seems to me that this is the highest level of Zen, and I will probably never grow up to that."

"Amazing!" apparently I will never grow up to it either. To perceive every moment of life with its various 'surprises' as a reason for joy? This was the highest level of equilibrium indeed.

"Well, are you going to get acquainted with them or not?" asked Paul.

"How do you think?"

"Then take off your helmet. I'll time and put it on you as soon as the safe period comes to an end. They communicate with us via the transmission of thoughts. They know how to "hear" absolutely everything that you're aware of. Their 'reading' range is twenty meters. If it's difficult for you to formulate a clear answer in your thoughts, then you can pronounce it out loud. And ask Arthur to teach you how to meditate. This is of great help when it comes to mastering mental conversations. But now it's necessary not to strain much. Try to feel comfortable. They'll understand and adjust."

Due to the constant mental 'noise', it was possible to communicate with the Lonquies for only five minutes, once an hour. This slowed down the work with the wards terribly, but the martial healers couldn't help it. A longer "conversation" could lead to the loss of consciousness due to overloading other individual's emotions. And in case of cardiovascular problems — even to death. Which, apparently, happened to Anthony.

I took off my defense and a real cacophony hit me. In front of me, there was a flying dragon with beautiful blue-green skin. It seemed to flutter the northern lights on it, bewitching with overflows of magic fire.

"Hello Helga!" I heard a voice inside my skull. The strangest thing was that I couldn't understand what kind of voice it was — low or high, pleasant or not. It wasn't intrusive — this might be the most accurate definition. And, at the same time, the voice was distinct.

"Hello!"

"I'm the leader and from now on I will be the only one to talk to you so that your mind doesn't get confused by our curiosity. We all want to get to know you, but days matter nothing in comparison with the peace of mind. We'll have our time."

"Thank you for your concern!" I couldn't formulate my answers in my mind, therefore, as Paul advised, I didn't push myself too hard and simply spoke out loud.

The reality around me blinked, rippled and changed. I was standing in the spring forest. The greens were bright and juicy, as if after the May rain. Paul and the rest of the Lonquies disappeared somewhere. Only the leader was still hovering in front of my face. But the mental 'noise' didn't vanish, even though it has become muffled. Apparently, the dragons tried to control themselves so as not to disturb us.

"Creating illusions is like writing a wonderful picture. You apply every stroke using all the wealth of colors and brushes of various shapes and sizes. This is the kind of creativity that we love to do in our free time. Therefore, I have fenced us off, so that the other Lonquies will not distract your gaze and attention."

"Do you know how to draw pictures?"

"No. We have nothing to hold the brushes with," it seemed to me that the little one smiled. "But we considered this image from one of your colleagues, and we liked it very much. However, I see that you're in a bad state of mind.

You're worried about something that is not necessary to even think about."

"Girls generally like to worry," I smiled.

"You're very balanced, Helga. And still doubt is gnawing at you. Allow yourself to bathe in it once, look at each facet, find the benefits and evaluate the harm. Dive into it fully and feel all the bitterness of the worst option. Cry out and feel the joy of being able to do it. And then imagine the sweetness of better variation and live through it as well."

"What for?"

"It will quench the fire of emotions a little and give patience a chance to overcome the withering bitterness. And you will see that soon everything will fall into its place, already predetermined a long time ago."

Perhaps this was the best conversation that has happened to me in the last month. I had no one to talk to about my real doubts. I used to trust my Mother with my secrets, but now the nuances of my work have parted us. I couldn't touch any of the topics that bothered me, without lying. Therefore, it was better not to talk about them at all. With the Lonqey I didn't even have to say the things that tormented me out loud — he read everything in my head, as in an open book. And that was cool.

I suddenly realized what kind of voice was in my head. It was full of kindness and real wisdom. And an understanding of why Paul was so fond of spending time with little dragons came to me immediately. Our conversation was like praying in a church. But in contrast to church, the higher mind gave me the answers.

No, I'm not trying to blaspheme. I'm trying to describe my own feelings during the first meeting with the Lonquies. I was interesting and important, they cared and worried about me, my state of mind wasn't insignificant and didn't leave them indifferent. I felt amazingly calm and joyful.

But that condition lasted for only a few seconds. I was overwhelmed by other being's diverse emotions and thoughts. I heard snatches of mental conversations. The Lonquies were talking about me and about Anthony, about Paul's fears, about his work, about some old person who would leave soon and because of that it was necessary to prepare a new body for him, about some girl with scissors, about patterns on the skin and about food. It was very difficult to endure. Then someone put a helmet on my head, and everything disappeared. Only the leader remained, hovering in front of me while the crowd of dragons was at a distance.

"Five minutes have passed," said Paul. "How was it?"

"Amazing! I want more!"

"In an hour, " Reincarnologist said sternly. "You can rest for now. Think about what you'll study next time. Did you manage to consider their magic field?"

"I didn't even think about it," I said, stunned.

"Oh you! Muddler," Paul joked. "That's not a big deal. You're not alone in that. The Lonquies make a stunning impression on everyone. What did he say to you?"

"That I'm a fool and my doubts are in vain."

"Is that what he said?" the guy cheered up.

"Of course, not! I've translated his words into a simple and primitive language for you."

Paul pushed me in my shoulder in a friendly manner.

"Well, go get your Zen."

Chapter 20

On Tuesday, Dun and I were standing in the hallway next to the Grenon's sector and discussing what Lina had said before about Anthony. And also for the first time ever I dared to talk to Professor about the death of the child. Over the last days, I have managed to release the stress, my emotions and bitterness have subsided too, but I still felt the need to tell him about what I experienced that day.

"I can't imagine what Alex had to go through during the conversation with the child's parents," I said, looking at Professor's shoulder.

"Unfortunately, secrecy has its terrible price," Dun told me sadly.

"We have to do something about this. I mean hiding wards from the world's population. Such secrecy is nothing but trouble."

"Maybe we can divide the Clevres somehow, in order to leave one part with us for the sake of research and to transfer another part to a sanctuary suitable to let people know about them. But the Grenons don't want to split up. And the Lonquies told us that they're satisfied with their life in the Department. They don't aspire to leave this place for somewhere else. After our organization took custody of them, people have finally stopped killing the little mentalists."

I opened my mouth in surprise. Who would think of killing cute small dragons? They're santient after all!

"Fairy Tales about dragon's wealth didn't appear out of nowhere," Dun grinned unhappily. "I'd rather say that they came out of the blue, because the Lonquies have no material wealth. Our little wards say that they had once communicated with some weird old man. It was about a thousand years ago, which by the standards of the little mentalists was quite recently. And the old man turned out to be not just a philosopher, but also a noble storyteller. And he was famous for his love of metaphors. He composed the parable of the Lonquies' wealth, referring to the magical gift, culture and mind of the dragons. But his tribesmen didn't understand this metaphor. Since then, the Lonquies began to have some very big problems with surviving."

Oh, yes, I could imagine! Considering the fact that dragon-crumbs don't have fiery breath and cannot devour an intruder. . . They, of course, have a weapon — they can kill a person with their mental strength or simply scare an aggressor. I suspected that the detail about the fiery breath of dragons has emerged merely because of their suggestion. But you can also find your tricks on such weapons.

"What barbarians we still are!" I exclaimed angrily.

"The attacks ended about half a millennium ago. Since then, humanity has grown a little wiser. But the Lonquies don't want to lose their secrecy."

"And I can totally understand them. How's Paul doing?"

"He's okay now. These days, of course, were bad enough for him, but, it seems that he has accepted that there is nothing he could do in both cases. By the way, the dragons-mentalists helped to convince our friend. I don't know what they told him, but he calmed down a little. We have to keep our eye on Lina now, so she doesn't tell him about tsikus."

"Don't worry, I warned her and her colleagues about that."

"I've always said that you're very smart. And beautiful. And that white coat was really sexy. I don't even know what fits you more — this coat or your wetsuit. I saved this white coat for you. Will you put it on again?"

I blushed. What should I answer this with?

"Dun, why are you embarrassing the girl? Don't pay attention to him, dear, he starts saying stupid things because of his own excitement."

I turned to this voice and saw an elderly woman of small complexion with long black hair, gathered into a tight bun at the back of her head. She was wearing strict dark blue trousers and a jacket of the same color with a stand-up collar. The stranger's outfit was very slender and made her look elegantly harsh.

"Mom?" Professor exclaimed in surprise. "What are you doing here?"

Dun was completely different from her. He had probably just inherited his appearance from his father. The woman clearly possessed much more genes from the inhabitants of the Yellow Archipelago — her skin had the corresponding shade, she had black hair and her eyes were narrow.

"Your director called me for a substitution. Your mom's still good for this job, though she's already retires," the woman cheered up in response to a question and turned to me again. "Hello, Helga!"

"How could you know my name?"

"Well, I haven't yet forgotten how to read," she pointed with her finger at my name tag. I was embarrassed. "You're such a cute little red fox! Just like our Kitsune."

I knew who she was talking about. The martial education included a class on evil spirits and it was part of my mandatory program. Kitsune, or the sacred foxes of the Yellow Archipelago, were sentient werewolves. Although they belonged to evil spirits, they were excluded from the list of beings dangerous for humans. Some inhabitants of the Archipelago considered them a much more ancient sentient race than humanity. I thought that the Kitsune settled on our planet along with the Lonquies but they were lucky to be completely alien to us on the magic and therefore the Department wasn't interested in werewolf foxes at all.

Kitsune lived in the mountains of the Yellow Archipelago's largest island. They ran on four legs in the form of huge foxes of different shades, or walked on two legs in a humanlike manner. They were reluctant to communicate with people, although they understood our speech and some of them could even respond with short barking phrases. There were legends saying that at the dawn of time people were fighting with werewolf foxes, trying to destroy this race completely. Apparently it was when the Kitsune decided to learn our language in order to understand their enemy's plans. As I said, werewolf foxes were now considered as sacred beings, and no one dared to touch them.

"Helga, this is my mother. Mom, this is Helga."

"You can call me Izumi Sifu, little one," the woman winked at me. Yeah, little one! I was almost a cut above her head. I was wondering why everyone around me suddenly began to call me that?

"Since when did you become a Sifu?" Dun was surprised.

"Since I've been training neighbor boys in martial arts," the woman replied cantankerously. "You'd know that if you showed up home more frequently. You haven't visited your parents for three months. Where's your conscience? Where's your conscience, I'm asking you!"

"I should keep an eye on both of you from now on!" Dun muttered under his breath, but Mrs. Izumi heard her son.

"Your maman is quite capable of keeping an eye not only on herself, but also on the two of you. And on your shameless Paul either. Actually, I'll keep an eye on him and the Lonquies until the end of this troublesome period. It's been years since the Department had experienced such a nasty time!"

An hour later, I was changing in the locker room before entering the gym. And suddenly I heard two women approaching conversation. From the voices I recognized Inga and Izumi Sifu. What made me hide in the nearest shower cubicle and close its door? Was it an instinct, curiosity or fear? Our shower cubicle didn't have these stupid transparent doors and walls — the Department respected the privacy of its employees at least during water procedures. Therefore, I was not scared about women finding me.

"Inga, I'm worried!" said Mrs. Izumi, entering the locker room. "God forbid my son freaked out the girl."

"As far as I could understand, Helga is not the one to be freaked out easily," said the trainer. I chuckled under my breath at these words, because she was right. "Only spiders can frighten her."

"That's so lovely!" Dun's mother was excited. "Just great! Every woman should have her own little weakness."

I would have never thought that my phobia could be turned into dignity! I thought that I have to tell Lina about it, she should also seek some kind of fear. I was wondering whether Izumi Sifu had any weaknesses.

"Well, she's not the freaky one but he can offend her," continued Dun's mother meanwhile. "You should have heard what my rascal told her! He's just like his father."

The old lady's voice clearly sounded with laughter. Apparently, she remembered her youth.

"Izie, your rascal is already thirty-four years old, he has the title of professor of medicine, a black belt in martial arts and a bright head."

"I know!" Dun's mother said proudly. "You can't wash out genes with soap. But he has too little experience in such things. He'll do something wrong, and we can kiss Helga goodbye. She'll leave the Department and will be as good as gone, such a cute little red fire."

"Yeah, that's true, she has the fire. Izie, well, since she's still here, I think it's not so easy to offend her. You can't follow your son and hold his hand, like if he's a small one."

I snorted gently, imagining this picture. To tell the truth, I still couldn't think of Dun as of someone's son. I got used to perceiving him as an older, much smarter person. Dun was my supervisor, my Professor, and not a 'rascal' who can blurt something out to a 'girl' like me.

"Inga, tell me what's going on between them?"

Well, we have come to the delicate topic here. Now the trainer would share all the rumors circulating at the Department. At least I should also listen to what they were saying about us.

"Izumi, how do I know? I don't even leave the gym too often. They're visiting us at different times; they had crossed in my presence for five minutes only once on her first day, when Paul brought the girl to meet us. Dun spends a lot of time in meditations and sparring. If Reincarnologist prefers boxing, then your son is engaged in your traditional art. Helga does a standard warm-up, throws knives and pulsars at the target, and then exhausts herself on a treadmill or does exercises to develop flexibility. Twice a week I train her in martial arts. There's nothing to talk about. The girl, by the way, should come soon, you'll see her for yourself. Rumor has it that she called your son to the range to be next to her during the bomb explosion. But I don't know if this is true."

Yes, security guards and healers, with whom we flew to the range, turned out to be reliable people, otherwise the whole Department, including Inga, would have known about our joint flight. In general, the paucity of information that the trainer has had surprised me. Apparently, on the first day I made a completely wrong conclusion based on Lina's words. Perhaps it was just the girl's provocation, which had been meant to find out something particularly piquant from me.

"I'll have to see it myself," Dun's mom said vexingly. "I was hoping you'd tell me. Whatever. It's even more interesting to look than to hear."

Women came out of the locker room, and I got thoughtful. The new factor in the form of Izumi Sifu didn't please me. Firstly, it was quite incomprehensible from the overheard conversation what she was experiencing for? Was it for the sake of our personal relationship with Dun or for the benefit of the Department, which I could potentially leave? Secondly, the appearance of another person, who was watching our 'dances' with special attention, didn't inspire me at all. Especially considering the fact this person was Dun's mother. The line that I had to walk on now became even thinner. So I just had to worry about how not to 'cut my feet'.

Oh, God, this time was so bad for personal relations! The entire Department was under a serious threat. In my mind I constantly went over all the information that was available to me. And now I had to strain myself harder so that I would neither blurt out anything to Mrs. Izumi nor blush eloquently at the wrong moment.

I got out of the shower cubicle, quickly finished changing and went to the gym. Izumi Sifu was standing opposite to Inga in a fighting position. The trainer was taller than her opponent, but she didn't seem confident. All of the gym visitors have crowded around the fighters. I stopped at the entrance.

Opponents bowed to each other and started to jump on the mat, holding their hands in a fighting position. In one second there was a jerk with two angry shouts and then Inga was lying on the floor, and Mrs. Izumi was holding out her hand to the trainer. Everything happened very quickly, but I saw how Inga went on the offensive, trying to kick the opponent with her foot. And she paid for that move — Dun's mother managed to grab the trainer's foot in a grip, spin it and throw Inga on the mats. While helping her friend to get up, Izumi Sifu saw me.

"Helga, come to us, dear!" she called. "Inga says that you wanted to improve your martial art skills. Is that true?"

"I'm afraid that my level is so low compared to yours that there's nothing to talk about," I bowed to Dun's mother in the manner of the Yellow Archipelago's inhabitants.

"Don't be afraid, little fox, I won't hurt you," she cheered up. "I don't offend my son's friends. You can ask that shameless Paul over there. He's such an impudent — decided to compliment me on my hairstyle. I wish there would be something to praise! He should find a girl and make compliments to her. How long can he stay unmarried?"

"There is already a girl," I quickly decided to turn the attention of the elderly lady from myself to Paul. "But she has been thinking whether to marry him."

But Izumi Sifu was much harder to trick than Lina.

"What is there to think about? She should agree! But let's check your skills. Don't worry, I have taught my sons since they were three years old. It's unlikely that you will do worse than my three-year-old munchkins."

"So Dun has a brother?" I emphasized the main thing in this speech.

"Yes, dear. My older son left for the Yellow Archipelago and has completely forgotten his parents, such a rascal. Aw, what a sly fox. You decided to talk a pensioner out? Go attack me!"

An hour later, I was completely exhausted, sitting in the dining room and eating. Izumi Sifu had knackered me down to dry, and now I was idly wondering what to do next.

Speak of the devil! My tormentor went into the room and came to me.

"Helga, may I pour you a cup of our restoring tea? My grandmother used to brew it for my grandfather. Dun neglects it, rascal, he's too lazy to obtain and prepare the components, then to brew them in a thermos. Although with his gift it's not difficult at all. If you drink it now, you will feel better right away."

I didn't refuse. Izumi Sifu poured the drink into the cup slowly, as if preparing a real tea ceremony. She gently unscrewed the cork, smoothly lifted the flask, carefully tilted it down. I admired her honed movements. The tea was delicious. I could clearly feel ginger and luinse (a magical plant that restores strength) in it, but I couldn't recognize the rest of the ingredients. The elderly woman fetched a small rice bun somewhere from her purse, deftly placed it on a small snow-white saucer and laid a napkin next to it. That definitely was not a snack, but a holiday. And Dun's reluctance to engage in preparation of the drink became understandable. If you spend so much attention on serving tea, then soon you will not want to drink it. Such a ceremony can be done for a loved one or a good friend, but one would not bother to do it for himself.

After the tea my head cleared a little.

"If you like it, I'll tell you the recipe, you'll make it and give it to your friends. Do you already have friends here?"

"Yes. Paul, Lina, and a few martial healers."

"That's great! So maybe you'll treat my son, because he doesn't want to make this drink himself."

"I'm not sure I can do everything as beautifully as you do, Mrs. Izumi," I decided to note the art of my interlocutor. I could imagine how wretched my attempts to treat Professor will look like against the background of the bewitching actions of his mother.

"Ah, little fox, that's nonsense!" dismissed Izumi Sifu. "It's always a pleasure to take something from your friend's hands, even if it's a bitter magic cucumber, not to mention the reducing tea. And no matter the package it was presented in."

Could she read thoughts? I didn't think so, of course, but who knows.

"You have a very nice suit," I decided to confess to my interlocutor in my own slight envy of her style.

"Thank you, dear! This is our traditional cut. But it won't fit you — you'll be too alienated in it," said Dun's mother. "You should wear lighter and more cheerful colored clothes. Just like the ones that you have on right now. Great taste! Are you going to visit the Grenons now?"

I imagined the upcoming conversation with Dun under the supervision of his mother and shuddered inwardly.

"No, I think it will be better to visit the Lonquies today. Moreover, Paul asked to substitute him for a couple of hours while he's working at the laboratory."

"Yes, I'd substituted him today before the training too. Let's go, I'll accompany you so that you can tell me what kind of girl this impudent has finally found. How do you feel? Is it better now?"

I nodded. The tea has really helped me to recover quickly, and the rice bun completed my meal and was the very last piece that brought me a feeling of satiety. In the little mentalist's sector there was no need to swim, which means that additional physical efforts wouldn't be needed.

We went down the corridor, I told Izumi Sifu a short story about Lina that explicitly raised the mood of the woman.

"You see, my dear, the boy has been all alone. There are no parents or any other relatives. It's not good when children are left to their own devices. Take the same Lina, as I understand, she has an older brother here?"

I nodded.

"And Paul has no one. So he needs a wife."

"And how do you think, up to what age do children need care?"

"Honey, a person should never be alone. There's no right age for loneliness."

I didn't have time to respond to this funny statement, because security Chief with two guards came around the corner towards us.

"Helga. Mrs. Izumi," he bowed to Dun's mother in the manner of the Yellow Archipelago's inhabitants. "Are you going to visit the Lonquies?"

"Look how significant you have become! So, you're a big boss now," my companion winked at the security Chief. "And I can remember those days when you were a handsome young air specialist."

The man smiled. No, it seemed that this woman considered everyone here to be boys and girls who need her supervision. However, her joy and guardianship have been warm and amusing rather than straining. Mrs. Izumi has even said her favorite "shameless" and "rascal" with friendliness and tenderness, which completely neutralized the negative meaning of these words. Dun's mother has always danced on a thin thread of care and tact, staying away from matters that were not her business and, at the same time, showing that she was there, remembering and appreciating everyone. If I had not overheard their conversation with Inga in the locker room, then I would have never suspected anything.

"Yes, sir, we're going there," I answered security Chief's question.

"Please, ladies, be careful. We have a sudden failure of electronics supply of the surveillance cameras near the Lonquies' sector. Therefore, we can't see what is going on from security desk. I sent two guards to be on duty there until a specialist fixes the equipment. But be careful. Put on your magic shields right now."

I felt uncomfortable. It was a new emergency and it happened near the wards' sector again. Izumi Sifu clearly thought the same thing. We thanked security Chief for his care and went on.

"Nasty time!" my companion muttered under her breath. "Nasty!"

"I'm starting to think that the Department is always full of emergencies," I complained.

"Oh, no, dear! Everything is usually quiet and measured here. Computer guys work with rumors, martial healers — with wards, medics — with flies. And all of them periodically run to swim with the Grenons and have fun a couple of times a month at a party organized by legend specialists. And security guards sleep at their desk."

It was very interesting to me. Was she telling the truth about the usual silence in the Department, or was it just to prevent me from escaping from here, frightened by a life filled with troubles?

"So, that's the legend specialists who organize parties, huh?" I clarified some new information for myself. Since I've never been able to participate in such an event, I didn't know the nuances.

"Who else? They're something like a PR department, modern for nowadays. So they deal with rumors and communicate with the press, if it's necessary, and are engaged in corporate culture."

"Is everything relatively quiet here indeed?"

"In my experience the only turmoil had happened when we decided to conduct an experiment and introduce the baby piggy to the Lonquies," answered Izumi Sifu. "We told the little mentalists about this meeting and calculated every action. There's no sense to warn the Clevres, as you can see. We chose the youngest and the most calm piggy. These two species have a different rhythm of life, so we decided to arrange a meeting in the evening, when the Lonquies are already awakening, and the Clevres are just getting ready to sleep. What blew into the little mentalists' minds that day? They had never admitted. Maybe the dragons just wanted to have some fun, little wretches? But when they saw the Clevr, a din rose and one of the Lonquies created an illusion of a huge fire-breathing dragon. Can you imagine a three-ton scared pig in the kids sector? The Clevr had messed artificial mountains to smithereens, broke the glass, jammed partitions and rushed down the tunnel directly to his own sector, stepping on my colleague's foot. Fortunately, we managed to save it. But our monthly bonuses were lost that day."

I laughed so loud that tears streamed down from my eyes. A three-ton furry pig in the Lonquies' sector, frightened by the dragon, was probably something. It was a big luck that the Clevr didn't kill any little mentalists. The dragons had probably just flown up. It was good that all victims ended with the subsequently saved foot of one of the experimenters.

"Had you not been working here for a long time?" I asked my interlocutor, when we entered the Lonquies' sector and put on mental protection helmets.

"Well, I'd prepared Dun, and then left. Almost ten years passed since that day."

"Do you miss your job?"

"I miss it very much, especially swimming with the Grenons."

"Can't you come to the Department to spend some time with them?"

"Oh, I can imagine this almshouse. It will be such an amazing nursing home for bored senior citizens."

I burst out laughing. Mrs. Izumi shook her head.

"No, little fox, we all have to learn how to live without this joy. I've been training boys. I found my own wards. It's as pleasant as swimming with the Grenons. Children can really warm your soul."

I hoped she wouldn't start talking about grandchildren. However, as far as I managed to understand, Izumi Sifu would never stop to such a hint.

"And didn't Dun resist working in the Department?"

"No, dear, he has been delighted with the Grenons since his childhood. When the first initiation took place and it became clear that he had inherited the gift of a martial healer, I introduced him to the wards immediately."

It turned out that Professor and I have had an absolutely same story of falling in love with our job."

Upon seeing us, Paul rejoiced. He was rushing to work in the laboratory and therefore eagerly awaited the replacement. But the last instructions for me took another ten minutes, after which Paul and Izumi Sifu left the sector. Apparently, the woman was expected in another wards' sector. When the door opened in front of them, I saw that on the sides of the entrance there have already been two security guards in helmets of mental protection. I heard Natalie's voice. The second guard was a stranger to me.

The Lonquies have also rejoiced at my appearance. One of the little dragons landed on my shoulder. He was golden — his skin shimmered in all shades, reflecting the light and creating charming streaks and lines. It was like a candlelight dancing some intricate dance. I started the timer and carefully took my helmet off with one hand so as not to disturb the little ward.

A mental noise fell upon me. The Lonquies were living their own lives, each of them experienced some emotion. Somewhere nearby one dragon was passing knowledge to another one, with curiosity, pride and joy emanating from there. On the other side, three individuals were creating a joint three-dimensional illusion and arguing over the details. The creative fight was in full swing with all the corresponding passions. Somewhere in the rocks an elderly slender individual was suffering from poor health and his grunt were inspiring thoughts of eternity, the imminent transition, and a new body. Emotions and thoughts were coming from all sides, and it was very difficult to endure it for more than five minutes. I tried to focus on the dragon sitting on my shoulder.

"Something strange and menacing is happening in the Department," the dragon said. "Izumi has appeared here. It's not good."

"We'll do our best to restore the balance," I said aloud. I still couldn't mentally form clear messages, some fragments of a completely different kind were constantly mixed in. I've trained, and even began to go to Arthur for meditation, but so far it has turned out badly. So it was better to speak out loud for now. This would help the mentalists to filter out my thoughts from what I really wanted to tell them.

"Just be careful yourself," the little one answered. "Many individuals here have taken care of you, but don't let this knowledge stir your mind with a fog of confidence in your own safety. The enemy can be in any guise, even hiding behind a friend's smile."

"Whom exactly can you call innocent?"

"All the martial healers, security Chief, Director, his deputy and Julie. We had no opportunity to check the rest of the employees."

My list has included the same people, plus with a probability of ninety-nine percent, there was also Lina.

"Lina? Is this the individual that Paul has so many emotions towards? It's like a creeping multi-colored fire that warms up, burns, shines, and sometimes even kills, but is never extinguished."

"Yes," his words and images were so amazing!

"Call her here for a couple of minutes. We'll check her. We want to meet the individual that Paul has so much fire towards. Such a flame needs to be protected so we can't let the black night of doubts muffle it even for a tiny moment."

"Okay!" of course, I was sure that Paul himself didn't doubt the girl for a hundredth of a percent, but I thought that Lina would be delighted to meet the dragons. So why not make my friend happy, since the Lonquies were inviting her themselves?

The checkup of the employees was an extremely important topic, but I couldn't concentrate on it in any way. The trinity of the creators have finally agreed and made such beauty that it was simply breathtaking. The illusion of a rainbow fountain was living, passing from state to state and attracting the sight. It seemed to me that it was the Lonquies who gave humanity the knowledge about volumetric illusions and moving photos. I felt that I was beginning to lose the essence of what was happening around me, that I was being drawn into the fountain and that I absolutely didn't want to resist and emerge...

The watch vibrated on my hand, as if squeezing it and reminding me: 'Be careful!'. Vibration drove me out of a trance state, and I instantly put on my helmet. The mental noise had stopped immediately, the illusion of the fountain disappeared, and my head began to clear up. The dragon on my shoulder shifted from paw to paw, but decided not to fly away. Apparently, it was more comfortable for him to stay with me. I took my phone out of my pocket and dialed a message for Lina: 'Come to the Lonquies' sector, they want to meet you. Don't tell Paul'.

Five minutes later, the phone vibrated and I saw a friend's incoming call. The dragon rose from my shoulder and flew somewhere not far away. I had to open the door outside for Lina, because the girl didn't have access to this sector. I hastened to press the necessary combination of keys on the lock, the door opened and my frightened friend ran inside the room.

"Helga! Hurry! They all are lying on the floor there!"

I put a mental defense helmet into Lina's hands and ran out of the sector. The second martial healer stuck his head out, not leaving the Lonquies territory. Two security guards were on the flour. Their coffee mugs were lying nearby. Their drinks were spilled over the tile and walls. A little further down the corridor, at the exit from the blind zone, another security guard was lying. I recognized this third employee, because he was the one who had flown with us to the range.

"Don't leave the sector and be alert," I shouted at the colleague. "Look after the girl. I'll check everything here now, and you call the guard from there, please."

The healer nodded and closed the door. I checked the heart rate of all the guards and made a quick health scan. All three were in deep sleep. Darts were sticking out of each body, apparently having some sleeping drugs in them. Security Chief with some of his guys rushed to me, and I noticed Ron behind them. Julie had already gone home, because it was after midnight.

"What happened?" security Chief shouted, still running.

"They're sleeping," I briefly informed him. The man breathed a sigh of relief.

"Who found them?"

"It was my friend, whom I invited to visit the Lonquies' sector."

"What for?" security Chief looked at me in surprise. Ordinary employees usually didn't go to the Lonquies.

"They asked me to."

"What the hell is going on here?"

I couldn't find an answer to this question. I also didn't understand what was happening in the Department. What was the point of sedating security? To get closer to the Lonquies? But we were still there. And we're constantly alert while on duty, always walking under the thin magical shields. Nobody could get us with such darts. Putting security guards to sleep was not logical.

"Yes, that's not logical," Chief agreed, and I realized that I had spoken the last sentence aloud.

The victims were sent to the laboratory to sleep in comfortable conditions. It was possible to ask the healers to neutralize the effect of drags, but the management decided to wait until the guards would wake up themselves. It was better for their bodies. A video surveillance equipment repairman appeared after this incident and the whole night shift of security was standing under the magic shields in a small corridor and controlling the repairment process, which luckily did not take much time.

When I entered the Lonquies' sector, they already knew that no one had died and nothing particularly terrible had happened. Lina was sitting behind the glass without a helmet and with a blissful look on her face, gazing somewhere at one point and stroking the belly of a pearl-blue individual. The dragon was clearly enjoying her touches. It was weird to see a little mentalist in such a state — it seemed to me that the wise and ancient creatures simply couldn't behave like that. But it turned out that I was wrong.

"How long has she been there?" I asked my colleague, nodding at Lina.

"For four minutes. Don't worry, I keep my eye on the time. Who would have thought that they can spread like a puddle in joy?" my interlocutor was clearly also struck by an unusual sight. "We had to let someone like Lina come here a long time ago. To let visit the dragons to someone who doesn't suffer from excessive reverence at our little friends. Maybe we would learn something new in that case?"

At the end of the set time, I went behind the glass and put a helmet on my friend's head. The girl woke up, looked at me, continuing to scratch the dragon's belly, and asked:

"What happened there?"

"I don't know. Someone sedated the guards using darts with sleeping drugs. The security were all wearing helmets, so the Lonquies couldn't understand their physical condition at the time of the incident. Apparently, two guards were standing on duty when the third one brought them coffee and then left. At that moment someone got him. The location of the darts in the bodies indicates that the attacker shot from the common corridor, but it's not clear who was sedated first. If it was the one who brought coffee, then why did the other two not notice the shoot and didn't raise the alarm? If they were the first ones to be attacked, then how could the third guard miss the shooter? We're waiting for the victims to wake up and tell us about what happened."

But security Chief wasn't successful in his attempt to find out something coherent from the guys. The Lonquies confirmed Lina's innocence, but the victims themselves didn't manage to notice the attacker. Only a third guard, who brought coffee, repeated one thing again and again: 'It's the fault of someone from security guards' and 'Everything happened so quickly'. Ron was trying to pull something else out of him, but the guard was apparently in shock, fixating on the same phrases. The management decided not to torment the employee.

The duties said that their colleague brought them coffee, but they didn't have time to drink at least a sip. They didn't hear when the third guard's body fell, because they were wearing helmets. Perhaps the attacker had also held his first victim, so that he wouldn't create too much noise. The victims converged in testimony. Their veracity was confirmed by Ron, who was checking their auras. In general, by morning it was clear that nothing was clear.

Wednesday and Thursday passed very quietly and calmly. I wasn't used to it, and that's why I felt that this was the calm before the storm. Because of this feeling, I was constantly looking around, being very uncomfortable. But no more surprises seemed to happen. Every day I was training my martial arts skills with Izumi Sifu, mastering a few more secret technologies of the Department and had even once swum with the Grenons. But nothing particularly interesting came to me this time after swimming. Apparently, my nervousness took a tall on me.

On Friday morning, right after the end of the night shift, Director called me to his office.

"Helga, you show very unconventional abilities. Your creative approach to solving problems allowed us to react and find answers quickly. The Lonquies splitted the journalist in half a minute, and it turned out that it was his editor-in-chief who had sent him on a mission to our botanical garden. The reporter didn't know where the editor had got the tip from. It is necessary for us to find it out. Considering suspicions around the death of Anthony and the incident with the guards' sedation, quite unequivocal conclusions have arisen. I'm afraid we have a 'rat' with huge teeth here. Julie will test everyone for loyalty again, but it will take too much time. It would be faster to direct the entire stuff team to the Lonquies' sector, but I can't risk the sanity of innocent employees' minds. So we have to spy."

"I'm afraid I don't quite understand---"

"On Sunday evening, the editors will arrange an event — a charity concert. There will be several mental musicians, the sounds and emotions gala there. You and Dun will go to this concert undercover. We found out that the chief editor is a connoisseur and a great lover of vintage wines. If Dun succeeds, he'll be able to drink the editor and know the truth."

"Why does Dun need my company?"

"He needs the most believable legend. Our best expert has advised your couple. Dun will be playing the role of a very rich man, accompanied by a beautiful woman. I also consulted with Julie. She didn't go into details, just said that we can count on you for sure. Our object is an aura specialist so he'll see all the blatant lies immediately, and in that case he won't admit to himself on a gunshot."

"Is Dun a rich man?"

"Girl, none of us are poor here. You don't know that because you've been working for a limited time here. You'll understand the situation when you get your first salary."

"But why us? It seemed to me that this should be done by security guards. I saw that we have a married couple here."

"We need a water magician who can evaporate alcohol from his blood in order not to get drunk faster than the editor does. And in that pair, the husband is an air magician. Don't you want to go to a concert?"

"Oh, I'm sorry," I said, feeling embarrassed. "I really want to! I just still can't begin to work directly with the wards. I've been doing something else here for almost a month. I visit them so rarely. In addition, I doubt my spy abilities. Also, I have this habit of asking questions, figuring out everything I can."

"Ah, you, little warrior," Director was delighted for some reason. "Helga, you have your whole life ahead! You'll have a chance to work with the wards. Believe me, you'll even get bored. Events like this are extremely rare here. If only they had never happened! You don't really need to spy, just enjoy the concert. The rest will be done by Dun. The Department needs your help."

"Why don't you think that I'm a rat?"

"Firstly, these weird events had started before you began to work here. Secondly, you would hardly offer us such options for solving problems if you were not interested in the security of the Department. Thirdly, your loyalty was confirmed by the Lonquies. So here's some money for a dress, shoes and all those lady things. You should have a good night's sleep on Saturday because on Sunday night you'll need your full concentration. I give you a day off after the concert, you can come to work on Tuesday. Izumi will replace you on duty. And I beg you — watch Dun. I have no one else to entrust his safety to."

"Yes, sir!" I blurted out half-jokingly, took the envelope and left Director's office. If it was my will, I would never take my eyes off Dun. But the will was not mine. And now I had to call Lina to ask her for help. I had to choose the outfit but I have never bought dresses for such events.

Chapter 21

I realized how insidious Lina is on Sunday evening, when I saw Dun's reaction to my appearance. The girl obviously decided to take revenge on me because of Paul, but I didn't even suspect something was wrong when I bought the outfit. Lina convinced me this was exactly the type of dress that is supposed to be worn by a wealthy and respectable lady at charity events. The first doubts flashed through my mind when my Mother became excited upon noticing my reflection in the mirror.

"You're so beautiful! This color and cut really suit you! Daddy, come here, look at our girl!"

Dad went into my room and froze.

"You're more beautiful than your mother is," he finally gave out unprecedented praise. "Sorry, darling."

"It's all right," my Mother laughed. "I totally agree with you! Helga, was it Lina who helped you to choose this dress?"

"Yes," I nodded. "I know nothing about such events, but she already has experience."

"Remind me, where are you going with your fiancé?" my Father became interested.

"To a charity concert, dad. We'll fight for money for the hospital equipment."

"In that case, I'm sure you'll succeed."

I turned back to the mirror. The dress flowed with dark green silk and really fitted to the color of my skin and hair. And the high cut was exactly of such a length to open my leg and at the same time to hide the hip cover with my throwing knives. Drapery made it possible to hide outlines of weapons on my leg. The image was completed with shoes of the same color on a stiletto heel. Walking on them was not very convenient for me, because of how tall I was, and I wasn't used to putting on heels of such a height. Lina and I had even had a fight while choosing the shoes. I said that I would be higher than Professor, but my friend said that Dun wouldn't care, and that all I need is to seduce the editor anyway. As a result, the girl just bought the shoes and put them in my hands, not taking any objections. Honestly, I felt extremely grateful to her for this. Stilettos were perhaps the only thing I've never allowed myself to wear, even though I've always wanted to. Riding back home from the store in a taxi, I was stroking this amazing green leather. And the rest of the Saturday, and then all the Sunday I trained to walk in my new shoes, while holding a posture. Now I was happy that there would be no need to dance, run and walk a lot. A concert is not a ball.

Dun was lost for words when I came out of my parents' house. He was looking at me without moving for about five minutes, and then he just silently offered me his hand and we got into an expensive car parked near the house. A familiar water magician winked at me from the driver seat. It was he who froze the targets for me in the gym.

"The Department has transport for such cases," the security guard explained in response to my questioning look. "The management has to visit different meetings. It's not good for Director and his deputy to fly through the air. Today I have to drive you two to the concert hall so you can respectively come out from a posh car. Unfortunately, I can't wait for the event's end because I will need to take the deputy director to the government quarter. Can you get home by taxi?"

I nodded and looked at silent Professor. He was looking very handsome today too. No, he's always handsome, of course. But today he was handsome in a fashionable suit!

In the maternity hospital, I used to see Dun in a white coat. In the Department he walked around in plain jeans and a T-shirt; during cool nights, he put on a sports jacket. I saw him in a suit and tie for the first time and couldn't say a word too.

However, it was necessary to relieve the situation so I pushed my companion in his side with my elbow in a badass way. I definitely learned this from Lina. Such a movement always defused the situation.

"Do you know what kind of concert we're visiting tonight?"

Dun finally revived.

"The editors are presenting a new band," he said, clearing his throat. "It seems that they have great designs on these newcomers. So, if this concert is successful, they will sign a contract with the musicians to earn money. If the evening ends well, the editor will get drunk because of excitement, if it ends badly, he'll drink because of grief. In any case, we'll be welcome with our gift."

Professor took a bottle of wine from a car refrigerator.

"I may be a little out of my depth here," I complained.

"It's expensive, old and good," Dun said briefly.

It turned out to be a short trip and very soon we were standing at the building's entrance in front of the receptionist.

"Mr. and Mrs. Lee," Dun said, and the guy let us in with a bow.

"Lee?" I was surprised.

"It's my grandmother's maiden name. And at the same time, it's a surname of one rich and influential family. They are our namesakes. It's very convenient that I almost didn't have to lie. Half truth is not so visible. The registrar didn't suspect anything."

"Is he an aura specialist?"

"Helga, were you born yesterday? Only the aura specialists are eligible for such positions. If the employer is poor, he has to buy lie detectors and metal detector frames."

Wow! Given the cost of the frame and the lie detector, I could count the income of this registrar! But the frame is bought only once, and the aura reader needs to be paid constantly. . . I decided not to think about this. We went into the hall.

Our concert halls are built according to a special principle. All the most talented and expensive musicians are mentalists. This ensures the completeness of emotions transfer — music is complemented by exposure. Of course, somewhere at a disco in a nightclub or at a student's wedding, one weak specialist would be enough to warm up the crowd, add some fun and slightly stir up lazy guests. But such halls are only open for strong, talented and skillful musicians to perform. Therefore, the spectator seats are always located in separate booths or lodges on several tiers up. Downstairs, in the very center, there are musical instruments. Most respectable and expensive seats are on the first tier. The closer the musician, the stronger the impact and the more respectable (or more expensive) the seats.

A manager took us to the second tier, and I breathed a sigh of relief. Who could know what to expect from this band? Medicine teachers told us about cases of excessive exposure that led to death. Usually elderly people with a weak heart couldn't stand it. But for young and healthy too strong influence could end badly as well. Therefore, all mentalists passed the full course of training and in ordinary life were obliged to restrain themselves or to take on a special screening amulet.

There was a small table in the lodge with a vase of fruit on it. A decanter with some water and a box of napkins were standing near the vase. We sat in comfortable chairs. Next to his chair Professor put a bag with the bottle. I looked down over the railing and saw a gorgeous grand piano, lightened with spotlights. There were two tabourets near the musical instrument.

"When are we going to get the editor?" I asked my companion, deciding to temporarily suppress my curiosity about the number of seats near the piano. All the same, I'll find out the details soon.

"We'll decide it according to the circumstances. It will be either at intermission, or after the concert. Don't worry, he's not going anywhere. The show begins!"

A light in the hall went out, there was only the beam of one single spotlight, which shone directly on the piano. Two figures in concert suits suddenly appeared next to the instrument. Are there two of them?

"Yes," Dun answered, and I realized that the last question was asked out loud again. I should do something about it, otherwise I'd blurt out a word that shouldn't be said. "The band consists of male and female pianists. They are four-handed musicians. Rumor has it that the mental impact is surprisingly rich and emotionally directed at each viewer in the hall."

It was very interesting to me. I've never seen anything like this before. Two mental musicians at once, obviously having approximately the same strength, otherwise they wouldn't be able to ensure a uniform impact. Yes, and they have a different gender. Were they twins like Inga and Arthur?

Meanwhile, the pianists sat down at the instrument, opened the lid and laid their fingers on the keys.

"'Without you'," an emcee, hidden by darkness, proclaimed the name of the composition, which began the evening. Sad, slightly philosophical music flew out. I started to feel the first emotions of the mentalists, which were difficult to separate from mine. A woman saw her beloved one off for a long and dangerous trip and was already yearning him, looking in his back. A man was leaving behind the most precious thing he had in his life, but he knew that there was no other way for him. Emotions rose, intertwined, forming a beautiful and extremely touching song with music, which made my heart ache.

It was now clear why there was a box with napkins on the table. I learned how to control my feelings at school, but there was a moment when it seemed to me that I couldn't bear this wild strain of longing. Tears could give it all away, and it would be easier for me to listen to the music, but nonetheless I was not ready to cry, although I was almost on the verge of it.

"'When the sun goes down'," the emcee announced again, and I breathed a sigh of relief when I heard a relaxing melody. During this composition we plunged into a hot night of southern islands, where all life begins only with an onset of darkness. Carefree and unobtrusive joy was streaming down the hall, as if we were in a light euphoria, dancing along with the performers, enjoying absolute freedom from conventions, from the heat of the past day, from obligations and heavy thoughts. My sensations were enhanced due to the contrast with the previous composition. I really wanted to jump up and spin in dance, but the small lodge didn't allow for this. It was perhaps even more difficult to prevent myself from wanting to dance than from crying earlier. The musicians were undoubtedly talented.

"'Four-handed Tango'," announced the emcee, and I freaked out. Tango is accompanied by a rather passionate music, and it's very difficult to listen to it without own emotions. In the darkness of the lodge it was impossible to understand how Professor was feeling now, but I tried to quietly move away from him. I was just afraid of myself in such a situation.

This time the piano was accompanied by double bass and cello. There was such a high level of passion that it threw me into a fever. Two lines of emotions — male and female — were simply tearing my body apart. It was really an explosive mixture: enjoying a beautiful dance, the delight of the skill and strength of your own body, eroticism, the desire to seduce a partner and having to restrain yourself because the tango hasn't ended yet. And most importantly — all the transmitted feelings were laying on my own experiences and intensifying because of it. My tango with Dun was also in full swing and it was completely unknown how it would end. I remembered the practice of breathing concentration, which Professor taught Lina, and tried to distract myself, but I didn't succeed. The external emotions didn't let me to. How could this couple play in such a state at all? They didn't just broadcast all this passion; they experienced it!

Dun reached for the table and poured water from the decanter into two tall glasses. I saw the outlines of his hands in a faint diffused light which was penetrating our lodge from the outside. I was watching his acts and imagining these arms around me, him stroking my cheek, running his fingers through my hair. . . In panic, I grabbed the glass filled with water by my companion. The first sip brought a little relief, and I tried to concentrate on the coolness of water I was drinking. Alien emotions slightly receded into the background, and then the composition ended.

"In most difficult moments just drink," Professor said hoarsely. "You'll feel better."

"How do you know?" I asked him in the same sagging voice.

"I've already been at such events, although today it's a unique case."

"'Lullaby'!" announced the emcee again. Oh, yes, children were definitely conceived after such tangos. A violin entered the game, playing an unspeakably beautiful solo. The main emotion here was tenderness to a child. A man was keeping and caring for his child and its mother, and a woman's heart was overflowing with love for her baby and at the same time pride for her husband. Tenderness was pervading all around me, it seemed that the hall was filled with pure and totally uncomplicated love. I felt this for the first time, because my personal life experience was not enough — I had no children. But I really wanted to go back home and immediately hug my parents. And I also felt a burning desire to become a mother myself.

Then I couldn't restrain my emotions and reached for a napkin. Tears were flowing down my cheeks, but at the same time I was in heaven. I didn't want the lullaby to end, I was bathing in it, as if it was a moonlight or warm waves of the sea. Dun squeezed my hand, and my happiness became complete.

"'Children of the fire'."

This new melody was already much closer to me. I was just at that age when you think that you can and will do anything. When you walk with your friends before dawn, you play the guitar by the fire, you look from under your eyelashes at your former classmates who suddenly become adults, and you feel carefree in that moment. In such an age all doubts and worries will begin tomorrow, and today there's only this carelessness, only night and only friends.

During the intermission, Dun suggested that we go out for a walk and breathe. According to him, physical activity could allow us to break free from this obsession faster and to prepare for the second part of the concert. We used this opportunity to find our current facility.

In vain Lina thought that I would have to impress the editor. He was old and bald like a billiard ball. Apparently, it was only possible to impress him with alcohol, which, fortunately, was in our lodge. The editor had the appearance of an avid wine lover, but with attentive prickly eyes.

"Elle and Dun Lee," Professor introduced us, telling only half of the truth again. I looked at him with enthusiasm. The names seemed quite consonant with the surname. And putting my nickname in first place, Dun didn't cause even a shadow of doubt that this surname was mine either. If only Lina could learn to talk like that with aura specialists! However, I thought that she would learn it from now.

"Are your protégés twins?" I dared to ask a question that tormented me all evening. The editor laughed joyfully.

"No, young lady. They're not twins. Many people asked me this question today. They have such a coherence of suggestion, don't they?"

"So, are they a couple?" specified Dun.

"And not a couple. Each of them is married to another person."

"So how is such a coherent performance even possible?" I asked in surprise.

"Nobody knows. They personally say that they're just kindergarten friends. But people don't believe that. Probably, they're lovers."

"Whatever is their relationship, these guys still are a real piece of luck, and I'm ready to invest a little money in their project," Dun said. "My companion is an imperturbable woman, but these musicians could drive even her to tears. It says a lot to me."

"I hope you were crying not out of grief?" the editor was worried.

"It was out of happiness," I smiled shyly. "I couldn't restrain myself on a lullaby."

"Oh, lullaby, yes! Both musicians have recently become parents. The composition was created right after that. I always cry upon hearing it too. I'm too old and sentimental now. My grandson was born last year. Do you have children?"

"Not yet," Dun said, putting his arms around my waist. "But, please, accept our congratulations on the birth of your grandson! We invite you to our lodge after the end of the concert. Let's celebrate the heir's birth and the success of your protégé with a bottle of twenty-year Pickar wine."

The editor perked up.

"Where did you get such a rarity? That's incredible luck!"

"My family was involved in this winery. After its merger and reprofiling, we still have some reserves," said Dun, and he obviously wasn't lying! I have been learning more and more about Professor. "I keep it for special occasions and I consider today's concert one of them."

After receiving a warm assurance of a mandatory visit from the editor, we made another circle and returned to the lodge in time for the beginning of the second part.

"'The Maple Waltz'."

And there was a new wave of tenderness, and the bitterness of separation, and flour, and creativity, and happiness, and curiosity. Compositions changed, emotions were intertwining and complementing each other, allowing listeners to experience the fullness of life in one evening. I thought that I should invite my parents to such a concert. And it was also necessary to slip tickets to one doubting girl.

Chapter 22

Dun was having a lot of fun. His right arm was around my waist, and I was supporting him with my shoulder and slowly dragging him up the stairs. The guy was singing a frivolous song to the entire parade, waving his left hand and stumbling constantly. The air smelled with alcohol.

"Gosh, Dun, please, can you sober up at last?" I asked him.

"I d-d-don't wa-a-ant!" Professor answered with a braided tongue, refusing to do me this favor. I was hissing, muttering under my breath and dragging him up. "A-a-and you're so-o-o-o beautiful!"

"Beautiful, beautiful, Dun. You're handsome," he won't remember my words tomorrow, anyway.

"Am I?" a happy drunk smile appeared on his face. "I d-d-didn't know that."

"Don't lie!"

"You have ne-e-ever told m-me that!"

"As if you don't know the colleagues' opinion about you. Can you just sober up?"

"No! A-a-and you're not only beautiful, you're so-o-o sexy."

"Oh, my God! Dun, you'll feel ashamed tomorrow."

"M-m-me?" Professor was surprised and suddenly stopped on the stairs. I couldn't budge him. The alcohol smell got even stronger. I tried not to inhale deeply. "Never! Listen, but we s-s-succeeded, d-didn't we?"

"I don't know, actually. We found out that there was an anonymous call indicating the approximate time and place. We have no specifics. Let's go ahead!"

"Why?" Dun was surprised again, moving on. "The r-r-rat is in the Department. We'll find him! Or her."

"How could you know that this person is in the Department?"

"A-a-a-a---" Professor swayed and nearly threw us both forward. "A-a-anonymous call! Here, open the door."

A drunken smile appeared on Dun's face again. He was handing me a key to his apartment, next to which we were standing. I turned the key in the lock, put a thumb of his hand on the button and forced him to turn his head to the iris reader. The door opened, and I dragged Professor into his apartment, pulling off his jacket.

"Where's your bedroom?"

"I like your train of thought!" my companion said in a completely sober voice and slammed the door behind me, pressing me to it. My purse fell somewhere under our feet.

"Dun, what are you doing?"

"I just want to kiss you, what else?" he stroked my cheek. "Why are you so scared?"

"I'm not scared."

"So kiss me. I'm sober, I smell good, I have a nice suit on, and I'm crazy about you today. Give me your kiss and I'll let you go."

What a tricky one! He knew that I had also drunk this amazingly expensive wine. He made me drink it! When would I get smarter? But he was so close. And smiled at me. Oh, Dun...

"Staying alone with you is an impossible mission," Dun was whispering in my ear a little later. His tie was lying on the floor, his shirt was wide open. I was standing in his arms without my hairpins and bolero. A holster with Dun's pistol got lost somewhere, just as my hip cover with knives. The dress has already been half-zipped. "And today I managed to lure myself. You're breathtakingly beautiful. You're insanely sexy. And these pianists with their crazy tango added fire. I tried my best to hold on all evening. I was concentrating on our damn task. Why haven't I brought you to a concert before? Or to a dance."

"We had no time for this. And I didn't have such a dress."

"Well, damn it. Let's take it off completely?"

"What are you doing? You'll tear it up!"

"Hush-h-h! I'll buy you another one. It will be even more sexy. Come here!"

After some time, I dared to recognize the obvious thing aloud:

"It was great."

"I know," Dun smiled with some smug smile. "I heard."

I was embarrassed and began to free myself from his arms.

"Where are you going?"

"I have to go home. Where is your bathroom?"

"Did I say something wrong?"

"No. I just have to go home, and you need to report to the Department about our results and get enough sleep before the night shift."

"I'll see you off."

"I can get home myself!"

"In that dress?" Dun nodded at the scraps of my clothes, lying on the floor. Hmm, in this kind of an outfit I definitely couldn't get home by myself. "Let me call a taxi though, if you don't want me to accompany you. I'll give you my t-shirt and shorts. You'll look funny, but decent. The shower is there."

It seemed to me, or was he offended? So what? I decided that I would think about it tomorrow, now I had to have my time.

After turning off the shower I wrapped myself in a towel and left the booth. Dun wasn't in the bedroom — his voice was coming from somewhere else in the apartment. I thought that Professor was calling me a taxi. Shorts and a tank top were lying on the bed. I quickly dressed up, finding my underwear that had accidentally survived in the fragments of the dress, and went to the corridor, glancing briefly at myself in the mirror of the wardrobe in the hallway.

Dun was completely wrong. I didn't look funny in spite of a decent outfit. His clothes suited me, notwithstanding the fact that the top was clearly a little bit too large.

Professor appeared at the kitchen door with a phone in his hand, dressed in a spacious dark kimono. At that moment I was braiding my hair, going to tie it with a strip of fabric, barbarously torn from the remnants of my dress. Honestly, I wished to open the door and run away quietly, but I understood that such behavior would be the height of idiocy and infantilism. I gazed at Dun, looking in the mirror reflection. Somehow it was easier that way — as if there was an invisible barrier or some kind of an intermediary between us.

"Well, it suits you," Dun smiled.

"Thank you!" while I was taking a shower, I tried to calm down and now was able to smile carefree in response. In the end, nothing special happened, what was the reason to freak out? "Do you know where my shoes are?"

"You'll find them in the bag, alongside your purse and knives. Will you take them on?"

"No, I'll get to a taxi barefoot," I imagined how ridiculous I would look in his shorts, his top and my stilettos.

"Let me carry you out, huh?" Professor offered. I was wondering why did he suddenly begin to ask me? Previously, he just grabbed and carried me without my permission.

"Dun, please, don't. I love to walk barefoot. Your house has a clean entrance, fine stairs. Sometimes it's even a pleasure to feel a cool surface under your feet."

"Won't you catch a cold?'

"It's the end of May, and it's not so far to go."

Professor only silently waved his hand, like saying: 'as you please'. He took my bag, opened the door in front of me and escorted me to a taxi.

"Just, please, don't think stupid thoughts," he asked me, looking straight into my eyes. Then he touched my lips with a light kiss and walked me off to a taxi that has just arrived. "Have some rest."

The car door closed, and the taxi started to move. I waited until we turned around the corner, and Professor was left behind, and then I groaned and put my head on my hands.

"Is it so bad?" a woman's voice came from the driver's seat. I looked up and saw makeuped eyes in the reflection of the rear view mirror. Despite the fact that it was a very early morning, there was enough artificial lighting to draw the appropriate conclusions — I was lucky to ride with a female taxi driver. A quick scan revealed that she had a weak mental talent. The woman has read our emotions in addition to my exotic look and the scene that happened between me and Dun.

"Well, I can't say that it's so bad," I decided to be frank. The car raced through the deserted streets of the predawn city, I was looking for words to answer. Whom else could I be so frank with, if not with an unfamiliar taxi driver who will never see me again? "It was just so not in time, and it seems, I did a very wrong thing."

"Can love really be wrong?" my interlocutor asked with interest.

I was silent for a moment. Honestly, I didn't expect such a question.

"No, love is right, but I'm not sure that it is it," I finally uttered. "Did you hear what he'd told me?"

"And what had he told you?"

"He advised me not to think stupid thoughts. There's nothing to fantasize about, apparently," sometimes you just want to hear from someone a refutation of your fears and disappointments! And the taxi driver didn't let me down:

"But maybe it was 'don't question my actions and torture yourself with it'?"

I thought about it. There was some meaning in words of my night companion, of course. And this meaning was encouraging and even soothing. But I couldn't get rid of the doubts in my mind. Everything was incomprehensible and unclear, ambiguous again. Even now, even after this hot night.

"It's the most inopportune time for love now."

"There is no inopportune time for love. We're at your place."

I looked around and saw that we really stopped at the parents' house. It turned out that Dun had already paid for the cab, and I got out of the car, remembering to grab a package with my belongings. It would be a shame to forget my valued possessions.

I was hoping that my Mother was asleep, and I wouldn't have to blush in front of her, but, putting the bag on a nightstand in a hallway, I heard a door open in my parents' bedroom.

"The clothes suit you," my Mom said, giving me a careful look. I felt a hot wave of embarrassment flooding down my face, neck and ears. "Let's go together to a sports store someday and choose a similar outfit for you. Where's your dress?"

"It died bravely in an unequal battle with our feelings," I looked into my Mother's eyes. Damn it, I was already an adult!

"The worthiest death," my Mother grunted. "It's neither the first nor the last one. Are you hungry?"

"I'm sleepy," I admitted honestly.

"Okay, go to sleep then."

It was the strangest conversation I ever had with my Mom.

Chapter 23

The phone rang six hours later. Despite the promised day off, Director urgently called me out at work. I rushed over, for the first time having gone all the way alone. I have only managed to grab a thermos with the restorative drink from Izumi Sifu and a bag with my Mother's bagels, which she gave me at the last moment. I was preparing tea components yesterday, trying to distract myself from the thoughts about the upcoming concert. But they were poured with boiling water right in the process of feverish gatherings. At the entrance to the Director's office I met Dun, and he was just as worried as me.

"We've got information that polar explorers saw something strange at one of the poles in the eternal snow. According to the description, it looks like a frozen baby Clevr," Director brought us up to speed. "Dun, you're a water magician. Take Helga, she has a fire gift. Check it out. We were lucky and there's a polar day now, so it will make the work easier for the two of you. If it really is a baby Clevr, you should gently melt it out so as not to scald it with steam, and then deliver it to the Department. I'm giving you transport and a security guard who's also a fire magician."

"I can take another fire magician, but not a martial healer," Dun said, and I looked at him reproachfully. "Why should the Department risk two of us at the same time?"

"Your argument is clear, but pointless, Dun, don't be silly. I understand that you have well-founded fears especially given the last search for the wards, but the situation is completely different now. In addition, Helga needs to train and gain experience in our activities. And this search is also a part of the martial healer's work. Such messages periodically come from different parts of the planet and I don't need to tell you that a big percentage of them turn out to be true. And yes, if there really is a baby Clevr, then it will be necessary to clean up the polar explorers' memory."

"Are there any selfies in the net?" I asked.

"Not yet. They have strict instructions about such a situation there. According to the protocol they immediately called us. So, you must go until any selfies leak out indeed. I can give you only half an hour for gathering. And take an unscheduled transfer of supplies to polar explorers, it was just delivered to your plane. Get the necessary equipment at our warehouse. Helga, call your parents. The security guard is already waiting. If you need something, ask polar explorers, they will give you any tool or thing they have. Go! Go! Go!"

We ran out of the office, I dialed Mom on the way.

"Helga, what's going on?" I heard her alarmed voice on my phone.

"Don't worry, mom! We're just having a difficult labor case here. A very big baby is being born," I said and almost didn't lie. "I don't know how long it will take. I can spend this night in the hospital."

"Helga, I'm worried!" she was chattering.

"Mom! What can happen to me in the hospital? I'll turn the phone off."

"Is Dun somewhere nearby?"

"Yes, Mom. Okay, bye," I disconnected.

Was Dun somewhere nearby? Yes, he was! But he, apparently, decided to avoid me. Just look at him, he wanted to take another fire magician instead of me. Or maybe not a male fire magician, but a female? He got what he wanted and decided to cut me off now? Bastard!

I was angry while a warehouse employee handed me my outfits and clothes for a frosty winter. I got a weapon in addition to standard equipment for very cold weather.

"Why do you give me a gun?"

"I have to do this according to the protocol. Magic is not unlimited, and the situations can be totally different. Weapons are required. Are you a martial healer?"

"Yes, I am."

"So, you know how to use it. Who else is flying?"

"Dun and some security guard."

"In that case, probably, it wouldn't be necessary. But keep it ready."

"Do you have throwing knives?"

"Yes, they've ordered them specially for you, but it will be inconvenient to use such a weapon in winter clothes. Grab your jacket and a backpack, and then go to the plane. I think it would be better for you to put it on there to avoid sweating."

Yeah, shoes have already roasted my feet. I collected extra heat and slowly dissipated it in space so as not to create a pulsar and not to overheat at the same time. Dun was already waiting for me on the plane. He helped me with my things and gave me a way to a window.

"It's hot here," my companion complained.

"It will become cold soon," the security guard cheered up, sitting in front of us. "I'm Kurt, by the way."

"Yes, I remember. We flew to the range together," I nodded to him and turned to Dun. "I can help you with extra warmth."

Professor held out his hand, I laid my palm on top of his and stretched out the excess heat, releasing it into the plane's tail. I took off my hand and put a mask on my face, activating a protective cocoon.

Two minutes later, we all breathed a sigh of relief, freeing ourselves from a load of compressed air.

"When you'll get some extra heat next time, tell me about it and I'll help you again," I told Dun. Somehow my anger dissipated together with the excess warmth.

"How do you do this?" the security guard became interested.

"Don't you know the method? All fire magicians have been taught it at school."

"We were taught only about how to do pulsars that are about collecting and concentrating but not about dissipating."

"Give me your palm and track my magic flows."

Kurt was following my actions with interest and at the end kissed my hand as a sign of gratitude for the training. I looked at Dun, but he was sleeping, crouched in his armchair. I carefully leaned its back to make it more comfortable for Professor. Apparently, he fell asleep instantly, not even having time to get more comfortable. I wanted to touch his cheek and to run my fingers into his hair, but I didn't dare to do this in Kurt's attentive sight.

"Let him sleep. Today's night was difficult for me too. I was on guard at the Grenons, they were naughty. Our wards are anxious lately," Kurt said. "My wife told me on the phone to recover on this flight, while there is time for that. Do you want to sleep?"

"I had a bit of rest, I don't know if I can fall asleep right now. I'll read my book for a while, and then maybe I'll take a nap for the future either."

"In that case watch the situation. Wake me up if something goes wrong, I'll take control of the plane."

Six hours later, we landed at the continent's military airbase. From here to the pole we could travel only by a helicopter. Thirty minutes before landing our plane, I woke up my companions, and men put on their backpacks. Dun took care of mine. Our flight had lasted for about an hour. Professor was sleeping again. I understood that he didn't really wake up when we relocated from the plane to the helicopter. Apparently, after my departure at dawn, he didn't have an opportunity to go to bed immediately. Probably, he was reporting to the managers about the results of our joint investigation. While Dun was resting, Kurt and I were quietly whispering. Basically, the security guard spoke about strange cases in his Department working practice. And more about his children. He had two daughters, both very beautiful and talented. One girl was a fire magician, like her dad. She was going to work in the culinary industry. The second girl was a weather specialist. She wanted to work in tourism.

"You remind me of my youngest daughter," Kurt told me. "She's the same smart as you are, but a wallflower."

"Thanks! I was also a wallflower for a long time," I smiled timidly.

"And we also had a son," Kurt's eyes filled with pain, and his voice sank. "But he died during the labor. Magical fields of my wife and our baby boy went apart in some wrong way."

I covered his hand with mine and squeezed it with sympathy. I knew that such cases happened during childbirth, and no one could do anything here. I was not a mother yet, but I could imagine my companion's grief. We didn't continue the topic. In order to distract my interlocutor of this painful theme, I took out a thermos and my Mother's bagels from my backpack. We should have arrived soon, so I touched Professor's shoulder.

"Do you want some tea?" I asked him. "If so, then get a mug out of your backpack."

Dun perked up and quickly pulled it out.

"Will I finally get something you cooked from your hands?" it seemed to me that even his drowsiness instantly flew from him. Was he really that happy?

"It's only tea for today. These bagels were backed by my mom."

Professor readily held me out his mug. Of course, I didn't succeed in pouring the drink as smoothly and beautifully as Izumi Sifu did. But for some reason I was sure that she couldn't do this art either in a helicopter, flying over the northern ocean. Dun inhaled the steam coming from tea and looked at me in surprise.

"Is it really our restorative drink?"

"Not quite it. I added something by myself."

"Mom gave you a recipe?"

"She persecutes me every day in training," I complained to Professor. "And after that she solders me with this delicious tea. I added something new for the magic reserve, and it changed the taste a bit."

Dun took the first sip, then the second one. I held him out a bagel.

"It's unusual, but I like it very much," Dun praised. "Was it the magic cucumber that you added? I can feel a spicy bitterness in the taste."

"No," I shook my head. "It was something else. A magic cucumber cannot be boiled — it will become useless immediately. I'll tell you about a new ingredient later. And now you have to eat, a lot of time has passed from our takeoff, and you probably haven't really eaten anything since last night."

"It's really delicious, Helga!" Kurt praised, diverting our attention from last night. "And the bagels are good as well. Say my compliments to your mom."

"You have to eat too," Dun intervened. "We're almost at the destination."

At the pole we were met by one of the polar explorers, taking on receipt the cargo we'd delivered. He went to accompany us to the place where they saw something weird.

"It's over there," he waved his hand in the direction of one of the small peninsulas consisting of rocks and ice and protruding into the ocean. "There is a cave in the rocks, and the ice near it. Your object is in this ice. I must go back now. I hope you'll let me know about your finding later."

"Thanks!" said Kurt. "We will."

We went in the indicated direction and had walked for a long time. It was faster to fly, but it was hard to do with our backpacks, and we didn't want to spend our magic reserves. A cave in the rocks was found quite quickly although we spent some more time to make sure that it was single here. Then guys made a temporary camp in it. They created an ice wall from snow, melting it and freezing again. I saw how a fire magician and a water magician could work together, carefully looking at the coherence of their actions. The colleagues' wall was with a small gap through which we squeezed into the cave. The gap was covered with a special material. Kurt made a bonfire inside the room.

"You can go and work now," he nodded to us. "Helga, I'll replace you when you get tired. And I'll cook dinner while you two are melting ice."

Chapter 24

I have been sinking ice for several hours. Dun diligently diverted water into the ocean so that it didn't freeze again nearby, interfering with our work. We haven't talked, afraid to disturb concentration. The ice around us was greatly reduced, but nothing except small debris appeared on the surface.

"That's weird," Professor muttered under his breath periodically. After some time, I gave up.

"Let's ask Kurt to go after the polar explorer. Maybe we chose the wrong place for seeking?"

We stumbled to the cave, being out of strength, and found a completely empty room. There were nor traces of Kurt, nor our belongings, nor supplies in the cave. Is it worth saying that the fire wasn't burning too?

"Damn it!" Dun swore. "Wait here, please, I'll be right back. Just don't sit on the stones, they're cold."

"I'll warm them up."

"Be patient, I'll bring some pieces of wood now, so you can light a fire and then warm them up before you sit down."

Ten minutes later Dun brought some wooden garbage, which we drew from eternal ice half an hour ago.

"Can you light it up?" he asked me.

"It's necessary to rid them of excessive moisture first, otherwise they won't give enough warmth."

"Heat it up, and I'll take water out."

We managed to start a fire with the remnants of magic, and the situation ceased to seem so frightening. However, there was still nothing to eat, and all the events were too weird.

When it got warmer in the cave, Dun took field rations out of some pocket of his jacket.

"Where did you get it?" I was surprised.

"Before leaving the helicopter I stuffed my pockets with some things from my backpack. I always do that, it's easier to carry luggage in such a way. Kurt and I took part of your load, so I decided not to tell you about this. Here's your part," he handed me half of the meal. "Are you tired?"

"Awfully!" my legs and arms were shaking from weakness, and my head was spinning from hunger. I sank my teeth into my biscuit.

"You can rest and eat now. I'll go to the station for help."

"Don't leave me here alone!" I asked.

"And this girl is calling herself a martial magician," Dun joked.

"I'm a healer! No one asked me if I wanted to be a martial magician!" I was indignant and then pleadingly continued: "Dun, please, I'm afraid!"

"Helga, we must hurry, we may have problems here."

"Let's go together!"

"Don't go crazy. You barely keep on your feet, and the way to the base is long enough. Take off your weapon and have rest. I'll be back as soon as I can."

Professor left the cave, and I trudged after him, overcoming my weakness. And so I just managed to see a bright flash in the polar station. The explosion was so powerful that we were thrown onto the rocks. Dun covered me with his body. The view was completely absent for me. I could only hear rumbling and felt the shaking.

"Are you alive?" being in a panic I asked Professor when it was all over, and I jerked at the terrible thought that had crossed my mind.

"I am," Dun croaked. Hearing his voice, I almost burst into tears of relief. "But, it seems, my hand was badly hurt. I can't feel it. And there's unbearable pain in my leg."

I tried to get out from under him very carefully. Unfortunately, due to the voluminous winter clothes, I didn't manage to avoid pulling him. Professor was constantly hissing through his teeth in pain. Pieces of ice and blocks of stones were lying around us. Left hand of the guy was hurt by such an ice block, and his right leg was broken near the knee by a piece of rock.

"Wait, please, until I melt the ice and set you free. Then I'll do a state scan and try to fix your leg. Hold on and don't twitch."

I carefully melted the block that pressed Professor's hand and threw its remains to the side. The piece of rock, which broke Dun's limb, having done its dirty work, bounced to the cave, so I didn't have to spend time on it. Professor screamed and rolled over onto his back.

"Don't twitch!" I yelled.

"And you don't make noise. Get a first-aid kit from my jacket's pocket. There is a folding tire for such cases and a few syringes with a stimulant. You'll have to puncture one of them yourself, if you're going to splice my leg. In addition to the rations it should be enough to restore my strength a little."

"What a well-stocked man!" I admired and began to unpack the bag with a portable first-aid kit. "My things were missing with my backpack. Here are four syringes with a stimulant, I'll inject you one doze now."

"Don't do that. It's better to leave it for the time when we get out of here. Find a small flask with alcohol in my third pocket. Let me make a sip so I can withstand the pain of straightening my leg."

Can you believe this?! What else could he have in his jacket? I wouldn't be surprised if he got a helicopter out of the fourth pocket. I unscrewed a cork from the flask, drifted a sip myself for courage and put the alcohol into his healthy hand.

"Let me make you anesthesia---"

"Please, don't. First of all, scan me, then straighten my leg, and if there is still some magic left in your body, try to grow my bones together at least a little. I'm also out of magic charge, but I'll try to start accelerated regeneration as far as possible. But it's necessary to make at least some connections for this, even if they're weak. Don't waste your energy on anesthesia, please."

"Hold on! I'll try my best to make everything quickly," I promised and joked for the first time: "And gently."

Dun laughed, taking another sip. It was precisely the moment that, in my opinion, was perfectly suitable for me to straighten his leg. Laughter turned into a groan and then a wheeze. I splintered and collected his broken bones and damaged tissues with magic. I fixed tears and added pointing anesthesia. But I didn't have enough strength for more.

"Wow! It was you who saved my leg before, but this time it's my turn to collect yours."

"When was the last time I told you that you're beautiful?" Dun was thick of speech. Uh, I could see that — he was drunk.

"Well, tonight," I grunted, additionally securing the tire with an ordinary bandage. "Did the polar wind blow off your memory?"

"N-n-no, I ca-a-an remember," it seemed to me that the guy broke into a smile. He remembered the events of the night, apparently. "Bad for me! It's necessary to tell you this more often. But you're not just beautiful, you're---" Dun fell silent. I looked up at his face. He was sleeping. Wow! He got out quickly. Apparently, regenerative magic had such an effect.

"Are you kidding me?! How can I hold you into a cave? Well, at least it's not so far from here."

I was muttering under my breath and jerkily, trying not to drag his sore leg over the stones, was lugging the patient into the cave. After each jerk, I had to rest and master the strength. I'm not a weak woman, and training does its job, but after hard work it was very difficult for me to pull such a muscular body. The bonfire in the cave was still burning, and it was relatively warm there. I just had to move flame and coals aside, exposing the hot stones. Now I needed to unfold heat evenly across the floor that was enough for two people. I did that with my last sparks of magic and laid Dun onto this warm surface, putting my tired body near him. It was comfortable that the stones were warmed up here, because I had been worrying about Professor's back, which was located on the ice while I was setting his leg. At least our jackets were equipped with a magic heating system. So I hugged Dun and fell asleep instantly, although it wasn't a good idea. I should have guarded us with weapons, but the tired body simply knocked my consciousness out. And even stimulants didn't help it.

It's still not the end, but thank you so much for reading my book! After ending, can you, please, be so kind and leave a review on the book's page? It will be a great gift for me and other readers. Best wishes and happy-endings, Anna, the author.

Chapter 25

I woke up because of Dun's move. Professor got up and pushed me away. It turned out that in a dream my body unconsciously pressed against Professor in search of warmth, and his sudden movement pushed me to the side. My watch showed that no more than half an hour had passed. This fact was confirmed by the bonfire, which was still burning nearby. I saw a stranger behind a flame and flinched. Dun was aiming at him with a gun in his healthy hand.

"Please, calm down," raising both of his palms up, said the stranger. "I mean you no harm."

"Who are you?" Professor asked tensely. The gun in his hand was slightly shaking. Apparently, not all alcohol has worn off his blood.

"I'm one of the expedition members, an atomic specialist. We found a radioactive source here, and now my job is to study this place. I was far from the station when I saw your helicopter and the three of you. I decided not to interrupt my work for lunch, like my colleagues did, so I saw one of you returning with three backpacks. I suspected that something bad has happened, but I didn't have the time — the explosion was so hard that I got almost hurled into the ocean. There's nothing left at the station," he hunched over.

"What about your colleagues?" I asked, and Dun put his gun down.

"No one survived, Ms--- They all were inside having lunch. But I saw that your helicopter flew away prior to the explosion. And on the site of the station there were only some random pieces and blood left---"

The picture described by the nuclear scientist made me cringe. Dun closed his eyes for a moment.

"Helga, where are the stimulants? It's time for me to take one more dose."

"You can't do that with alcohol in your body," I tried to object.

"I'll remove the remnants of alcohol through the pores of my skin. You shouldn't have let me sleep."

"She did the right thing," the polar explorer intervened. "You could do nothing in your state for half an hour and I just came here while you were restoring. Moreover, I know where the station helicopter is.".

Dun perked up, and I was ready to cry with relief. Professor hardly took off his glove from his injured swollen hand and asked me to help him with the healthy one.

"My fingers don't bend," he said.

I took off his second glove, and Dun spread his open palms up. The air smelled distinctly of alcohol. Napkins from the first-aid kit allowed me to wipe off the remaining moisture from my companion's skin and, at the same time, to disinfect the injured hand. Dun still had little magic charge, so his regeneration was slow, but the wounds on his hand were no longer bleeding. It seemed to me that now was the right time to inject the stimulant to ensure accelerated healing.

"How do you feel? Can you walk?" Professor asked me.

"If there's no need to drag you, I can go."

"You won't have to help him, Ms.," the polar explorer intervened again. "I'll transport your husband through the air, if need be. And there's some food in the helicopter. It's not so far away from this cave."

"He's not my husband. But thank you for your help, I couldn't have done it in this condition."

"Oh, I'm sorry, miss."

"Don't you dare say something!" I exclaimed, seeing Dun open his mouth. "Gather your strength and let's go!"

"As you wish," Professor muttered offendedly.

I shouldn't have lost my temper, of course. It was much wiser to listen to what Dun would say to my remark. Perhaps in that case I would have found out something new. But I just didn't have the strength for that either. My emotional resources were empty. Physically speaking, I also barely kept on my feet, so it was better to leave the clarification of our relationship for better time.

The helicopter was located very close to the cave and we used it to get to the military air base. The dispatcher confirmed that our plane with a security guard on board flew back to the capital city about an hour ago. Dun showed his ID to the dispatcher, and we were taken to the leadership of the air base to report about what had happened at the station. After that Professor asked a transport to the Department. I was silent, only blinking in surprise when we were given an ultrafast military aircraft. Using it, we definitely had a chance to reach the Department before or simultaneously with Kurt.

My conscientiousness began to torment me when we were in the helicopter. How could I lose my temper at all? Why did I have to make this remark about a husband? This clearly offended Dun. I needed to apologize.

"That's the trouble with this fracture!" Professor muttered under his breath after our takeoff. "Even with accelerated regeneration and your treatment, it will take about fifteen hours and a lot of food to recover."

"That's not a big deal, we'll come back and put you right into the regeneration box. You'll be okay in twenty minutes," I tried to persuade him like as if he was a little boy.

"Helga, who'll give me those twenty minutes?! This security guard left us after blowing up a polar station with thirteen people! We can't even warn the management because our cellphones are at the Department and their radio station is quiet. I think Kurt has damaged it before the flight!"

"Dun, forgive me, please, for this flash," I finally decided to speak with him about that, trying to turn his thoughts off the bad events. Professor looked at me. His eyes were cold. He was definitely offended.

"You've told the truth. I'm not your husband, you've refused to marry me," He turned away. I had to do something about it and quickly.

I got under my companion's sore arm, gently hugged him, kissing on his cheek.

"I'm so, so sorry! It was just a terrible day. I don't know what came over me," I whispered in his ear.

Dun hugged me and kissed me back. His gaze got warm, and he resolutely said:

"Baby, you have to rest now and restore every grain of strength. And, please, don't try to catch Kurt on your own."

Unfortunately, I couldn't promise this to him.

We were sleeping during the flight back to the Department. I woke up half an hour before arrival and began to think.

I couldn't let Dun go out of the plane for battle. His leg was badly injured, there were a lot of tiny bone fragments. It was impossible to fix them in such a good way that the patient would be able to move as if his legs were healthy. In addition, the situation with Professor's hand wasn't clear yet. It was pretty swollen and didn't bend. Dun said that he had scanned his condition, and the hand just got a great hit, and because of this there was such an edema. In any case, the best thing was to put the guy into a regenerative box, so that magic, in cooperation with science, could do their job, delivering the necessary trace elements to the sore spot and healing the injured areas. But this stubborn man will never let me deal with the bomber alone. Therefore, it was necessary to leave Professor in a drowsy state in order to hand him over to doctors immediately after landing.

I quietly got out of the chair, so as not to wake Dun up, and went into the cabin, where the flight was controlled by a military pilot sent with us by the leadership of the air base. I tried not to think about what kind of thrashing Professor would suit me for what I was going to do now.

"I need a first-aid kit. Can you please tell me where it is?"

"Does the guy feel worse?" the military man was worried. "Here it is."

"No, no, not so bad. It's just necessary to add a little more bandage on his broken leg," I took out a bag with a standard first-aid kit and went back to the salon. There I quietly opened the lock and breathed a sigh of relief, finding a syringe with short-acting anesthesia in the bag. Twenty minutes would be quite enough for Dun to wake up in a regenerative box, instead of trying to be a hero with his broken bones. It was safer, of course, to lull him with my magic, but he could feel such an impact before everything was finished, and I was afraid that he would wake up. I decided not to risk it.

Before landing, I carefully rolled back the sleeve of Professor's sweater. It was good that the plane was warm inside, and we took off our winter polar jackets. Dun moaned in his sleep, but I stroked his hair and he fell silent again. Being very accurate, I made a point magic painkiller at the site of the future injection, so as not to disturb the patient with manipulation, and injected anesthesia. Then I monitored Professor's condition, took off his shoes, and then locked him in a protective cocoon.

The plane landed right in the hangar of our own base, and doctors were already running towards us. I handed Dun into the hands of a healer from the regeneration laboratory, briefly explaining what happened, what was done and what else needs to be done. He promised to put the patient in recovery immediately. The plane took the direction of the military air base. Now it was necessary to find out urgently what was happening in the Department, where was Kurt, and what did all this mean. I had no good thoughts about the entire situation.

Lina hurried to me. We flew back just in the midst of a night shift.

"Elle, you're alive! Thank God! What about Dun?"

"His leg was broken, and his hand was badly bruised. I hope that he's already in a regeneration box, or at least on the way to it. What do you have here?"

"The security guard came five minutes ago. Alone. He was gibberishing about someone who had attacked you, blowing up the station at the pole. He also told us about your disappearance, saying that he survived by miracle and barely managed to drop into the plane, literally at the last moment. Our specialists are frantically gathering an expedition to find your bodies. Elle, what happened there?"

"Lina, I'll tell you about it later. Where's this guard?"

"I guess, they all went to the conference room."

"Okay, now you have to run to our guards and take them there. Say to them that it was Kurt who blew up the station and left us there to freeze. If we're not in the conference room, then they should find us, come hell or high water."

"Elle, are you going there alone?"

"Lina, run to the guards! I'm a martial healer equipped with a fire and a gun. I can handle it! Just pour some of your magic into me, please, because I got a half empty reserve."

The girl helped me with my charge and rushed towards the security service. I hurried to the conference room located next to the Lonquies' sector, from where the growing alarm seemed to come. As I expected, Kurt was not in the conference room, there was only unconscious Ron, who had a big hematoma on his head. The door to the dragon-mentalists' territory was ajar.

I tiptoed to it and peered through a narrow gap. Kurt didn't look in my direction, he was busy tying to a chair an elderly martial healer, who was now working with the Lonquies. The bomber has a mental-protective helmet on his head. The wards were fluttering on their small wings behind the glass and tried not to "make noise" so as not to disturb me. On the floor, near the cabinet with helmets, Dun's mother was lying. I quickly scanned her from a distance and realized that she was alive, but unconscious like Ron. Her condition wasn't very critical, despite her position. How did they all manage to miss the attack?

I tried to squeeze as quietly as possible into the door slot and to cover it behind me so as not to attract the bomber's attention. When I turned around, Kurt was aiming at me with a gun.

"Stay there, Helga! This isn't a pulsar, you'll not catch it. A bullet's a bullet — magic has almost no effect on it. Even a shield won't protect you completely."

I froze. The security guard walked behind me, still holding me in sight, and locked the door from the inside.

"Kurt, what are you doing?"

"I'm saving humanity from these little vampires!"

"Are you crazy?"

"Don't come closer, Helga! These things need to be destroyed! My son died because of them! Because of them, and this idiot who was transmitting abilities to children that year!"

"Kurt, this didn't happen that way," I tried to speak as gently as I could. "The transfer technology is absolutely safe.

I'm telling you as a doctor. The infusion of magic into the general flow of a baby can only give it additional strength during the process of labor, just like nourishment. It's impossible to kill a child this way."

"Shut up!" the security guard yelled hysterically. "Mental magic cannot be safe! I saw what these things did to that reporter! My boy's magic field simply didn't accept such type of energy, and he died. And now everyone involved in his death will die, including him."

Kurt pointed to the tied martial healer. It was interesting to me, was it really he who transferred new knowledge to newborns that year or the bomber, like every crazy person, simply decided to execute the first one?

"My wife told me that I'm mad," Kurt continued, meanwhile. "Oh, sure! She has daughters, and that's enough for her. You, women, like when you grow in numbers. And I need a son!"

Behind the crazy guard's back, the Lonquies were silently crying for the deceased baby, sharing grief of its father. They were crying for the mind that had left the man. For these magical creatures the mind is the most important thing. They are so wonderful! How could one go ahead and call them "things" or "vampires"? The Lonquies are much better and more spiritual than people! However, if the bomber thinks that his wife was not bothered with the death of her own child, then hardly anything can be done here.

"Kurt, take off your helmet, please. The Lonquies are crying for your son. They say the baby will be come back as your grandson. You'll be able to raise him as a real man. Look at your hostage, he also can feel it."

A tear actually flew down the face of an elderly healer. I knew that he had an adult son and a little granddaughter.

"They can say anything for the sake of their lives," the security guard laughed. "And this one is just scared for his destiny. No, Helga, the helmet is my defense."

Well, my opponent was crazy, but not a fool.

"Kurt, let the man go, and we'll talk," I made another try. What a pity, that I didn't have the negotiating skills and my life experience was a little taut. Maybe at least I would be able to distract him and win some time until somebody breaks the lock? "Why did you kill Anthony? That was you who killed him, right?"

"I tried to take his place and get closer to these things. I needed time to get all the necessary components for the new bomb and then destroy them calmly. However, this bitch Julie decided that I'm a bad guard for them. I only exposed myself in vain."

And there was no guilt in him about the life taken, no doubt, nothing but anger and hatred.

"I had to arrange an additional re-enactment of the attack on the guard, in order to avert suspicions from myself," Kurt said meanwhile. "It was unpleasant, of course, to stick a dart into my own shoulder, but they immediately stopped giving me sidelong glances."

"And what was that with the pole?"

"You think I haven't seen your abilities?" the man frowned. "We had blown my first bomb on a range together. It's a pity, I didn't take into account that these vampires can manipulate the minds of the botanical garden's visitors. Everything had been so well-calculated! I chose the time when there were no people in their sector, I put my bomb at a break from patrolling the territory. But they dragged a stupid onlooker and forced him to inform the guards of the botanical garden. I just didn't have time to blow it up. But this one will be explored for sure."

"Was it you who poisoned a Clevr?"

"Yeap. Who else? And the publisher was informed by me. I hoped that it would be possible to publicize the activities of the Department, and that it would simply be demolished by angry parents. It had to help me distract attention from myself in order to construct a new bomb. Everything went pretty well when these huge pigs trampled a boy. I thought that rotten activities of the Department would certainly be revealed after that."

"Kurt, can you hear yourself at all? The child died, and you're rejoicing that?"

But the crazy security guard didn't hear me. He continued to mutter, becoming looking like a madman more and more:

"But this idiot reporter didn't even think of switching his camera to silent mode. I poisoned a Clevr for him, so that there was more time for taking pictures. And he screwed everything up. It's always necessary to do everything by yourself! So I'll blow this beauty now."

"Kurt, wait!" I screamed. "You never answered my question about the pole."

"I saw that you can catch fire and extinguish it. This time I wanted to neutralize all the factors. I was thinking about how to lure you out of the Department. And then the Higher Powers helped me — a baby Grenon was found. You rushed off right away. I thought it was a great option to solve the problem. I talked to my classmate who used to work at the polar station and owed me, and then got you out of the Department at the right time. But why are you here now? Ah, it doesn't matter! I made a new bomb, much more powerful than the first one. So that there will be no even a scrap of these small bastards."

"Did you kill your friend too? Did you blow him up with the others at the pole?"

"No. I just threw him out of the plane with a parachute. I even saw when the parachute opened."

"Why didn't you just shoot us, Kurt?" I asked.

"You have too much in common with my youngest daughter. I have told you that. I didn't want to kill you, only to keep you away from the Department until I destroy these things. Get out of here, Helga!"

"No, Kurt!"

"Then you'll die with us."

There was a click, and time seemed to stop. Very slowly a flower of fire began to unfold on the site of Kurt's body. I was surprised to understand that everything around me got severely slowed down and that I was in time. I managed to release my fire and catch the explosion in its trap. I guess, all of my abilities have sharpened in those extreme conditions, and I finally mastered the science of Grenons' time controlling. But the bomb was too powerful. My magical potential was not enough to keep the explosion in the cocoon of my fire gift. But I realized that I just couldn't give up. I'd rather perish from exhaustion than the wonderful, wise and surprisingly kind Lonquies would disappear forever. I thought about Dun, and it seemed to give me extra strength. I heard when the lock on the sector's door clicked. Apparently, security guards, finally, broke it up. I managed to encapsulate the fire in a temporary trap, and it got dark. The last thought in my fading mind was: "And I never told Professor that---"

Chapter 26

I was sitting in a meadow full of terribly bright light. Why do all of us say that there's a river and fog when you die? It's nothing like that! There's a meadow. It's unbearably green, sparkling and full of life. Thick May grass alternates with wildflowers of incredible beauty. Magical plants grow mixed with ordinary ones, creating a delightful pattern. The insects that I hated are crawling across the grass, butterflies and dragonflies flock around me, and this is not scary, but rather very joyful. A striped spider ran down my leg and for the first time in my life I didn't feel a desire to kill it with a knife. And that's all because the meadow was full of Love, and this Love was in every blade of grass, in every little fly. How can you be afraid of such a miracle? The energy was so palpable that I felt I could almost touch it with my fingers. This was a very interesting sensation for a healer. I thought that this must have been the place where all my colleagues drew their magic gifts from.

But something bothered me, not allowing to enjoy the fullness of magic and happiness. I looked around and saw a red thread that was coming from my chest. One edge of it started in the place where my heart was, and another one was lost somewhere in the grass. And if everything around was filled with Love, then this thread embodied a pure deadly Yearning.

"He's persistent!" an admiring voice came from somewhere. "Just look how persistent he is! And he hasn't even closed his eyes for all these days. Should we give in, or what?"

I turned my head and saw a girl of about five years old with huge scissors in her hands. Smooth ebony skin contrasted sharply with golden hair and green eyes. A simple silk chrisom fitted her well. Bare feet stepped on the grass without touching it. The girl approached me slowly.

"Who are you?' I asked.

"Oh, these martial magicians! They always need to know everything!" she waved scissors with irritation in a dangerous proximity from me.

"I'm a healer!" I stumbled back to avoid myself and the red thread from being caught by this huge tool. I wouldn't let her cut anything until I figure out what's going on.

"Oh, yeah. You can fool your friends, but not me," the girl cheered up. "Who's holding you there?"

"I don't know," I said, thinking. "I can't remember. Who can hold me? And what is this place?"

"Listen," the girl said in a confidential tone. "We don't usually let people return. Since you came to us, the next step is only reincarnation. The clones that you're trying to develop are a piece of cake compared to what we do. You can use cloning for organ transplantation, but don't meddle in our sphere. If we don't give permission, there will be no resurrections. And we usually don't allow it, because life must be protected as it's the greatest Gift. If we allow you to clone people, you'll begin to kill them lightheartedly."

I was confused, and the girl continued.

"But in your case three factors came together. First, we need someone to send our instructions regarding the clones to the people down there. Second, the Lonquies were pleading for you. They never plead for anyone, so apparently, we have an extraordinary case here. You're the savior, who rescued the whole population from death. And third, He (the girl pointed a finger up into the sunlit sky) loves when there is Love involved, is that clear?"

I shook my head. I understood nothing. Who is He and what does love have to do with it? For some reason, at that moment someone's words resurfaced in memory: 'There's no inopportune time for love'. Who said that? When? Where? The girl got angry at the sight of my negative gesture.

"What else can be unclear here?! Do you want to come back? Is there anyone waiting for you? Can you promise us to send our words about the resurrection to your colleagues?"

The girl held out her hand and an hourglass appeared in it. Time was passing, I focused on myself.

It was so good here! Love was surrounding me. This feeling on earth had no equivalents to be compared to. As if all the positive emotions have come together at once, and I was swimming in them. I didn't want to go back. There was no room for fears and worries in this meadow...

The girl lifted the scissors, getting ready to cut the thread, and then I felt as though I plunged into an ice hole.

"Dun!" I exclaimed, and the girl, in the literal sense of the word, kicked me! I swear, she kicked me! And I flew out of a meadow into my own body like a bullet.

***

I opened my eyes and understood that I was lying in a cloning box. I tried to raise my hand to my face and realized that it was very hard for me to do it.

"Don't rush," Paul's voice came from speakers. "It's not your body, but your soul that needs to get used to it."

"Don't scare her, necromancer!" hissed Lina next to the guy. She didn't even hesitate to call her fiancé that word, this is how angry she was at him. "Don't listen to this fool, Elle. It's your body. It's cloned, but it's yours."

"Lina, kick him for me," I said, barely moving my tongue. "I'll hit him later too."

"Speech functions are normal! Hearing is normal! The memory is in its place," came Paul's joyful voice. "Helga, you can even bite me now. You're alive!"

"How long should I be here for?" I asked. "I'm hungry! And where's Dun?"

"Dun, she is thinking about you," Paul laughed. "But thoughts about food came first. Gastrointestinal function is in order."

"I'm here," Professor rustled in the speakers. I hardly recognized his voice. What happened to him?

"Paul, let me out!" I was seriously alarmed. To hell with my pride and independence. What's the matter with my beloved Professor?

"Calm down, Helga! You must lie here until all your functions are connected. Just concentrate on moving your limbs slowly. And there's one more thing--- Do you feel your magic?"

"I do! Paul, I'll not just bite you, I'll torture you for a long time, if you don't tell me how long I should lie here for!"

"It depends on you, but I think that it's about half an hour. Your recovery speed is really stunning! And be careful with your arms and legs here. The supply tubes aren't disconnected from your veins yet. Master your new body, and we'll cook some broth for you."

I needed Dun, not broth! But I had to endure and to work on my body. Fingers were the first, then toes, then wrists, feet, elbows, knees. I scratched my nose, turned on my sides, hiccupped, tilted my head back, licked my lips, made alternately all the sounds that I knew and waited for the IV feeding tubes to be turned off. And all this happened alongside with Paul's comments about my functions being in order. My body responded quite easily and quickly. But I didn't doubt it, considering everything that happened in the meadow. The lid opened twenty-five minutes later. Lina was the first person that I saw, and she instantly threw a white coat over me. Unharmed Dun was standing nearby. He was very thin, unshaven, with bruises under his eyes and with hair as if sprinkled with salt.

"What happened?" I asked in horror.

"What happened? What happened?! You were dead! You died, that's what happened! You gave away all of your magic, and it pulled out your internal organs with it. I saw the remains of you! I almost got crazy because of this sight! And the damn plasma is still soaring over there!"

Hmm, I can imagine. But we saw more terrible things here.

"You've turned gray. Why?"

"Because I love you, you shameless woman! How could you leave me here alone? At some desperate moment, I thought that if the thread breaks, I would lie down next to your box, fall asleep and never wake up!" he hunched over. It seemed that his last exclamation had taken all his strength. It was possibly true, because I didn't know how much time had passed, and what he was doing here while I was in that meadow.

I sat in the box very slowly, turned to Professor carefully and put my feet on the floor. I just couldn't do it faster in my condition.

"Do you know why did you manage to resurrect me?" I asked Dun, looking up at him.

"No. Why?" he said tiredly and even somehow indifferently, staring at the floor.

"Because I love you too, Professor!" I said, hugging him. "I've been loving you for many years. I love you so much that even the Gods took pity on us and decided to let me come back to you."

We were kissing again as if we were on the hospital roof that night in April. Paul was joyfully jumping around us, tugging the equally joyful Lina at her skirt. The laboratory was small, but someone was constantly looking into the little windows of the door, outside there was a noise and people's exclamations. I suspect that the entire Department had come to look at us. And I was the first to break the kiss again, whispering in Professor's half-opened lips:

"Sleep!" and then to Paul: "Help me, I can't hold him for long!"

The guy grabbed Dun's limp body, carefully put him in the box to my place.

"That's good!" said Reincarnologist. "He hadn't slept for almost a week while we were working on you. He was holding on our magical recharge and stimulants and didn't eat to avoid falling asleep. Dun was afraid that the connection with your soul would break, and you would die completely if he closed his eyes. I'll call Alex now, he'll transfer your boyfriend to a regeneration box for restoration. But how did you manage to get him asleep so quickly?"

"All questions later! I can eat a horse!"

Chapter 27

I sat back in my chair with my stomach full and listened favorably to the Lina's incessant talk.

"Director unlocked the door with his key the moment you caught an explosion and fell down. There were only your limbs and head on the floor. It was a terrible sight. Dun almost fainted when he saw your remains after we had released him from the regeneration box. Paul diverted his attention, telling him to hold the thread."

"Oh, yeah!" interrupted Reincarnologist. "I realized that if I didn't distract my friend, we'd have had to clone both of you here. And who would keep his thread?"

"And that bomb's plasma is still hanging in the air near the Lonquies' glass. A temporary cocoon has encapsulated it in stasis," continued Lina. "The dragons had been urgently evacuated and the management still thinks about what to do with this huge power now. God forbid to accidentally touch it and destroy the temporary cocoon."

"It's just necessary to call the Grenons and ask them to levitate it somewhere into a safe place," I shrugged. "How could Julie overlook Kurt?"

"She says that he had been singly when he came to work here," answered Paul. "There could be no suspicion of his disloyalty. He loved to spend time with the Grenons and even proposed some ideas a couple of times based on simple observations. Kurt's son died only two years ago. Apparently, it was the same moment you came to work at the maternity hospital, and Dun was the healer who used to give new skills to babies."

So, I was right in my assumptions. The elderly martial healer was just a scapegoat for Kurt. On the other hand, it turns out that we were incredibly lucky that he hadn't recognized Dun, otherwise he would have probably killed him during the flight to the pole. Reincarnologist, meanwhile, continued to recount:

"It was a late child, a long-awaited boy for Kurt and his wife. All these changes in the security guard began after the death of this baby. But you always pay attention to your closest circle in the last place, and Kurt rarely went far from the guard post as his shifts were mainly at the entrance. And he didn't come close to the Lonquies who caused such violent bouts of hatred in him. Even for round-the-clock duties at the wards he was accidentally sent to the Grenons. When you've given away all your magic, Julie had a heart attack. She was the second whom Lina called after you've opened your eyes and remembered us."

"And who was the first?" I looked at my friend.

"Your brother," he said.

My blood ran cold.

"Parents---"

"Paul sent a couple of our doctors to them immediately. Your father suffered from a stroke, but your mother, bless her, got a grip and gave him first aid. Our guys have put them to sleep and placed them into regeneration boxes until the situation is be clarified. We eliminated all the consequences of your dad's stroke and managed to cure your mom. Your brother was trying to come here today, but I said that all three of you will be home tomorrow and asked him to be patient."

I exhaled and felt my hands shaking.

"Paul, how could you know that it's Dun who should be asked to hold my thread? Why not my parents?"

"I could see it in him. It's in the looks and the absence of them, in facial expressions. Of course, both of you are tough nuts to crack, but we have three aura specialists in the Department, not counting two reincarnologists," Paul patiently explained to me. "We don't meddle in the business that is not our own, because ethics doesn't allow that. But we can see love right away. The aura doesn't show the object of love, of course. When Lina suddenly lit up, I was restless for three days. I thought she'd met someone on the side while working the day shifts. But when two people with such bright auras appear in the same building, when they look at each other like you and Dun, everything is clear. Now, as I understand, I have the right to hand your Professor over to you. You thought that it was you who were swept by the emotional wave in the gym the other night, but Dun was overcome by a tsunami of feelings every time he looked at you. It's so good that you rarely crossed paths at work, otherwise I would probably be blinded by your emotions."

'Don't shine around here, Dun!' said Julie on my very first night in the Department. Why didn't I pay attention to it? Listening to Paul, I recalled all my doubts, all the harshness and shortcomings that I caused because of my own nervousness. Dun said to me immediately: 'I was exhausted!'. He cared for me, and he rejoiced at any sign of attention from my part, and his kisses were so sweet. But instead of believing him, I had a fair share of suspicions. I was remembering all my stupid actions, including the morning escape from his apartment. What a blessing that I had common sense not to run away quietly! And that I had strength to apologize on the plane. I put myself in Professor's shoes and was horrified. If I was bogging down in doubts about his feelings, how was it for him? I felt embarrassed and sad.

"All this time I couldn't help but wonder what if this was for the sake of my loyalty?" I confessed gloomily to Reincarnologist.

Lina giggled, poking the guy with her elbow in the side.

"It turns out that I'm not the only blind one here, Paul!" it was a weird feeling, but these words of my girlfriend immediately defused the situation and improved my mood.

"God, what crazy things I've done! Poor Professor!" I repented aloud.

"I said to him immediately: 'Hold on to her! You'll definitely pull Helga out! I can see it clearly'. I had to hint at it, otherwise Dun wouldn't have managed to keep your thread. And he calmed down right away. It became evident that all of his doubts had left his aura. And he pulled you out, he really did," Reincarnologist told me while pulling Lina to himself, but I objected:

"But he didn't pull out Sophie."

"Sophie didn't love him," Paul grunted. "Was it Lina who told you about her and Dun? You shouldn't have listened to her, because she wasn't there when this whole story unfolded."

"And have you been there?" pouted the girl.

"Yeap! 'Dun's ha-a-andsome'," Reincarnologist mimicked his fiancée, and I realized that Lina's opinion of Professor was known to the whole Department. "He became so attractive to the opposite sex after the tragedy with Sophie. You, girls, love the sufferers! When I came here, he was still quite a rockie. Dun is three years older than me. And his appearance is quite ordinary. Maybe he's a bit more attractive, how do I know? I'm not familiar with these things. I remember exactly that the beauties weren't so crazy about him. Especially Sophie. He loved her, but she didn't love him back. This girl had simply allowed Dun to go after her and that's all. I can even remember when she had told her girlfriends that he was mediocre in bed."

To say that I was surprised would be an understatement. Lina became interested:

"So, have you found out whether it is true? When?"

"After the concert," I mumbled, blushing.

"So I didn't recommend that dress for nothing! And...?"

I blushed even more.

"And we can see that he's not mediocre," Lina giggled.

"Don't be envious," Reincarnologist told her and continued. "And everyone went crazy when he returned half a year later. 'Dun's so cute, Dun's so hot'. Ugh!"

"Don't be envious," Lina cheered up again, reiterating a mocking joke to her fiancé. "So, Elle, we put your remains on a medical table and started to make a craniotomy---"

"Why?" I made my eyes big.

"In order to preserve your personality and memory, why else? One Lonquie had told this to Paul the day before this explosion. Apparently, he had foreseen the situation. And Paul also thought about it immediately, taking into account that incident with brain of the cloned boy. Dun was sitting on the floor under the operating table and was told to concentrate on your soul thread. I don't know what he was thinking about at that moment, but it's good that he didn't look while we were working. Such visions wouldn't be good for a man in love, you know? In general, your brain was connected to life support systems, and the rest of your body was built up around it. We were shaking each time it was necessary to make the next system of organs autonomous. But everything went well: your new heart started beating, your lungs were breathing---"

"Dun's mother was very worried for you," said Paul.

"How is she?"

"She was recovering in a regeneration box. It was evident that her heart was breaking for you two, but she escaped and went home. I've already called her too," said Lina.

"And then we dragged you back," Paul entered the conversation again, "and you weren't coming. Dun was completely exhausted, holding on merely because of his stubbornness. I looked at him and saw his eyes had already begun to roll back, and then bam! — you were there. And your soul got in so smoothly, my heart was relieved!"

"But Dun did faint," Lina said to me. "He was off for about five seconds, I didn't even have time to react. And then he woke up, and Paul said to him immediately: "She's here!" and your boyfriend fainted for another five minutes. I didn't touch him, just checked him from distance and let him rest. When he woke up again, you've just opened your eyes."

I cringed. I wouldn't wish this on anyone. My poor Professor! Can you believe this? Despite everything, he didn't accept a drop of doubt even for a second. One slight hint of a friend was enough for him. It was right to call him persistent. Now I had to go sit next to him and stroke his hair, so that he could see me as soon as he opened his eyes.

"Guys, help me get back to the lab, please," I asked friends, because my brain was working, but I had to train muscles of my new body to regain my fitness. "I made this month really hard for Dun because of my stupid doubts. So, I need to make it up to him as soon as possible."

"Wait! Where are you going?" Paul was indignant. "Dun will wake up no sooner than in three hours, you still have time to mend the situation. And your confession was enough for him, I saw it. You promised to answer our questions! How did you manage to get him asleep so quickly? This is a complicated process, and he was simply in euphoria."

"Guys, I was in such a wonderful place! Everything there was filled with the purest energy of Love. You seemed to be constantly in the arms of caring parents, with no worries, fears, or pains. I can now draw this energy from there and heal almost all diseases. And Dun was completely exhausted so he needed only a tiny jolt to get asleep," and I told my friends about everything that had happened in the meadow.

"And you came back here from this amazing place?!" Lina exclaimed in surprise.

"Love feels even stronger here."

In the hallway of the laboratory department, Paul told Lina:

"Go back to the dining room for now, I need to talk to Helga in private."

Lina turned around, and Reincarnologist opened a door to an empty laboratory. Until this moment, the guys have supported me from two sides, helping me move slowly but surely towards the desired sector. Colleagues came across to greet me, being delighted by my lively appearance. I was attempting to smile, and it turned out better with every time. When Lina left, Reincarnologist brought me to a chair, sat me on it and suddenly fell on his knees in front of me.

"Paul, what are you doing?"

"Helga, I'm sorry! I could only get you out. She's gone."

"Who?" I was seriously scared. Who else could die if everything was fine with my parents?

"Her thread broke down immediately, she left first and in an instance, I managed to only see the trace of her departing soul. But this is understandable, she simply had nowhere to return too."

"Paul, you're scaring me! Who are you talking about?"

"I'm talking about your daughter," said Reincarnologist with terror.

"It can't be true," I said in surprise. "People don't have unwanted pregnancies nowadays."

"Maybe you both wanted this," the guy groaned. It seemed that his guilt and self-flagellation were so palpable they could be touched.

Events of that very evening flashed in front of my eyes — tango, lullaby. . . Dun was already at that age when a man starts to want to have a family and children. . . And Paul was chattering at that time:

"We had your brain, your DNA, a cast of your aura and a unique pattern of your magic field. But there was nothing to recreate a baby from. She was still a small drop at the time of your death. I could do nothing."

I put my hands to my face.

"Does Dun know?"

"No. I haven't told him. These days were too difficult for him. Helga, I'm so sorry!"

"For what? It's not your fault at all. Your strength and knowledge are not unlimited," Kurt managed to take revenge for his son by killing my baby.

"Helga, don't cry, please! She will be back. I can see it. And the Lonquies have also confirmed it. You're alive and fine, Dun will be okay in a couple of weeks. And when you are ready, she'll definitely come back."

Epilogue

Paul and Lina got married six days after we gave them tickets for the concert of those pianists. My girlfriend rolled her eyes up and said that she had agreed to marry Reincarnologist while still being in the concert hall. She mentioned bachata instead of tango, but the result was the same. At the wedding, Victor presented Lina with a huge toy tiger, which has incredibly amused me and Professor, and also embarrassed the groom.

Dun and I didn't rush to register our relationship. After those events we both didn't need any confirmation of our feelings to each other. I have just moved to his apartment, and we were enjoying every minute spent together. I could never breathe in enough of the summer wind, look at the stars sky, rejoice with my friends. My death and miraculous resurrection made the recovery of my physical fitness last for a long time, that is why I was training with Inga during my working hours. For the rest of the shift, I either swam with the Grenons, which also helped to restore my strength, or sat behind the glass at the Lonquies' sector, making jokes about the ebony girl with the scissors. The little dragons turned out to be masters of having fun, which I also didn't expect from them. My attempts to improve my martial skills with Dun had failed. Professor was laughing all the time, seeing a highly focused look on my face. I was immediately offended, and the training usually ended there. Once I still managed to catch Dun precisely during such moment of fun and hit him. But after that, this kind of luck never happened again. Then I decided to ask my boyfriend's mother to mentor me, and that has finally started the process.

The Lonquies, by the way, lost their excess mental power over me. After visiting a wonderful meadow, I could fuel my gift from there and form a partial mental shield at any time. In just a couple of days, I learned to make a defense that allowed blocking emotions while leaving the possibility of mental communication. The little dragons could still scare me or inspire some kind of hallucination, but they weren't going to do this to their friends. And the danger that forced us to constantly wear shield helmets was gone. The first person I taught that new skill was Paul. After him, the rest of the martial healers also mastered this new technique. Now helmets were needed exclusively by outsiders. Working with the Lonquies became really easy. This way, I was not only increasing my muscle mass, but also bringing value to the Department. But I didn't manage to repeat the trick with the encapsulation of fire with time. Security guards tried their best to make me do this, they even drove me to a range a couple of times, until Dun became utterly indignant. I couldn't encapsulate fire with time anymore. Apparently, the affective state played a decisive role the other night.

Reincarnologist was sent to transfer new knowledge to the children. He flew back to his country and Lina followed him. Director calmly let the girl go on an indefinite (albeit unpaid) leave, joking that he was waiting for the guys back with a new addition to their family. Lina was embarrassed. I knew that the "addition" was already on the way. That is why Paul was present at his baby's birth and transferred new skills to his first-born. It was easier for his wife to cope with the chores of motherhood under the supervision of her husband's parents. I was missing the guys terribly, but I understood that this separation was necessary and that it wouldn't last forever.

The directory of cloning and resurrecting people was officially closed after my report, which looked more like crazy nonsense. Paul was standing nearby at that moment and nodded in confirmation of confirmation of my words. Director listened carefully to me and decided to do what the ebony girl had ordered.

"If you're right, then we'll only keep wasting our resources by conducting work in this direction," he was a rational and prudent manager. "This direction's very promising for us, but it's really controversial according to ethical standards, so we didn't report it before obtaining any reasonable positive results. So, I guess we can suspend it altogether."

And the journalist, by the way, wasn't injured that day. I don't know what Kurt's sore imagination has conjured, but the Lonquies simply made the reporter believe that he was talking to his seniors, and the guy immediately gave in. He said: 'Why are you asking me? You sent me there'. Our employees quickly drew appropriate conclusions from this. They said that the mentalists had not only carefully obliterated the journalist's memory, but also gave him some kind of a gift. Now the reporter is having a dazzling career as a very highly paid photographer with a special perspective on the world.

Dun and I got married two and a half years after my rebirth. Our friends came back, and we planned everything without any rush, discussing the details with relish. On the eve of our wedding, I decided to finally tell Dun about our daughter. Surprisingly, his reaction was calm. He only said: 'We'll call her'.

Mentalist pianists were invited to perform their Lullaby at our wedding. Mom was crying, Dad was hugging her. My brother's wife sobbed nearby, pulling my nephew's head to her chest. Izumi Sifu didn't want to cuddle with her husband, gazing at me instead. Only Lina had no time for the Lullaby-induced worries. She was constantly running after her son, catching him in the bushes, then under the table, then in my lap. However, I was sure that she had her own emotions to deal with — our friends were expecting a baby girl.

And our daughter came as soon as we called her.

August 2019

Thank you so much for reading my book! Can you, please, be so kind and leave a review on the book's page? It will be a great gift for me and other readers. Best wishes, Anna, the author.

You can find the book's page, scanning this QR-code:

I'm working on the second book of the 'Dance' series. It will tell you the story about Helga's son Eric. Please, follow my Amason or Facebook page to know more about it.

All the money, earned on this book will help me to control my 1 type diabetes and tell you new interesting stories because...

Once I went blind . . . And then I wrote my first novel . . .

My name is Anna. All my life, I have loved to read. Books saved me from disappointment and loneliness, from fatigue and pain, from tears and self-doubt. Books inspired me to perform my own feats, helped me to relax, and educated me on a par with my parents and teachers. There were no problems with interesting literature when I was a child - my mother used to find more and more new stories for me at bookstores and libraries. But as I grew up, it became much more difficult to find an interesting plot for me.

The thing is that I prefer to read fiction with a love line and a happy ending. I believe that there is enough grief in our lives, so books and movies should have a happy end. But at the same time, I don't like generic romance novels; I want to read a plot with intrigue, a detective line, or a fight-against-evil line. Such literature inspires me to accomplishments, charges me with positive emotions, and helps me to believe that life is wonderful!

I went through many authors, read domestic and foreign writers. Some of them disappointed me with their syllable, some were poorly translated, and some books gave me the impression that I had already read something like this before. After all, the older we get the greater baggage of watched films and read books we have under our belt.

As a result, the works of two dozen writers settled in my library. In their plots, all components converged: there's a love line with a happy end, there's intrigue, they are easy and interesting to read, and they give positive emotions. However, this was not enough for me even for a short relaxation before bedtime. I wanted more and more new high-quality and at the same time entertaining stories. I needed them to help me to rest after my hard work. I had my own handmade gift making business.

But one day a misfortune happened - I'd gone blind for half a month. The thing is that I have been suffering from type 1 diabetes since my childhood, and one of my eyes had almost lost sight a while before, and the second one went blind due to a sudden hemorrhage. I'd been following all the doctors' instructions, laying all days with an eye patch and thinking a lot. What if I go completely blind? In that case, I won't be able to do my business work. What will I do? How can I make my living?

And in a month after the hemorrhage, I woke up in the morning with the feeling that I had just read a piece of my ideal book. I had a dream that left a feeling of clear joy and inspiration. I sat at my computer and wrote my dream down, creating vivid images - the beginning of the story. Thanks to my four years of experience in journalism, I did it easily. But the pounding feeling of incompleteness, the desire to find out what would happen next, pushed me to write again. I emerged from the sweet rapture of creativity in two weeks. A finished novel in the genre of lyrical fantasy, written in accordance with all my requirements about love, adventure, detective story, and a good ending, had been written to the end. And the plot for the next novel had already matured in my head.

But there was the trouble - I couldn't afford to plunge headlong into writing. I have to earn money for my permanent medical needs. My husband supports the family, taking care of all the expenses for food, utilities, education of our son. He helps me with buying medicine as well, but his abilities have a limit. It would be unfair to impose these costs on him too.

"Well, that's enough for now," I thought, returning to my business. "Who said that someone else except me would be interested in my novels?"

But dreams didn't want to wait. They didn't accept any reasoning. My soul demanded to write further. It was supported by readers who suddenly liked my first novel. And

I, suppressing the voice of Creativity inside me, suddenly fell sick. Vision deteriorated again.

I hesitated, wrote down pieces of plots, and left them half-finished. And every time I promised myself that this novel would be the last one. But in the end, I had to surrender to the mercy of the winners - my stories and my readers, who demand them. I continue to write, taking into account the people's wishes, making changes to the already finished manuscripts, improving them, making new novels more and more interesting. I realized that even if I go completely blind, it would not be that scary for me. After all, thanks to the software for blind people, I can still write my stories. And thanks to the positivity that I put into my works, my vision somehow stabilized a little. And now, I invite you to read some of my plots in order to get positive emotions, to experience inspiration, to feel that life is wonderful!

You can find other books by Anna Molman here: https://www.amazon.com/Anna-Molman/e/B08F3TP9N5

Anna Molman's page on Facebook:
https://www.facebook.com/molmananna

Printed in Great Britain
by Amazon